They strike from the shadows when they're least expected. They wear the face of innocence— appearing to be perfect victims or so unremarkable as to remain unnoticed. They kill for gain, from bloodlust, or because they cannot escape the demands of their masters. Whatever their reasons, whatever their methods, they are a terrifying and fascinating elite corps in the annals of fantasy— and in this book you will find some of their stories:

"Hang Ten"—She said she hanged people for a living. He told her he surfed for his. But which of them would prove better at *hanging ten* . . . ?

"Fealty"—He'd fought in the Crusades, sworn to obliterate the unbelievers. Now he'd been sent forth once again, but this time something seemed terribly wrong . . . .

"Breia's Diamond"—The Necromancer had hired Breia and her comrades to make a series of kills but the payoff would prove beyond their expectations . . . .

PLACES TO BE, PEOPLE TO KILL

More Journeys of the Imagination Brought to You by DAW:

UNDER COVER OF DARKNESS *Edited by Julie E. Czerneda and Jana Paniccia*. 14 all-original tales of the true powers that work behind the scenes—the covert masters of time, space and destiny. . . . From an unexpected ally who aids Lawrence in Arabia, to an assassin hired to target the one person he'd never want to kill, to a young woman who stumbles into an elfin war in the heart of London, to a man who steals time—here are unforgettable tales that will start you wondering whether someone is watching you from the shadows or changing your destiny at this very moment. . . .

IF I WERE AN EVIL OVERLORD *Edited by Martin H. Greenberg and Russell Davis*. The 14 original tales in this volume run the gamut from humorous to serious, fantasy to science fiction. These are stories for anyone who has ever played the role of an Evil Overlord, or has defeated an Evil Overlord, or would like to become an Evil Overlord. After all, isn't it more fun to be the "bad guy"?

ARMY OF THE FANTASTIC *Edited by John Marco and John Helfers*. 13 original tales of battles fought by magical creatures in fantastical realms, and our own transformed world. . . . Includes stories by Jean Rabe, Rick Hautala, Fiona Patton, Tim Waggoner, Alan Dean Foster, Tanya Huff, Mickey Zucker Reichert, and more.

PLACES TO BE, PEOPLE TO KILL

edited by
Martin H. Greenberg
and Brittiany A. Koren

DAW BOOKS, INC.
DONALD A. WOLLHEIM, FOUNDER
375 Hudson Street, New York, NY 10014
ELIZABETH R. WOLLHEIM
SHEILA E. GILBERT
PUBLISHERS
http://www.dawbooks.com

First Printing, June 2007
1 2 3 4 5 6 7 8 9

ACKNOWLEDGMENTS

Assassins: An Introduction copyright © 2007 by Brittiany A. Koren

Exactly by Tanya Huff, copyright © 2007 by Tanya Huff.

Bloodlines by Jim C. Hines, copyright © 2007 by Jim C. Hines.

Hang Ten by Jean Rabe, copyright © 2007 by Jean Rabe.

Fealty by S. Andrew Swann, copyright © 2007 by Steven Swiniarski.

Breia's Diamond by Cat Collins, copyright © 2007 by Cat Collins.

While Horse and Hero Fell by Sarah A. Hoyt, copyright © 2007 by Sarah A. Hoyt.

Deadhand by John Helfers, copyright © 2007 by John Helfers.

All in the Execution by Tim Waggoner, copyright © 2007 by Tim Waggoner.

Money's Worth by Bradley H. Sinor, copyright © 2007 by Bradley H. Sinor.

Substitutions by Kristine Kathryn Rusch, copyright © 2007 by Kristine Kathryn Rusch.

Drusilla by Ed Gorman, copyright © 2007 by Ed Gorman.

The Hundredth Kill by John Marco, copyright © 2007 by John Marco.

For Jim and Ed:

With sincere thanks,

—B.A.K.

CONTENTS

ASSASSINS:
AN INTRODUCTION

Brittiany A. Koren

AH, THE ASSASSINS! Characters so well loved for their deviousness and slyness. So what do assassins do when they finally get that well-deserved vacation? In this anthology we will explore the places they visit, and go deep into the depths of their minds. What makes them the elite killers that they are? Are they misguided? Is it fear for their own or someone else's life—kill or be killed? Or is it an occupation passed down from one generation to the next?

We'll show you the events that lead assassins to be who they are: being in the wrong place at the wrong time; greed; love; or the chosen path of the honored sentinel or spy. We'll show you that assassins are human just like you and me. They walk among us, never knowing, but always suspecting, that someone might turn on them.

Assassins come in all shapes and sizes, and one never can tell who the next great assassin might be. Some are witty and coy like Tanya Huff's Vree, the sister in the Vree and Bannon team. And some are surprising, like the character in "The Hundredth Kill" by John Marco. We are fascinated by these people who live on the edge and in the dark. Life is too precious to be trifled with, and the assassin takes life very seriously—as in Jean Rabe's "Hang Ten." It is a duty in some cases, as in Tim Waggoner's "All in the Execution," and we also see it with Ed Gorman's Aarak in "Drusilla." Some assassins kill for acceptance—"Breia's Diamond" by Cat Collins—or for love—Bradley Sinor's "Money's Worth."

Others, however, try to start over, to leave that dark life behind as Jim C. Hines shows us in "Bloodlines," but can they ever get away? Does their past life ever stop haunting them? Even in the afterlife, their services may be requested, as is the case in S. Andrew Swann's "Fealty" or in a somewhat different fashion in John Helfers' "Deadhand."

And yet some not quite in the typical assassin mode, taking lives for reasons not their own, as in "Substitutions" by Kristine Kathryn Rusch, are unlikely candidates for the role, doing what they must. Some may not even realize they could be a killer, as in Sarah A. Hoyt's "While Horse and Hero Fell."

Whatever their reasons, we continue to be entertained by their stealth abilities and put on the edge of our seat with the suspense of each new adventure. We hope you enjoy reading the tales from these authors about the cursed, the not so lucky, the hopeful, and the bred assassin. They've made me laugh, cry, and kept me up at night, afraid that I might be the next victim. But most of all, these authors have given life to incredible assassins and taken them to far away places where you'll want to be—and to people to kill.

EXACTLY

Tanya Huff

Tanya Huff lives and writes in rural Ontario with her partner, Fiona Patton, an unintentional Chihuahua, and six and a half cats. Her latest book from DAW is *Smoke and Ashes*, the third and last Tony Foster novel, and her next book will be a new installment in the *Valor* series. When she isn't writing, she's weighing the pros and cons of raising trout in her flooded crawlspace.

"ASSASSINS," COMMANDER NEEGAN declared in the rough whisper that was all an enemy arrow had left of his voice, "do not take leave."

"But it won't *exactly* be leave," Marshal Chela reminded him.

"They will be away from the army but not on

target." A dark brow rose. "I fail to see the difference, Marshal."

"They won't *exactly* be on target. There's the difference, Commander. Governor Delat is convinced she's got an Ilagian sorcerer pretending to be a carpet seller. She thinks he's the vanguard of an Astoblite invasion since Prince Aveon welcomes both Ilagians and sorcerors to his court."

"Why would Prince Aveon invade the South Reaches?"

"I don't know. Maybe he's looking for vacation property. The point is, Governor Delat has demanded we do something about her problem—which may or may not be the result of an overactive imagination. Vree and Bannon will go to the South Reaches *as if* they were common soldiers on leave, and they'll use their unique skills to determine whether or not this Ilagian carpet seller is a sorcerer working for Prince Aveon. If he turns out to be what Delat fears," the marshal continued, "they'll send a message back with one of her couriers, and I'll send them new orders. If not, they can come back to barracks having spent a pleasant few days in a nice little resort town on the emperor's coin. You have to admit, they deserve a bit of a break."

Neegan's expression suggested he had to admit nothing of the sort.

"You know Shonna took leave in the South Reaches when she won all that money betting on that fight Oneball had with Keenin last year."

"I know, Bannon."

"She said it was the best five days of her life. Full body rubs with scent oils. All the food she could eat. All the wine she could drink. And the sex! She said South Reaches whores were more flexible than even you, sister-mine."

Vree rolled her eyes and shot her younger brother a look it was just as well he didn't see. "We're on target."

"Not exactly." He threw an arm across her shoulders. "And that means there's no reason we can't enjoy ourselves while we're finding out. Look at it, Vree." His voice brought her to the halt his arm hadn't—she'd walked right out of his careless embrace when he'd stopped. "The South Reaches. Isn't it pretty?"

They were standing on the Shore Road, on top of a hill looking down at the town.

"Pretty?" Vree repeated wondering if Bannon had gotten a little too much sun.

He grinned. "In a 'hey, look at all the colors' sort of way."

All the colors was no exaggeration. Even the expensive packed earth houses of the wealthy that fronted the white sand beaches stretching out on both sides of the small harbor were an astounding variety of pastel shades. The town itself had moved past astounding to unbelievable. Red, blue, yellow, orange, turquoise, and every shade of pink imaginable covered the wooden walls, the colors crammed close together and jostling for attention.

"There's a pair of Astoblite ships in the harbor. Maybe they've already invaded."

Vree frowned at the two vessels tied side by side at the north pier. "In those? They're probably small traders delivering exotic wines and . . ." Her frown deepened. Born in barracks and having spent her entire twenty years in the army, she was ill equipped to come up with another exotic example.

"Perfumed oils," Bannon offered when it became obvious she wasn't going to fill in the blank.

"You're fixating on those full body rubs, aren't you?"

"I hear they're very good for working knots out of stiff muscles," he said cheerfully as they started walking again. "We can't do our job if we're all knotted up."

"You can't do your job if you're lying naked on a slab."

"You'd be amazed at what I can do lying naked on a slab."

"I'm not that easily amazed," she snorted, hip checked him, and snickered when he had to dance to miss a pile of horse shit on the road.

The South Reaches had no walls and no gates, but at the edge of town the Shore Road passed between two pairs of heavily muscled young men in black uniform kilts and tunics. "The governor's guard," Vree murmured as they approached.

"Think they can use any of that hardware?" Bannon asked at the same volume.

All four carried short swords in black-and-silver sheaths and two daggers, one on their belts and one sheathed at the edge of their black greaves. Their collective size was impressive and drew many admiring glances from other, less discerning, travelers. They made Bannon, who was taller than Vree by almost a head, look scrawny.

Everyone else on the road had passed unchallenged, but a massive hand beckoned the siblings over to the east-side guard post. Since there was no easy way to tell what they were, Vree wondered if the guards were more perceptive than seemed possible and had realized they were a threat or if they were about to indulge in a little soldier baiting. She was betting on the latter and figured it was pretty much a sucker bet.

"So, what have we here?" The guard who spoke had the smug, self-satisfied air of a bully who'd aged easily into a brute. He waited until the other two guards crossed the road to join the huddle before continuing. "It seems we've stopped a couple of the Empire's brave soldiers. Looks like they're scraping the bottom of the barrel, don't it?"

His crew laughed.

"You two do a little looting and then decide to grace the South Reaches with your ill-gotten gold?"

"Actually, we spent all our ill-gotten gold on a couple of magic beans that turned out to be total crap." Bannon grinned at the glowering faces. "We're just here on leave."

"This is an expensive place. Let's see your

coin." The leader poked a sausage-sized finger at Bannon's shoulder and missed by a hair's breadth. Which was exactly how far Bannon had moved.

"No coin," he said, still grinning. "Just a letter of credit from our marshal."

At Bannon's gesture, Vree pulled the letter from her belt pouch and handed it over. She wasn't worried about it being destroyed, since she had every confidence in being able to take it from the big man's hand if he made the attempt. Of course, he wouldn't survive the attempt, so she hoped he was smarter than he looked.

He scowled at the piece of vellum, lips moving as he puzzled out the larger words. "Why would you two skinny grunts rate a letter of credit?" he demanded when he finished.

"Services rendered. At the battle of Bonkeep the two of us were personally responsible for the deaths of the enemy commander and his entire staff."

"Yeah. Right." But his gaze kept dropping to the letter. "Reeno, search their bags."

They were carrying the bare essentials, the sorts of things any soldier on leave would carry. When Reeno got a little rough with her kit, Vree murmured, "Gently," at him and, when he looked up, she smiled.

She caught her bag before it hit the road and didn't bother correcting him when he pretended he'd thrown it there on purpose. After all, from a distance "thrown there on purpose" looked very much like "dropped from nerveless fingers."

"There's nothing, Orin." Reeno barely looked in

Bannon's bag before giving it back. "Just, you know, clothes and stuff."

"No weapons?"

"Their daggers . . ."

"I can see that!" Orin glared at Reeno and then at them. "Letter of credit, eh? Maybe someone who deserves this ought to use it."

"You'll have to kill us to keep it," Bannon pointed out.

"Orin!" Reeno nodded toward the traffic still passing by on the road. Toward witnesses.

Orin pretended to crumple the letter up, but when neither Vree nor Bannon reacted, he thrust it back at Bannon. Vree hid a grin at his expression when he crushed air instead of Bannon's hand. "I'll be watching you."

"Not a problem."

"Not a problem?" Vree repeated as they moved out of eavesdropping range.

"Hey, at least I didn't threaten young Reeno's manhood."

"All I did was smile at him."

"Yeah, that's what I said."

"You told them that we were here as a reward for taking out an entire command staff."

"We did."

"But that's not why we're here."

He patted her fondly on the arm. "You really suck at this lying thing, don't you?"

"Forget it, Bannon." Vree wrapped her hand around her brother's arm and dragged him to a stop as he started up the broad front steps of the Cyprus Garden Inn. "We are not staying here."

"Too small?" He frowned up at the pale pink walls and wide louvered windows thrown open to catch the late afternoon breeze. "I was hoping for cozy, but—hey—elegant's fine if that's what you want."

"Don't be such a slaughtering smart-ass. This . . ." She jerked her head toward the two story building, conscious that they were under scrutiny from the inn's atrium. ". . . is too expensive."

Bannon touched his belt pouch where the letter of credit had ended up. "We're on the emperor's coin, sister-mine. And besides," he added before she could respond, "this place is used to soldiers who've had a run of luck. It's where Shonna stayed."

"You asked her?"

"I did. Now if you really want to stay in some bug-infested dive with sweet piss all in the way of . . ."

"Here's fine." Releasing his arm, she started up the steps. If it was good enough for Shonna, it was nothing more than they deserved.

"Still angry about her trying to gamble away your coin?" Bannon asked as he caught up.

"Sod off." Of course she was. And he knew it. And that was why he'd brought them to this inn. She'd be upset about how easily he could read her except there wasn't much point; a lifetime of training had all but taught them to think with one mind.

They had a pair of adjoining rooms at the back of the building, small but clean. Included was unlimited access to the hotel's bathhouse and one meal each day of their stay.

"I like the sound of the bathhouse," Vree admitted, going into her brother's room. She'd already tested the strength of the balcony railing and noted all lines of sight to her window. "It's hard to stay unnoticed when you stink of the road."

Stripped down to his sling, Bannon stared up at her from his sprawl on the bed. "I stink of the road?"

"We stink of the road."

"I just got comfortable."

"There'll be bath attendants."

"Easy enough to get comfortable again." He grinned as he stood and scooped up his kilt. "Lead the way, sister-mine. A bath, a meal, and visit to a carpet shop," he continued as she led the way down the backstairs. "What more could a man want—except maybe a full body massage with scented oils."

"We're working."

"Not exactly. Not yet."

Her bath attendant was as taken with Bannon as his was.

"Your man is quite the flirt," she sighed, absently passing Vree a soapy sponge.

"He's not my man; he's my brother and be my guest."

She preferred to wash herself anyway. The possibility of being temporarily blinded by accidental soap in the eye by a distracted attendant was too dangerous to risk in her line of work. Their line of work. Not that Bannon seemed to be worried. But then again why should he when she was?

Well, slaughter that. This was not-exactly her leave, too.

She had the kid for supper and roasted peppers and a sherbet made with ice brought down from the mountains at—if the price was any indication—great expense. Bannon grinned and saluted her with a raw oyster.

According to Governor Delat, the Ilagian had opened his carpet shop in the jumble of tiny streets close to the harbor. Painted a pale green, it was fifth in from the corner Fat Alley shared with the Street of Knives. Washed and fed, Vree and Bannon wandered toward it past market stalls and shops crammed full of items designed to separate tourists from their money. Everything that could have some variation of "I bought this in the South Reaches" stamped on it, did.

"Bannon, look at this."

This was a knife-seller's stall. This *specifically* was a dagger with a broad curved brass blade etched with a rough map of the South Reaches and the legend *Don't cut me out of your life.*

"What's that mean?" Bannon muttered as they stared at the blade.

Vree shrugged. "No idea."

The tang and the pommel were also brass, suggesting that the dagger had been made from one piece of metal while the weight suggested otherwise. The grip had been wrapped in leather strips died a virulent orange-red, small shells danging from the half dozen tassels. The sheath was a slightly darker shade and a double row of the same shells had been glued along its length.

"Ah, yes, there is nothing like a beautiful woman who appreciates a good blade." The stall's owner bustled around and laid a pudgy arm around Vree's shoulders. "That dagger is . . ." He paused. Swallowed. And started to sweat. "For a small woman, you have quite the grip."

"I don't like to be touched."

His smile wobbled and he snatched his arm back. "I'll remember that."

"Probably."

Bannon shook his head as they walked away, leaving the stall owner clutching his genitals and gasping like a landed fish. "I think you hurt his feelings."

"At least I left them attached."

Torches had been lit by the time they reached the carpet shop, but the narrow streets were still busy—probably because every second shop sold alcohol of some kind. Beer, wine, and the apparently popular something pink with a tiny spear

stuck through a pineapple chunk. Although clothing ranged from kilts to sarongs to breeches, they
were the only people in army blue.

"We may need to buy a change of clothes," Bannon noted.

"Something in black wouldn't hurt if we're
going to be climbing around at night," Vree
acknowledged.

"Do you *see* anyone in black?"

"That guard."

Bannon leaned out and peered at the guard who
was suddenly not looking their way. "Besides
him?"

Up and down the street, the clothing was as
bright as the buildings, many of the tunics printed
with birds or flowers or cats. "There is no slaughtering way . . ."

"We could probably get something in silk."

Silk. "Silk's a good strong fabric," Vree said
slowly. "You can bend iron with it when it's
wet. Useful."

Bannon grinned. "Very."

"I'm sorry, I couldn't help but overhear. You're
looking for a silk carpet?"

They turned together to face the middle-aged
woman standing on the other side of the pile of
rugs that nearly filled the front of the shop. She
was pleasantly plump with dark hair and pale
brown eyes and skin a little lighter than theirs.

"We're looking for Ilagian carpets," Vree told
her.

She smiled broadly and spread her hands. "Excellent. We specialize in Ilagian carpets." Hands still spread, she beckoned them into the shop. "In fact, my employer, Hy Sa'lacvi, is Ilagian himself and imports only the most beautiful carpets from his homeland. Although he isn't here tonight, he has taught me everything he knows. Now, this beauty . . ."

At first, Vree was impressed by the woman's knowledge. As time passed and every attempt they made to leave was somehow twisted into another examination of another stack of carpet, she began to grow annoyed. Although a variety of merchants intent on separating soldiers from their money surrounded the barracks and most camps, assassins were usually left to choose as they pleased. This woman almost had them convinced they needed a carpet. Bannon had gone so far as to give her the measurements of the area beside his bunk. Vree had her hand on her dagger hilt and had planned her strike—up under the ribs, slice through the heart, wrap the body in a red wool rug—when customers obviously carrying more coin entered the shop and saved them.

"At least we found out Hy Sa'lacvi has the rooms upstairs." Bannon picked up the pace as they reached the street.

"And that he isn't in them right now." Vree effortlessly slipped through a group of laughing matrons all dressed in shades of purple and fell into step with her brother. "Safer to search them when he's home, though. A sorcerer would set up spells to protect his rooms when he's not in them." A man, sorcerer or not, could be avoided. Spells were a different matter.

"Tomorrow, then."

He was thinking about full body massages, she could tell. "Tonight."

"We should wait until we're a little less obvious."

"Until *we're* less obvious?" Vree snorted as a pair of heavyset men in very short kilts, sleeveless tunics, and shell necklaces sauntered past. Fortunately, it was now full dark and the torchlight hid as much as it revealed. "Or were you referring to the guard watching us from over by the wineskin seller?" she sighed, trying not to listen to the fading sound of bare thighs slapping.

"That, too."

"Think he's going to follow us all night?"

"Seems likely."

"People seem to be avoiding him," she noted as they changed direction slightly. The pattern of the street eddied around the guard, even the very drunk maintaining a careful distance of more than an arm's length.

"Almost looks like they're scared of him," Bannon agreed.

"Well, who isn't afraid of a great big guy dressed all in black and carrying a sword? Even if he's not likely to use it very well."

A moment later they moved into the guard's personal space, the pattern of the street now ebbing around them as well.

"You were on the gate when we arrived," Bannon said after sweeping a slow gaze up the guard's body from sandals to helm. "Didn't catch your name."

"Keln." He looked confused; prompted to answer by fear, unsure of what he should be afraid of.

"You were watching us, Keln," Vree purred by his ear. By the time he turned to face her, she'd moved to the other ear and was asking, "Why?" He whirled around, but she was back beside Bannon when he stopped. "Why, Keln?" she repeated.

Keln jerked forward, then stopped when he realized they were suddenly flanking him. "Orin thinks you're troublemakers," he snarled.

"Us?" Bannon grinned. "We're not troublemakers, Keln; we deal with troublemakers."

"Not in this town."

"Wherever we're sent, Keln."

"Stop saying my name!" The big man pushed past them, shoving the rack of wineskins out of the way as he plunged into the crowd. Someone cried out in pain, someone else swore, and Vree caught the rack before it fell.

"Can't say we didn't warn him," Bannon sighed.

"It's easier when they know we're assassins."

"People avoid us when they know we're assassins."

"And that's easier." She frowned at a wineskin. "There's an image of a parrot burned onto this. Why would someone burn the image of a parrot into a wineskin?"

Bannon peered at the leather and shrugged. "I have no idea."

Shops and stalls that didn't sell alcohol closed up just before midnight. Hy Sa'lacvi returned just after. He was short, round, and wearing a long, bright orange sarong patterned with palm leaves. Half a dozen shell bracelets gleamed against one dark wrist. As a sorcerer, he made a believable carpet seller.

Staggering a little, like everyone else on the streets, Vree and Bannon started back toward their inn, lost the pair of guards watching them—Keln and the remaining unnamed of the four—and ended up a few moments later at the top of the stairs that led to Hy Sa'lacvi's second-floor rooms.

Moving silently to the open window, Vree tossed the Nighthawk moth she'd snagged by one of the sputtering torches in over the sill. No lights. No whistles. No moth suddenly aflame. It seemed this access, at least, had not been protected by sorcery.

As they crouched inside the room, waiting for their eyes to adjust, the moth fluttered toward them. It was almost back to the window when an enormous pair of white paws came out of the darkness and brought it to the floor. The paws were more impressive than the cat they were attached to as the long-haired calico whacking the struggling insect across the painted wood was distinctly short in the leg.

Vree caught Bannon's eye and made a face. No

one had mentioned Hy Sa'lacvi had a pet. In their business, pets were more trouble than guards and servants combined.

As the moth managed to get into the air and out of range, the cat bounded up onto the narrow table that ran down the center of the room. Vree heard glass containers chime. The cat whirled, leaped a stack of brass weights, raced past a row of bottles, and charged through a cluster of squat clay jugs.

Vree caught the weights.

Bannon caught the bottles.

Neither of them could get to the jugs in time.

The first one to topple hit the floor with a crack, spilling out a pile of yellow granules. The second hit the floor with more of a thud, the viscous fluid in it adding a soft splat. When the fluid hit the granules, there was a high-pitched whine, a loud bang, and a cloud of purple smoke.

As the two assassins slipped back out the window, they heard the cat sneeze and Hy Sa'lacvi yelling in his own language. From the roof across the courtyard, they watched the smoke billowing up into the sky.

"That's a lot of smoke without fire," Bannon murmured.

Vree nodded. "We can assume the sorcerer part is correct anyway." She grinned as the cat raced down the stairs to the courtyard and disappeared in the shadows. Glittering with purple highlights, Hy Sa'lacvi stumbled out onto the landing.

"Mirrin!" He had a thin blanket wrapped around

his waist. "Mirrin! Get here! I not angry, I just need see if you all right!"

Below, in the darkness, the cat sneezed.

"Fine! You be hurt, cat, I no care. I sleep now!" Pivoting on one bare heel, he stomped back into his rooms.

"Definitely a sorcerer," Bannon snickered. "Any one else would've been told to shut his slaughtering hole." Pale faces had shown in a few of the other windows overlooking the courtyard, but no one had protested being so rudely awakened. "I wonder why he called for Mirrin in Imperial?"

"He probably got her here and figures that's what she understands. We're not going to find out anything else tonight," she added, leading the way down to the alley. "We might as well go back to the inn and get some sleep."

"You can go back to the inn, sister-mine. I've got other things to check out."

"You smell like . . ." Vree leaned closer and lifted her brother's arm to her nose. "Limes. And you're greasy."

"Oily." He pushed his wrist through her grip and back again, the motion blatantly suggestive. "Harder for an enemy to get a grip."

"I doubt it was *enemies* gripping you," she snorted, releasing him and stepping away from the bed. "I've done a bit of recon. Orin and his friends are lurking in front of the inn."

"So? If they do anything more than lurk, we'll take them out."

"Just like that?"

"We're on target and they got in the way."

"So now we're on target?"

Bannon grinned, rolled out of bed, and reached for his kilt. "Now, it's convenient. I'm starved, let's go eat."

"It's almost noon."

"Which is when things start happening in this town."

"You think they're going to arrest us?" Bannon wondered, as he worked his way along the inn's buffet table, piling food on his plate.

Vree glanced out at the four guards in time to see Orin throwing a cup of liquid back in the face of a water seller. "No. I think they want that letter of credit."

"You think they'll take the first chance they get to jump us?"

"Yeah."

"Idiots."

"Do they think we haven't noticed them?" Vree wondered as Orin and crew nearly knocked over a sausage cart trying to keep them in sight.

"I don't think they think." Bannon gestured at the nearest alley. "You want to lure them to their doom?"

"No, let's see how long their attention span is."

They lost the guards in a crowded ale house, slipping unseen out the back and up onto the roof. It was a simple matter to make their way to Hy

Sa'lacvi's carpet shop without ever returning to the ground.

"I can't believe how close together everything is." Bannon stepped from roof to roof past a line of disinterested pigeons dozing in the sun.

"And how much of it seems to be held together by paint," Vree added, adjusting her stride as a board began to give underfoot. They had no fear of being heard, for those who slept on the upper floors were out serving or servicing the visitors to the South Reaches, and anyone still asleep wouldn't be staying so close to the harbor.

Hy Sa'lacvi was sitting in the courtyard behind his shop; an abacus, stick of charcoal, and a pile of parchment seemed to indicate he was doing accounts. While they watched, Mirrin leaped up onto his lap desk and knocked a mug of steaming liquid over the pile.

"I wish I understood Ilagian," Bannon murmured as the sorcerer screamed at the departing cat. "That sounds like some impressive swearing."

As soon as it became obvious he was going to start again with dry parchment, they dropped silently off the roof onto the landing and slipped into his rooms.

"A considerate person would have a note or something lying around," Bannon grunted a short time later. "Yes, I am the vanguard of an Astoblite invasion. Kill me." He stared at the purple stain on the floor. "And it's no slaughtering fun going through a sorcerer's things; you never know when something might bite you on the ass."

"I didn't find anything either," Vree sighed. "We're going to have to do this the hard way."

"You mean the boring way," Bannon protested as they climbed back onto the roof. The soft click, click of the abacus drew his gaze down to the courtyard. "He's not going anywhere for a while. Do we both have to stay?"

"For the love of Jiir, Bannon, you're still greasy from your last body rub!"

"Oily. And I was just thinking that now would be the perfect time for me to pick us out some clothing that would help us blend in a little better. It's what soldiers on leave do."

Vree glanced down at the pile of blank parchment and compared it to the pile Hy Sa'lacvi had already covered with neat lines of tiny numbers. He was clearly going to be a while. "Fine." She couldn't understand why being on vacation suddenly made people wear clothing they wouldn't be caught dead in otherwise, but it *was* what soldiers on leave did and that was what they were supposed to be. Shonna had returned to barracks wearing a bright yellow tunic printed with purple flowers. "Do not," she warned her brother as he turned to leave, "bring me back anything printed with parrots, kittens, or palm trees. And don't take on Orin and his crew without me."

Moving into the only available bit of shade, she sat and watched their target do his accounting.

Except he wasn't *exactly* their target. *Pity*, she thought, fingers curled around the pommel of her dagger. *We could have killed him last night and been on our way home by now.*

Maybe he's working out the numbers of Astoblite soldiers he needs for the invasion. If he is, I can kill him now.

Before she could move, the woman who'd tried so hard to sell them a carpet the night before emerged from the back of the shop and told him she'd sold the small red-and-gold rug. "Good. Good!" Hy Sa'lacvi added a note to one of the finished sheets and flashed a brilliant smile up at the woman. "Maybe this month we make enough to import more, yes?"

Maybe import more was a euphemism for more soldiers.

"Maybe you should import something that doesn't unravel when you move it," the woman snorted.

Or not, Vree sighed. She'd never spent this much time on a target she could have taken out within moments of first marking him. *Boring, boring, bor . . .*

Mirrin clambered into her lap and shoved her head under Vree's hand.

Over the years, she'd had every type of insect imaginable climb over her while waiting to take out a target. There'd been half a dozen snakes, a few lizards, and on one memorable occasion a rat that'd had to be fatally discouraged from snacking on Bannon's foot. Dogs were avoided and, as a rule, cats avoided them.

Mirrin demanded attention more insistently.

When Bannon returned, Mirrin was napping with her head on Vree's dagger, and Hy Sa'lacvi was just filling his last piece of parchment. The breeches he brought her were dark green silk that hung low on her hips and flowed over her legs like water. The sleeveless tunic had been block printed with large pale green fish.

"You never said no fish," he protested, blocking her blow.

He wore a similar style in dark red and gold— the vest lightly laced across his chest with gold cord, the whole thing fish free.

They ate in the ale house across the road from the carpet shop, Bannon having taking their letter of credit to a moneylender for some coin. As they ate, they watched Hy Sa'lacvi try to sell a carpet to a middle-aged couple dressed in matching sleeveless tunics and short breeches.

"Do they know how ridiculous they look?" Bannon wondered, eating a small onion off the point of his knife.

Vree shrugged and peeled another shrimp.

By the time they finished their meal—having switched their full tankards for the convenient empties of their neighbors, Hy Sa'lacvi had turned the shop over to his employee, pushed his way out into the milling crowds, and began walking toward the harbor.

Vree and Bannon followed, careful not to be seen by either their quarry or Orin's people. Given both crowds and darkness, it wasn't hard. Eventually, after a short stop at a bakery and a slightly longer one at a wine merchant's, they found themselves at the harbor watching Hy Sa'lacvi go into a warehouse near the North Pier.

"That's it. The Astoblite ships are tied up at the North Pier. We can kill him."

Vree stopped her brother's forward movement with a well placed elbow. "He could be seeing another trader about a carpet. We need to be sure."

"Fine." He rolled his eyes. "We'll sneak into the warehouse, get close enough to find out exactly what Hy Sa'lacvi is up to, and when we find out he's helping the Astoblites invade, then we kill him."

"That works."

There were four men and two women sprawled on cushions around a low table in an empty corner of the warehouse. One of the men and one of the women were definitely Astoblites. Three of the other four were South Reaches locals, and the last was wearing the distinctive orange-on-blue parrot tunic of a visitor. When Hy Sa'lacvi joined them, money changed hands and tiles were slapped down on the table.

Catching Bannon's eye, Vree signed, *No kill.*

He nodded and signed, *Stay?*

She signed back, *Maybe kill later,* mostly just to cheer him up, and they settled in to watch and wait for the tile game to become strategy and tactics. It never did.

"So tomorrow we tell the governor she was imagining things and head home," Bannon sighed as they headed back toward their inn. "Hy Sa'-lacvi is no more planning a slaughtering invasion than I am. And he sucks at tiles."

Impossible to argue the latter point as the Ilagian had, indeed, lost steadily all night. They'd followed him home, watched him climb into bed, discouraged Mirrin from following them, in turn, away across the roof, and were now calling it a night.

"I suspect the governor will want us to observe him for a little longer," Vree pointed out. "He can't spend all his time planning an invasion. Maybe this was his night off."

"So we're staying?"

"For a while." She grabbed his arm as he started to turn away. "Where are you going?"

"Big Eylla's place is still open. I can see the torches from here."

Since she couldn't think of a good reason to hang on to him, she let him go.

"You should come with me."

"No, thank you."

"Your loss." Walking backward, gracefully avoiding the other people still wandering the streets looking for entertainment, he winked. "You need to get laid more, sister-mine."

"Sod off. You, too," she added before the elderly man leering cheerfully at her could make the obvious suggestion.

Just before dawn, someone heavy heaved himself up onto her balcony. It sounded very much like he took out two or three other people on the way down.

Their second day in the South Reaches was very much like their first—except Bannon smelled faintly of cinnamon instead of limes. That night Hy Sa'lacvi had dinner with friends, ate sixteen crabs, drank half a barrel of pale beer, and threw up three times on the way home.

On day three, Orin attempted to shove Bannon into a cup-seller's cart, inexplicably missed, and somehow ended up crashing through it himself. The resulting shouting match was made funnier by the minor wounds Orin had taken. That night, they watched from the roof as Hy Sa'lacvi mixed powders and potions in his back room. After the first small explosion, Mirrin joined them.

When Vree returned alone to the Cyprus Gardens, heavy breathing and the creak of leather told her she had company in her room. She thought about taking care of it herself but figured Bannon would never forgive her for blowing their cover without him. Noting where each man stood, she backed away from the door, returned to the atrium, gave the information to the large young woman on duty, and let the inn's security handle it.

The intruders had swords out, but they weren't expecting crossbows.

"Who says assassins have no sense of humor," she murmured to herself as Orin and his crew were tossed down the front stairs loudly protesting that they were the governor's guard. Orin seemed to be bleeding slightly again.

"We need to deal with them," Vree muttered the next morning as she watched Orin shove that same poor water seller out of his way with a bandaged arm. Keln and the still nameless fourth kicked the man on the way by. "They're starting to annoy me."

Bannon glanced behind him. The four guards were barely three or four body lengths behind, shadowing them obviously, scowling, hands on their weapons, the noon crowds scrambling clear. "They look a little bruised."

"They've had a rough couple of nights. Come on." She led the way into a narrow alley between a candler's and yet another ale house.

Rubbing at a bit of sandalwood-scented oil in the crease of his elbow, Bannon shrugged and followed.

From the look on his face when he joined them, Orin had not been expecting an ultimatum.

"Sod off, and we won't kill you."

His mouth opened and closed. Two of his men laughed. Reeno didn't.

Vree reached into her belt pouch and pulled out a square of leather stamped with a black sunburst. "This is your last warning," she sighed and tossed it onto the packed dirt between them.

Reeno whimpered.

"I'm guessing he served," Bannon noted from where he was leaning against the candler's wall. "And these three got deferments for being in the governor's guard."

"Orin!" Reeno grabbed the big man's arm. "They're . . ."

". . . not armed with nothing but knives, and they're runty," Orin grunted. "Soldiers die on leave all the time, accidental like."

Vree smiled at Reeno who whimpered again and ran.

That night, Hy Sa'lacvi went to another tile game, and Bannon came back to the room smelling faintly of cloves.

"We can't keep this up indefinitely," Vree sighed as they followed Hy Sa'lacvi while he shopped.

"We could kill him."

"No," she flicked an apricot pit at a street performer. He shrieked and grabbed his crotch. The crowd applauded. "Our orders say we have to be sure."

"So?"

"So we force his hand."

*   *   *

They laid a black sunburst on the sarong he wore out in the evening. Mirrin looked up at them, yawned, and went back to sleep.

"He probably doesn't know what it is," Bannon reminded Vree when Hy Sa'lacvi returned to the shop in his sarong, apparently unaffected by the square of leather he carried in one hand. "He's a foreigner, remember? Don't worry," he added as the square was passed to the woman in his shop. "She'll . . ."

Her shriek could be heard clearly across the street in the ale house.

". . . know."

They got to their regular place on the roof in time to see Hy Sa'lacvi carefully stack the contents of his worktable into one covered basket and frantically shove a fistful of clothes and Mirrin into another. The calico kept up a steady protest as he pounded back down the stairs, through the shop, and into the street.

"Sounds like he's got a demon in there," Bannon snickered as they followed.

"Looks like he's heading straight for the docks," Vree pointed out.

"The Astoblite ships."

"He ran right to his co-conspirators."

"So we can kill him now?"

"Works for me."

Hy Sa'lacvi was in the cabin of the farther ship with the Astbolite woman he played tiles with.

His baskets on the floor at his feet, he was clutching her arm and speaking so quickly in Astbolite it sounded like one long, hysterical word.

"Speak Imperial!" she snapped at last. "Your accent is terrible at the best of times!"

Tucked in the shadows outside the louvered window, Vree doubted his Imperial was any better. Although she could hear separate words, hysteria gave them unintelligible inflections.

"Why are assassins trying to kill you?" the woman demanded at last.

"My carpets."

"What about them?"

"I sell cheap because pay no duty!"

"You're smuggling carpets into the South Reaches?" she asked as Bannon mouthed, *He's smuggling carpets?* at Vree.

"Hide them with sorcery!"

"Oh, give it a rest, you're no more a sorcerer than I am."

Which was when Mirrin finally got the lid of the basket open. Yowling indignantly, she leaped up onto the table, scrambled through the piles of paper, knocked over the lantern, and threw herself out the window.

The lantern landed on the second basket.

Clutching the furious cat who'd landed in her arms, Vree danced along the railings, leaped to the other ship, skipped past an astounded group of sailors, and was on the dock before the purple flames had reached the top of the first mast.

Bannon was a heartbeat behind her.

"At least there's no invasion," he said as they slid into an alley while bells tolled and people yelled and Hy Sa'lacvi and the Astbolite captain's voice could be heard screaming contradictory orders as the purple fire spread. "I think it's time we left."

"Past time," Vree agreed, wiping her bleeding cheek on her shoulder as Mirrin settled in her arms and began to purr.

"You going to take her back to the shop?"

She glanced at the burning ships. The purple fire had chased both crews onto the docks and seemed to be following them. "No, I think I'd better take her with us."

"What are we going to do with a cat?"

"Give it to Marshal Chela."

"Well, if we're bringing her something, we'd better get something for Commander Neegan, too."

"So the Ilagian sorcerer was not the vanguard of an Astoblite invasion although he might have precipitated one since Prince Aveon is likely to be more than a little annoyed about losing those two ships. Half of the South Reaches has been reduced to purple ash and rubble, three of the governor's personal security force are dead, someone named Big Eylla has sent me a bill for half a dozen full-body rubs . . ." Marshal Chela grabbed Mirrin just in time to keep the inkwell from going off the edge of her desk. ". . . and I seem to have acquired a cat. Did you have anything to add, Commander Neegan?"

"Just that this," he told her, holding the souvenir dagger between thumb and forefinger, and staring down at the dangling shells in disbelief, "is *exactly* why assassins do not take leave."

BLOODLINES

Jim C. Hines

Jim C. Hines has been writing for over a decade now, though he tries not to think about that. His humorous fantasy novels *Goblin Quest* and *Goblin Hero* are both available from DAW. His short fiction has appeared in over thirty magazines and anthologies, including *Realms of Fantasy*, *Turn the Other Chick*, and *Sword & Sorceress*. Jim lives with his beautiful wife and two wonderful children in Michigan, where he is patiently waiting for fame and fortune to arrive. They haven't shown up yet, but Jim remains hopeful. He suspects they took a wrong turn in Albuquerque. If you see them, please direct them to *www.jimchines.com* so they can get in touch.

TO ONE ATTUNED, the scent of dark magic was unmistakable, even through the sweat and dust permeating the stamp mill. Valerica Eminescu rested her sledgehammer on the floor and wiped dust from her eyes, wondering if she had imagined it. Already the tang of burning blood, sharp and coppery and hot as the devil's forge, had begun to fade. Her hand tightened around the handle of her hammer as she searched the crowded mill for anything unusual.

"You all right, Val?" asked Jim Daley, as he dumped another shovelful of crushed ore into the pans.

Before Valerica could answer, Jim's shovel clattered from his hands, and he lurched forward.

Valerica tried to catch him. Her fingers brushed his coverall, and then he twisted sideways, staggering like a man too drunk to walk. Another miner shouted, but it was too late. Jim fell against the machinery and didn't move.

There was no way for her to stop the riverwheel from rotating, lifting, and releasing the heavy weights of the mill. Designed to pulverize crushed ore, the stamps smashed down before Valerica had taken two steps.

She grabbed Jim's arm and dragged him back. Blood spurted from his ruined right hand, spraying Valerica and darkening the dusty floor. Jim stared dumbly at his hands. Splintered bone protruded from the broken fingers of his right. His left hand hung limp. The stamps had torn skin and muscle near the wrist, and already his entire sleeve was dark with blood.

Someone shoved her aside, wrapping a belt

around Jim's left arm, then twisting a sheathed knife through the belt to tighten the tourniquet. Another miner handed him a steel flask and forced him to drink.

Nobody noticed as Valerica slipped out of the mill, hurrying around back to plunge her bloody hands into the stream. It wasn't enough. She waded into the water, fighting the urge to strip off her bloody clothes and fling them away. Blood trailed downstream like smoke in the water.

"Control," she said through clenched teeth. Her hands twisted the denim of her overalls. The yearning hadn't been this strong since she left Romania, nearly ten years before.

She could almost hear her father's voice whispering, *"The blood burns with power, ready to be claimed."*

Valerica dropped to her knees and plunged her face into the water. The shock of cold finally purged the scent of magic from her nostrils. She remained there until her lungs threatened to burst, then sat back, gasping for air.

This was an accident, nothing more. The Red Eagle Silver Mine was a dangerous place. A sinkhole had claimed three men earlier this year. A cave-in had buried another group only last week.

Heavy footsteps crunched the rocks behind her. "What the hell is wrong with you?"

Henry Cooper had worked this mine since eighteen fifty-four, taking over as foreman a few years later. He was a God-fearing man with a temper hot as a smelting fire. A black bush of a mustache covered his mouth, and his bald head was damp with sweat.

"Is Jim—"

"Cussed fool will probably be dead by dinner." Henry crossed himself, then said, "I let you work this mine because you're strong enough to swing a hammer, and you don't complain. But this is dangerous work. Man's work. If you're going to run off and swoon every time—"

"I'm the one who pulled him away from the stamps," Valerica said.

"That so?" Henry folded his arms. "Old Clyde says it looked like you were the one who pushed him in the first place."

Valerica didn't answer. Against the word of a man, hers was worthless as pyrite.

Eventually, Henry shrugged. " 'Course, Clyde's half-blind, too." He turned and spat. "So if you're through with this little display, why don't you get back in there and start cleaning the pans."

As she returned to the mill, Valerica saw the other workers carrying Jim Daley downhill, toward the makeshift city of tents and cabins that surrounded the mine. Others ran out to help, and to learn who had been hurt.

Valerica ducked into the mill and did her best to lose herself in the work. She yanked the pans from beneath the stamps, then began to rinse away the pulp and mud. It was a mindless task, one that slowly allowed her to regain her control. By the time she began to draw the quicksilver from the bottom of the pan, shaping it into crude, fist-sized balls, she felt human again. The splotches of blood no longer called to her, or if they did, she refused to listen.

Valerica's cabin was a quarter mile south of the main camp, away from the others. She reached for the heavy canvas that served as a door, then yanked her fingers back. She might have imagined the smell this morning, but here the scent of fire and blood made her eyes water.

"Bill," she whispered. "Alina!" Valerica ripped the door aside. Stepping into her cabin was like walking through cobwebs. Foulness permeated her home, a shadow that clung to her skin and seeped into her lungs. "Where are you?"

She found her adopted nephew in the corner. Bill was half-naked and trembling, his eleven-year-old body curled into a ball. Thin lines of blood crusted his forehead, the Cyrillic characters barely legible. Others marked his chest, over the heart.

Valerica grabbed him by the arms. Without thinking, she smeared her fingers through the blood on his chest, severing the enchantment.

"Aunt V?" Bill coughed and looked around. "What are you doing here?"

"Where is Alina?" She held him still as she checked his body for injuries. The cuts were shallow, and should heal quickly. She licked her thumb and scrubbed his forehead.

Bill looked down at himself, and his face went white. "How . . . who did this to me?" He tried to squirm away, but Valerica held him fast.

"Let me go."

"Where is Alina?" Valerica shouted.

"In her crib!"

Valerica released him.

Bill's shirt was balled up in the corner. He slipped it on and began doing up the buttons. "She's been bawling all morning. I thought about mixing a bit of whiskey into the goat's milk, but she finally settled down." He pulled his suspenders up over his arms, then stopped, staring through the open door at the sunset. "Aunt V, what the hell is going on?"

Valerica was already moving into the other room. A set of bunkbeds stood against the wall beside the small crib Valerica had built almost a year ago. She knew it was empty the second she stepped into the room, but she tore through the blankets anyway. She ripped apart the lower bunk, then dropped to the dirt floor to check beneath the bed. There was no sign of her daughter.

Bill stared at the empty crib. "I didn't doze off. My word on it. I tucked her in, safe as—"

"Get out."

His eyes shone, but he blinked back the tears. "Don't be like that, Aunt V. I can help you search. Little Alina can't have gone far. The pup can barely crawl."

Valerica grabbed him. One hand twisted his collar, the other seized the seat of his pants. She dragged him from the cabin and set him down hard, facing the town below.

"You can help by going to church and praying for Alina."

Bill scowled, his face red. "You don't have to—"

"*Now.*" Perhaps a bit of power slipped into her words. Or maybe fear alone compelled him. Bill fled without another word.

"Forgive me," she whispered. Slowly, her anger turned inward, where it belonged.

Father Fanshaw had refused to allow Valerica into his church, ever since he learned of her relationship with Elizabeth. But he wouldn't refuse a frightened boy, and the church was the one place Bill should be safe.

Valerica closed her eyes. She should have known. With all of the commotion after Jim's accident, who would have noticed a lone figure making his way through the camp?

She *had* known. She had simply refused to see.

"Watch over her, Elizabeth," she whispered. "I swear to you I'll save her. Keep our daughter safe until I can find her."

It was a year and a half since Valerica had taken Bill's mother into the desert. Elizabeth hadn't understand at first, thinking it nothing more than a fancy picnic. There were so few chances to be alone, away from the gossip. But this morning Bill was in church, and the mine was shut down for Sunday worship.

The two women were a sight. Valerica was still

caked with dust and sweat from yesterday's work. Her loose miner's overalls hid a muscular body, and her black hair was tucked into a blue cap. By contrast, Elizabeth Bemis was a proper lady. She wore a black silk hairnet with beads and blue ribbons dangling down her neck. Despite the heat, she refused to remove her bonnet, nor would she soak it down with water from the canteen, as Valerica had done with her cap.

"Where are we going?" Elizabeth asked, taking Valerica's hand in hers and swinging them like a child.

"There." Valerica pointed. The blood spell she had traced on the cracked boulder was gone, washed away by the elements, but the power remained. Trapped by the magic, a coyote whimpered at the base of the boulder. The animal favored her back left paw as she paced, and her ribs were clearly visible against the dirty gray fur. Even without Valerica's spell, she would have died within a few days.

Valerica pulled out a razor she had borrowed from Elizabeth's cabin. She opened the blade and nicked her palm, then extended her hand so the blood dripped onto the coyote.

The coyote's legs collapsed. Her tongue lolled from the side of her mouth as she struggled to raise her head.

"What are you doing?" Elizabeth asked.

"Did you mean it?" Valerica tightened her fist, squeezing more blood into the dirt. "What we talked about last week, after Bill's birthday?"

Elizabeth stared. "That's impossible. You can't—"

"*We* can," Valerica said. "If it's what you want. There will be questions and rumors. Ugly rumors. Are you sure—"

"Yes," Elizabeth said firmly. She bit her lip as Valerica moved toward the coyote. "Are you going to kill it?"

"She's paralyzed. She won't feel anything." Valerica hesitated. "The spell will work better if we both . . ."

Elizabeth's hand closed over her own. They slit the coyote's throat together, making the death as swift as possible.

"How?" Elizabeth asked.

"The coyote lived a long life, and carried many litters." She wiped most of the blood from the razor. Blood sank into the engraving on the ivory handle, highlighting the initials *G. L. B.* Gary L. Bemis, Elizabeth's husband, who had died of influenza several years earlier.

Elizabeth pulled out a lace-trimmed handkerchief and began wiping the blood from her hand. "Is all magic so bloody for a *strigoi viu*?"

Valerica dropped the razor. "Where did you hear that term?"

"You whisper in your sleep sometimes," Elizabeth said. She put her clean hand on Valerica's shoulder. "When the nightmares take you. What does it mean?"

She stooped to retrieve the razor, never meeting Elizabeth's gaze. "The words are Romanian, the title for a child of power." Not a lie, but far from the truth. "You may wish to turn away."

Without waiting for a response, Valerica knelt and sliced open the coyote's stomach and chest. She peeled back the skin and cracked the ribs, shoving organs aside until she exposed the pink of the uterus.

To Elizabeth's credit, she never averted her eyes. She was pale and sweating as Valerica used the razor to reopen the nick on her palm, but when it was Elizabeth's turn, she held her hand steady for the cut.

They clasped hands, pressing together until their palms and fingers grew slick, and blood dripped onto the coyote.

Blood burns with power. Jaw tight, she ignored the words, repeated so often by her father in another land, another life.

"How does it work?" Elizabeth whispered. "Which one of us will—" Her eyes widened, and her free hand went to her stomach.

Valerica grinned and put her own hand over Elizabeth's. "You will."

Elizabeth's face was like the morning sun, burning away Valerica's fears. "I can feel her," she whispered, her voice soft with awe. "Valerica, it's a her. Bill's going to have a sister."

For nine months, Valerica had known joy. She deluded herself into believing she could violate the laws of God and never suffer. She and Elizabeth had *created* life. They had done no harm. Surely God would bless a child born in such love.

Alina was born in winter. Elizabeth lost consciousness shortly after the contractions began. She never woke up.

The quarter moon provided enough light for Valerica to make her way back to the stamp mill. After checking to be sure it was abandoned, she crept inside.

Even in the darkness, she had no trouble finding Jim Daley's blood. It called to her, stirring memories of that day with Elizabeth, the way the blood had coated her arms like a second skin.

Someone had washed away the worst of the blood, but enough remained, clotted in the cracks between the planks. Valerica opened her penny knife and used the blade to dig up clumps of bloody dirt, which she sprinkled in a small circle.

When she had enough, she pulled out a dented silver rattle, tarnished where Alina had gnawed on it. Giving the rattle a quick kiss, she placed it in the center of the circle.

An observer would have seen nothing. At most, one would hear a faint ringing as the rattle rolled to one side. Valerica picked it up, feeling a soft tug at her hand. She stood, wincing at the cramps in her legs. Outside, a glance at the moon told her only an hour had passed, but her muscles were tight and knotted.

She ignored the pain as the rattle led her uphill, past the miners' main camp. She stopped behind the cooking tent when she realized where Alina must be.

A place of darkness, where screams would go unheard. A place where one could work magic, unseen by the eyes of God and men.

Up ahead, the entrance to the Red Eagle Silver Mine was an open mouth, laughing as it waited to swallow her in darkness.

The cabin door was still ripped asunder when Valerica returned for supplies. Candlelight flickered inside. Valerica hesitated, but there was no trace of new magic. "Who's there?" she called.

Bill stepped into the doorway. "Now don't get all sore, Aunt V. I know you said to stay away, but—"

"No." Valerica stepped past him. She opened her trunk and grabbed a dark jacket, a handful of candles, and some matches. "Go back to the church."

"Jim Daley's body is down there, along with some whore who got herself stabbed." He tried to act nonchalant, but Valerica saw him shiver. "They say she's the third one this month."

She nodded, unsurprised. "You can't stay here. Return to town, and—"

"No." He folded his arms, and Valerica had to fight back tears. Standing like that, jaw clamped with determination, Bill was the shadow of his mother. "I want to help you find my sister. She's in the mine, isn't she?"

"How did you—?" Valerica swore. Alina's rattle had come from Elizabeth. No doubt it was the same one Bill had used as a baby. Valerica's spell must have called to him, too. "You're not coming."

"It's my fault she's gone," Bill insisted. "Let me help!"

"Bill, please." She forced the coldness from her voice. "The man who took Alina is worse than a murderer. He's probably the one who killed those prostitutes." The more blood he harvested, the greater his power.

"What does he want with Alina?"

Valerica closed her eyes. He would take Alina to live among the dead. He would teach her power others never imagined. He would give her the strength to defeat death, and he would damn her forever. He would make her *strigoi viu*, as he had done to Valerica. And he would use her to control Valerica, to punish her for her disobedience. "Let me worry about Alina. If you interfere, you will join Jim Daley."

"He didn't kill me before," Bill said.

Only because I would have sensed your death and come running. "You should thank God for your good fortune. If you return willingly to his grasp, he will make you beg for death."

Bill reached behind his back and drew a Bowie knife. The blade was twice the length of his hand. "I'd like to see him try."

"Where did you get that?"

"Don't matter. You didn't expect it, and neither will the bastard who took my sis."

Valerica grabbed his arms and shoved him against the wall. Years of working in the mill had strengthened her muscles, so she barely noticed Bill's weight. His dangling feet kicked her shins, and the knife point pricked her side, but she ignored it. Her right hand held him pinned. Her left twisted the knife from his hand and stabbed it into the wall beside his ear.

Bill's face was white. He was breathing so quick he couldn't talk. His panicked gasps reminded her of the coyote, right before she and Elizabeth had killed it.

"I know you love Alina," she said. "But this man will eat your heart while your blood is still hot. The only way I can save Alina is by destroying him. Alone."

"Who—" Bill swallowed and tried again, but the words didn't come.

"My father," Valerica said. As a child, she had been too weak and afraid to fight back, choosing instead to flee. Had she fought, he would have killed her . . . and Elizabeth would still be alive.

"What kind of man—"

"He is *strigoi mort*," Valerica said. "Living dead."

What she would become after her own passing.

Valerica had never won an argument with Elizabeth when she set her mind to something, and Bill was his mother's son.

"You need me," Bill said as he followed her toward the mine. "I've been running ice in those tunnels for a year. You ain't never gone farther

than the ore dump. Without me, you'll get yourself turned about or trapped in a sinkhole."

"If I need guidance, I'll ask one of the men."

"Those same men who say ladies oughtn't be
in the mine at all?" Bill shot back. "What are you
gonna tell them, that your dead pa ran off with
Alina?"

"When has anyone in this camp ever thought
of me as a *lady*?" Still, he had a point. Her spell
drew her toward Alina, but it couldn't guide her
through the labyrinthine twists of the tunnels.

"You're scared for me, I know," said Bill. "You
worry like my own ma. But that's my sister down
there, and no walking corpse is going to stop me
from getting her out."

"You don't know what he is." Valerica's father
had been buried facedown, with sharpened stakes
planted in the earth to impale his body should he
try to return. It hadn't been enough. Others had
tried to warn them, urging her grandfather to
burn the body, but he had refused. He hadn't believed, and it had killed him.

Valerica had thought she would be safe in
America, with an ocean between her and her father. The purity of water was one of the few
things his kind feared. Had the ship gone down,
or had he fallen overboard, it would have destroyed him. His body would have sunk quickly,
drawn toward hell. She had seen it once as a child.
Her father and his fellows had flung one of their
number into a pond as punishment for some

transgression. Like a twisted baptism, the immersion purified him, burning the very flesh from his bone.

She had underestimated her father's determination. *You are mine, little Valerica, to the last drop of blood in your veins.*

"Please, Aunt V."

Valerica bit her lip. If anything happened to Bill, Elizabeth's spirit would never forgive her. But without him, her slim chance to save Alina dwindled to nothing. "I'm sorry, love," she whispered. To Bill, she said, "You may guide me through the mine. When we are close, you will stay hidden." She raised a hand, chopping off his half-formed protest. "Promise me."

Bill scowled, but nodded.

They walked in silence toward the square hole in the earth. To either side, iron pumps rested over narrow air shafts. With the pumps shut down for the night, the air inside would be hot, bitter, and stale.

The rattle in Valerica's hand drew them down the ramp, into darkness.

Candlelight sent shadows flickering over the planks and timbers of the tunnel. The huge support beams locked together in an unending series of squares and triangles. Valerica's hand was sweaty on the rattle.

"You still haven't told me what your pa wants with my sister," Bill said.

"He wants me." Alina was born of dark magic, the strongest she had ever cast. That had to be what had drawn him from Romania. She had led him here. "He and his fellows taught me the black arts."

She glanced at Bill. His face was pale, but he didn't react. "So you're some kind of witch?"

"The name is *strigoi viu*, those who are cursed from birth." Her own evil paled beside the sins of those who returned, the ones who defeated death through blood and blackness. The ones like her father. "They teach their children the magic to escape damnation. To endure death and rise as *strigoi mort*."

She wiped her face. "He would have burned me on the pyre to stop me from leaving."

"Is that why he's here? To kill you?"

"To reclaim me." No doubt Alina as well. Her father's blood pumped through Alina's heart, too. She raised the candle. The tunnel leveled off here, opening into a loading platform. "We need to go deeper."

"To the right," Bill said. "The ladder'll take us down."

Bill had been right. Without his guidance, she would have been lost.

At the bottom of the ladder, she stopped to put a fresh candle into the holder. Wax dripped along the iron spike of the handle, singeing her callused fingers.

Bill pointed to a sign nailed to an overhead

beam. "We're at fifteen hundred feet. They closed this part down a week or so back, after the tunnel flooded."

Valerica nodded, remembering the men who had barely escaped. Many had burns on their hands and faces from the steam.

"When they finally got it pumped dry, they lost a blasting team in a cave-in. Foreman wants to tunnel around, go after a more stable part of the vein. Don't know why he didn't—"

Valerica grabbed his arm. "He is there. In those tunnels."

Bill swallowed.

"No matter what you hear, no matter how fear compels you, *do not follow*. If I do not return, run to the surface." She handed him the extra candles and several matches, as well as Alina's rattle. "Flee as if your soul depends on it."

She expected an argument, but he only nodded. Perhaps he could sense it too, the smell of decay and the heaviness of the shadows. The walls were hot and damp, as though Valerica moved through the bowels of an enormous serpent.

Valerica drew her penny knife and jabbed the tip into her forearm. A thin line of blood tickled her skin.

A small spell, undetectable against the stench of magic that filled this place. She used it to draw the shadows close, wrapping herself in darkness. Her candleflame took on a blue hue, invisible to any but herself. She saw Bill searching, proof her spell had worked.

Her father had the blood of his victims to fuel his power. Valerica had only herself. But she had slipped past him once before, in Romania.

These deeper tunnels were rough and unfinished. Loose rock and dirt made her footing treacherous. She moved cautiously, testing the ground before each step.

She smelled the fire before she saw it, an oily smoke that dried her eyes and filled her nose with the scent of burned meat. She glanced behind to be certain Bill hadn't followed, then moved closer. The tunnel split, veering off at right angles. Her father was to the right.

Knife raised, she moved closer. A knife blow wouldn't kill him, but her blood gave the blade power. So long as she struck quickly, before he could defend himself, she had a chance.

"Hello, Valerica." The dry voice plunged her into despair. "Come, let me look upon my only daughter."

Running would only anger him. Praying Bill would have the sense to flee, she stepped around the corner. Her father was unchanged. He wore loose trousers and an embroidered, off-white shirt. His face was the color of old linen. Even his lips were bloodless. Dirty tangles of black hair hung past his shoulders. He reached for her, and his yellow nails were like claws.

Valerica raised her knife. "Where is Alina?"

He nodded to a broken rail car leaning against the wall, up the tunnel. Valerica could feel his power reaching for her, like insects burrowing through her skin. She ignored it, hurrying past the small fire to peer into the car. She jammed the pointed handle of the candle holder into the wall between the planks and reached for her daughter.

Alina lay naked, sprawled in a bed of dirt and straw. Blood crusted her round cheeks and pale chest. Valerica lifted her. Alina didn't respond, and Valerica felt like her own heart had stopped beating. She forgot about her father, about Bill, about everything but the tiny, bloody body in her arms.

"Open your eyes, child." She scrubbed desperately at the blood. The cuts were too shallow to have killed her. She fought to keep from shaking Alina. "Please." She smeared her own blood over the cuts, using all of her strength to try to break her father's spell.

Alina whimpered softly, and tears blurred Valerica's vision. "You're safe now," she said, slipping into Romanian. "*Tu eşti în siguranţă.*"

"You thought I would harm her?" asked her father. "Why would I hurt one with such potential?"

Valerica ignored him, rocking her daughter against her chest. For the first time, she saw the shadows farther down, partly concealed by a bend in the tunnel. Shadows resolved into bodies as she walked closer. Bill's lost blasting team, no doubt. Lost, but not to a cave-in. Still holding Alina, she approached until she was certain they were dead. The chests were torn open and the limbs broken. She turned away.

"What potential?" she asked.

He smiled. Decay had taken most of his teeth, and the ones that remained were brown, whether from rot or blood, she couldn't say.

"You've done well, Valerica," he said. "Can't you taste the power in her blood?"

She backed away. He had swallowed the blood of her baby. That was how he had pierced Valerica's illusion. She wanted to vomit.

"But you've done nothing to prepare her for the darkness," he went on.

"Alina is innocent." Unlike her father, whose birth caul had covered his face like a mask. Even as a babe, he had hidden his face from God.

He laughed, a sound of genuine amusement that pierced her with memories from her childhood. "The girl is damned, Valerica. I can smell the darkness enveloping her. *Your* darkness. *You* damned her, from the very moment you created her."

"No." It was Valerica who had cast the spell. The mark was on her soul, not Alina's. "She was baptized the week after her birth." Father Fanshaw had insisted. Elizabeth had borne a bastard child, and he wished to cleanse Alina of that sin. Valerica had been all too willing to comply, even if she wasn't permitted to attend the ceremony. "She is pure."

"I can save her from the hellfire of damnation. *We* can save her. Would you deny her that protection?" Her father scoffed. "You know nothing, Valerica. I have faced death. I know the fate you would lay upon her."

She shifted Alina to her left arm and pointed her knife at his throat. Before she could take a step, the wooden handle twisted. Splinters drove into her palm, and the knife dropped to the ground, warped by his magic.

"You should have fled," he said. "But I understand. It is difficult to abandon one's child, yes?" He clapped his hands. At his feet, the small fire flashed, and suddenly Valerica felt Alina sliding from her grasp.

Valerica tried to catch her, but blood had turned Alina's skin slick. Valerica's fingers clamped around Alina's leg, slipped. Alina wailed as she fell headfirst to the—

The fire faded. Valerica staggered back, nearly dropping Alina for real. She clutched Alina as tightly as she could without hurting her. The *strigoi mort* were adept at drawing nightmares from the mind. After so many years, Valerica was unprepared for such an assault.

Another flare, and Valerica stood in the desert again, holding the bloody razor. But where the coyote had been, now Bill lay butchered on the rocky earth. She tried to look away, but the vision followed.

"Ah, yes, I almost forgot." Her father smiled as this second illusion faded. He licked his lips. "The valiant brother. Your baby's blood calls to him as well. Shall I show him the fate which awaits him?"

Before Valerica could move, the fire brightened

again. This time Valerica was unaffected, but Bill's terrified screams echoed through the tunnel.

"You could fight me." He pointed a bony finger at Alina. "Her blood is quite potent, Valerica. Your broken knife should be more than adequate to slit her throat."

Valerica shuddered. She returned Alina to the rail car just as another nightmare took her. She pressed her forehead to the wall, eyes squeezed tight as she watched Elizabeth burn.

He knew she wouldn't hurt Alina, but he wanted her to fight. He had the strength of the dead miners, as well as his victims on the surface. Nothing Valerica did could overpower him. He would wear her down until she had no strength left. Then he would take her. Her and Alina both. Bill, he would simply kill. Or more likely, he would taunt Bill's mind until he took his own life.

Valerica grabbed her candle from the wall. Too shaken to stand, she bent down to kiss Alina's forehead.

"Let them go," she said. She rested her arms on the broken car. Alina reached up to tug a lock of Valerica's hair. Valerica smiled and squeezed Alina's hand, then brought her own fingers to the base of the candleflame, where the fire was hottest. "I'll come back to Romania with you. I'll do whatever you ask."

The calluses dulled the pain for a moment, but soon the fire burned deeper, searing the nerves. Her arm shook as the skin of her fingers turned red, then black. Blood began to drip from cracked skin.

"Valerica, you are already mine, as is your daughter. Do you truly think I would accept such a bargain?"

Valerica looked up. "No." She pinched her fingers together, screaming as the pressure sent new pain through her hand and up her arm. Collapsing against the cart, Valerica drew the fire into her own blood, then flung it away, down the tunnel, toward the broken bodies of the blasting team.

"*Bun rămas*, father." Farewell. Perhaps this time he would stay buried.

He stepped toward her, and then thunder and light filled the tunnel. Her tiny flame had been enough to light only a single stick of the dynamite carried by those poor miners, but when it exploded, it triggered the rest. A wall of wind toppled the rail car. Valerica caught Alina with her good hand and rolled, covering her with her body. A futile gesture that would do nothing against the collapse of the tunnel, but she couldn't help herself.

Stone and dirt rained down, but the tunnel held. Alina burrowed her head into Valerica's chest.

Her ears rang, and she could see her father striding toward her, but she was too battered to flee. Blood welled from his chapped lips. His whispers charged the air with magic far more powerful than Valerica could fight. Then he stopped. In a single heartbeat, rage transformed to fear.

"Valerica!" he shouted, his bloodshot eyes wide. He backed away.

Water had begun to rise. The explosion hadn't brought down the tunnel; it had cracked the floor, breaking through to the water below. The fire disappeared in a hiss of steam and smoke, and the tunnel went black. By the time Valerica pulled herself upright, the water was already to her waist.

"Where is the ladder?" Panic gave her father's voice an edge she had never heard before.

The sharp scent of magic overpowered the salty, muddy smell of the water. The planks along the wall began to burn. Her father held one hand in the fire, maintaining the spell as he frantically searched for the way out. Spotting the ladder, he waded away from the wall.

He had only taken a single step when a surge of water knocked his legs from beneath him. He lurched back, grabbing the wall with his fingers and straining to keep his head above the surface. Valerica could see terror on his face. For so many years he had evaded death, mocking the laws of God.

He reached for her, and his arm was little more than bone. "Daughter!"

"*Bun rămas*," she whispered.

A moment later, he was gone.

Any satisfaction she might have taken from his destruction was lost in her fear for Alina.

Valerica raised her daughter over her head, trying to get to the ladder, but the water was rising too quickly. Alina squirmed and batted Valerica's hands. Over the pounding in her ears, Valerica could make out the sound of crying.

"I'm sorry," Valerica said. Her father's fire died, and Alina began to scream. She wanted to hold Alina close, but the water was already to her neck. "You'll be with Elizabeth soon. You'll be safe."

She lost her balance. Salty water scalded her throat and face. She kicked as hard as she could, desperately trying to keep Alina above the surface. Her stomach convulsed, and her body tried to gasp and vomit at the same time.

Alina kicked and twisted. She started to slip away.

"Please, God!" Valerica tightened her grip as she floated through the darkness. "Elizabeth, help me."

She knew Alina would die. She had known it from the moment she touched the flame. But not alone. She would die with Valerica, safe from the darkness of *strigoi* magic. And she would go to be with Elizabeth. But still Valerica fought, desperate to give Alina every last second of life.

A hand grabbed her wrist. She tried to twist away. How could her father still survive? The water should have destroyed him. She pulled harder.

And then a quiet, frightened voice said, "I've got you, Aunt V."

Valerica stood with Bill and Alina behind the church, near the back of the cemetery. It was the first time Valerica had visited since Elizabeth's funeral.

She coughed, then flinched, but Alina continued to sleep. Her cuts had begun to heal, and she seemed unharmed, aside from a powerful fear of being alone in the dark. Valerica prayed that would fade with time. Until then, she and Bill were scrounging every extra candle they could get their hands on.

"I want it to be here," Valerica said. She reached out with her bandaged hand to touch the small gravestone. "With her."

Bill nodded. "Shouldn't you tell Father Fanshaw?"

"He wouldn't understand. He thinks I'm damned." She chuckled. If Father Fanshaw had known the truth, he would have burned her alive.

"You've got my word," said Bill. "I'll cremate you myself if I have to. God willing, that won't be for a good long time, though." He stared at the grave. "Are you really cursed? I mean, would you really come back like *him*?"

"I don't know."

"What about Alina?"

Valerica shook her head. "Alina is innocent. The potential may be in her blood. But the power must be taught, passed down from parent to child. No one will teach Alina while I draw breath."

"Parent to child," Bill repeated. "He called Alina your daughter."

Valerica took a deep breath. Bill must have heard the rumors, but he had never once asked about her relationship with Elizabeth. "Yes," she said. "Elizabeth's and mine."

"Oh." He pursed his lips. "That's mighty strange." Clearly he didn't understand. Just as clearly, it didn't matter one whit.

She laughed, tried to smother it so she wouldn't disturb Alina, and ended up coughing again instead. Alina's eyes blinked open. Valerica hummed an old folk song, bouncing Alina until her eyes eased shut once more. "Yes, it is," she whispered.

"She's got my mama's face, but your eyes," Bill said.

Valerica grabbed him and planted a quick kiss on the top of his head. "Thank you." Gingerly, she lifted Alina and passed her into Bill's arms. "She needs to be changed. I'll be back shortly."

Bill made a face, but didn't argue. As he took Alina back to their cabin, Valerica knelt and pressed her hand to the headstone of her lover. "Thank you."

She leaned forward to kiss the dusty stone. For the first time in years, she felt free.

She felt alive.

HANG TEN

Jean Rabe

Jean Rabe is the author of eighteen fantasy novels and more than three dozen short stories. An
avid, but truly lousy gardener, she tends lots of
tomato plants so her dogs can graze in the late
summer months. In her spare time (which she
seems to have less of each week), she enjoys role-
playing, board, and war games; visiting museums;
and riding in the convertible with the top down
and the stereo cranked up. Visit her web site at
www.jeanrabe.com.

"I DIDN'T CARE much for Tobago Cays." Jillian rested her knitting in her lap and
turned her head so she could better see her
companion.

He was stretched out on a lounge chair mere
inches away, muscles gleaming from a mix of

sweat and suntan oil. She licked her lower lip
when she stared at his abs. Not the proverbial
ounce of fat on him, she decided, pronouncing
him at a little more than eleven stone.

"In the Caribbean, right, Tobago Cays?" His
voice was rich and melodic.

She nodded. "The Cays are beautiful, certainly,
but they are basically deserted. No one lives there.
Just a stop for tourists, snorkeling and drinking
and . . ."

He raised a blond eyebrow and smiled, the sun
glinting off his polished teeth. "I would love to
be on a deserted island with you, Jillian."

"We just met." She blushed and picked up her
yarn. Today she knitted with a worsted weight
spun from an Angora goat, mohair the label read.
A natural fiber, the yarn was "breathable" and
slightly elastic, yet warm. She slipped the stitch
from the left needle to the right, passing the pre-
viously slipped stitch. "I prefer working with
cashmere," she said to change the subject. "Expensive, especially if blended with the hair of baby
alpacas and some merino wool. But it is soft to
the touch. Or silk. I like the feel of that. I've
worked with silk yarns a few times, blended with
mercerized cotton to make it stronger. But this
mohair, it was the only black skein in the ship's
stores. I forgot to pack yarn."

"When you left for your cruise to Tobago
Cays?"

"No, I had a cashmere skein with me then.
Black, of course. But I worked all the way through

that. I was in such a hurry to make this cruise on
time that I didn't pack one . . ."

"Andrew. Just call me Drew."

"Drew." She smiled sweetly.

"So you cruise often?"

A nod.

"So you just came from the Caribbean, Jillian?
From Tobago Cays?"

She let out a sigh, apparently unable to get
away from the subject of traveling. She considered
leaving to escape it, just getting up and going to
another deck. But he was too easy on her eyes.
"A few weeks ago, as part of a cruise I'd booked
with a group—a knitting circle from Honesdale.
We were in Barbados or Martinique first. No,
Union Island, I think. Those Caribbean spots are
all a blur. Took a charter catamaran from Union
Island as part of the package to get to Tobago
Cays." She used her forearm to brush a strand of
hair out of her eyes. "Oh, the colors were lovely,
a veritable kaleidoscope of turquoise, green, and
gold reefs, the sky and water so clear. Colors I'd
knit a sweater with some day. But . . . there was
not a single village to be seen on the Cays . . ."

"Andrew. Drew."

"Drew. St. Vincent and the Grenadines ap-
pealed to me more. I think my favorite stop on
that particular cruise was the little islands south
of Guadeloupe. Terre-de-Haut is only three miles
long, but it's an especially romantic spot, with a
long lane shaded by bougainvillea. Unfortunately,
I was there with knitters, all women, and there

wasn't a single man under retirement age on that cruise."

"Good thing I bumped into you on this cruise. I'll save you from boredom and bald guys."

She patted his arm, finding it firm and muscular. "I did have a good time, Drew, in Terre-de-Haut. The highlight? An old cemetery with tombstones dating back centuries. The names you could read—barely—showed the island's Norman history. Conch shells, they decorated the cemetery and were meant to honor the island's sailors who were lost at sea."

"Surely there were better things to occupy you than graveyards."

"Death . . . the method of death . . . interests me," she said almost too softly for him to hear. Louder: "I remember a charming little village with an art gallery and a superb restaurant in Terre-de-Bas. Illes des Saintes . . ." She said this with an appealing, but failed, attempt at a French lilt. ". . . was lovely. Eight islands. Volcanic dots, the guide called them. Pointe-à-Pitre had some excellent shops. The best fishermen in all of the West Indies are said to come from Illes des Saintes. I spent one morning just watching them haul in their blue nets—*filets bleus*. One late cloudless night I lay on the sand and looked up at the stars. There must have been a million, all sparkling like diamonds on a black velvet dress."

"Have you packed such a dress on this cruise? You could wear it to dinner this evening with me." Drew swung his legs around so he was sit-

ting and looking directly at her. His gaze inched
from the tips of her manicured toenails, up her
shapely brown legs and lingered on her flat stomach. Her string bikini left little to his imagination.
His eyes traveled up farther, resting again, then
finally locked onto her unblemished face. "You
will join me for dinner, won't you, Jillian? I'd hate
to dine alone on my vacation—the first real holiday I've taken in three years."

She didn't answer him right away, knitting several more stitches so she could get to the end of
a row. She favored a mix of plain stitches in the
Continental style, using circular needles.

"What are you making? A ski mask? It looks
like a ski mask, but you've left no holes for the
eyes or the mouth."

"It's something like a ski mask." She finished
another row then put the piece, yarn, and needles
in her beach bag. She rose from the lawn chair
and rolled her shoulders, working a kink out of
her neck. Then she stepped to the railing and let
the water spray her. "Drew, what time is dinner
tonight?"

His smile reached his eyes, and he quickly
joined her at the railing. Drew was tanned, even
all over from hours surfing in the sun. He'd explained that as a professional surfer he regularly
"hung ten" up and down the coast of California,
but also worked Hawaii once in a while. He
wasn't sure she was paying attention, and he intended to mention it all again at dinner and after-
ward, impress her by telling her about the size

and ferocity of the waves he'd ridden. Maybe he'd show her one of the pictures he brought, tucked in his duffel for the wow factor.

"The first dinner service is at eighteen hundred, Jillian. So . . . you are joining me?"

"I'd be delighted."

She wore a black satin dress with spaghetti straps. The material clung to her, stopping mid-way down her thighs. The black leather shoes she wore were toeless.

They had a table by a window, and though it was set for four, they were alone for the early meal.

"She wouldn't go eight stone." Jillian looked at a reed-thin waitress threading her way between tables. "Nine stone, at least," she said of a waitress who was considerably more voluptuous.

"So you travel a lot, Jillian?" Drew poured her a glass of wine, a Merlot from a Sydney winery.

"In the past few years, sure. I've had to—for work." The surfer was so easy to talk to. Too busy with work, she hadn't enjoyed a man's company in so many months.

"I travel for work, too, catching the best waves. California. Hawaii. You?"

"England, Australia, South Africa." She rattled the countries off like items on a grocery list. "Japan, South Korea, India, Pakistan, Iran, Egypt, Syria, Jordan, Lebanon, Kuwait, and Bangladesh."

"I'm impressed. And now with this cruise, Singapore and Malaysia. We dock in Penang tomor-

row." He waited until she nodded that the wine
was suitable, and he poured more. "So what sort
of work takes you around the world?"

Her shoulders sagged for just an instant, accompanied by a sigh. She usually didn't discuss what
she did for a living, but he was so very easy to
talk to. Besides, if she told him the truth, he'd
either be repulsed and leave her alone or accept
her profession and win a second date. Either
would be acceptable.

"I hang people."

Drew had been sipping the wine, but now sput-
tered it up. "S–s–sorry. Did you say that you
hang people?"

She ran her thumb around the lip of the wine
glass. It hummed, showing that it was made of
crystal. "Yes, I hang people." Jillian took a swallow of the wine and held it in her mouth. The
taste filled her senses. She studied him over the
rim of the glass. He seemed honestly curious,
though perhaps morbidly so. Earlier she'd put
him at a little more than eleven stones. But he
had broad shoulders and probably went an even
dozen. All of it muscle. "Look, Drew, mine is a
very old profession. The Persians invented it more
than twenty-five hundred years ago—for men
convicts. Women were strangled at the stake, for
decorum I suppose. And the English embellished
it, starting way back with the Saxons."

He cocked his head.

"The English, for especially heinous crimes, sentenced a person to be hanged, drawn, and quar-

tered. They were careful with the knot and length of rope so the criminal wasn't completely asphyxiated. They needed to spare him for the worse ordeals. Barbaric. A simple hanging is the only way to go. You see, hanging is spectacular, visual, and should serve as a deterrent. It has none of the blood a beheading or firing squad would bring, and it is inexpensive and relatively painless . . . if done properly."

Drew shuddered, but gestured for her to go on.

"I first practiced my craft in the States, learning it from my father, he from his father. My dad taught me the history of it, too. In Britain, more than fifty-five hundred were hanged between 1800 and the mid 1960s. In the United States, about thirteen thousand men and five hundred women were hanged from the early 1600s to the mid 1990s. The first man ordered hanged by a proper court of law in the States was Jose Forrni on December tenth in 1852. The second was William Shippard, hanged on July twenty-eighth at the Presido two years later. They said ten thousand came to watch that one. In 1859, Tipperary Bill— William Morris—was hanged. A little more than a year after that, James Whitford. John Devine, called The Chicken, killed James Crotty and was hanged in May 1878 for it. And . . ."

"You've quite the mind for details, Jillian." His hand shaking slightly, Drew refilled her wine glass.

"But there isn't enough work in the States anymore. Through the years fewer and fewer states allowed hanging. Delaware stopped the practice a few years back. New Hampshire permits it now only if a lethal injection can't be administered. And Washington state . . . an inmate has to ask to be hanged, otherwise he gets the needle."

"So it's like being laid off, huh? Can't hang folks in America."

She giggled at that notion, and at the wine which was going to her head. Yes, Drew was definitely a dozen delicious stone. "Hanging is still the most prevalent form of execution in all the world. More than a hundred people were hanged in about a dozen countries in 2002. A year later only a few less. In 2004 . . ."

"So you've been traveling the world just for work?"

She drained the glass and let him pour more. "For the past year I've been cruising to countries where they still hang people. Well, I had to fly into Botswana and Zimbabwe. And I passed on Iraq. Saddam ordered a lot of hangings, but I wanted no part of that. Some other Middle Eastern countries, I flew into them, too. Hard to cruise into a desert. Ah, all the places to go and people to kill." She leaned back in the chair as the waitress—nine and a half stones—delivered their lobster tails. "It's a respectable profession, Drew, hanging."

He took a piece of lobster and dipped it in butter. "Probably more respectable than mine. People think surfers are bums."

"Hang ten?" She giggled. "I've hanged a lot

more than ten. I think I hanged eleven just last year alone."

Drew nearly choked on the lobster. He washed it down with a big swallow of wine and waved a hand. "Would you bring another bottle?"

A passing waiter, hefty for his short frame at fourteen stones, nodded.

"This bothers you, doesn't it, Drew?" No second date, she sweetly pouted.

"N–n–no. I find it fascinating, Jillian. Truly." He was quick to take another bite of lobster and finish the last of the wine. He kept his gaze on the table setting. A moment later, the waiter returned with a new bottle. Drew didn't bother to sniff the cork. "Terribly fascinating, dear Jillian. D–d–do you throw the lever that sends them dropping through the gallows floor?"

She forked a small piece of the lobster and took a delicate bite. She closed her eyes and savored it, then took a second, this time dipping it in butter. How many people ordered lobster for a last meal, she wondered. "No, not at all, Drew. I couldn't stomach that, actually flipping the switch so to speak."

"But you said you hang people." The wine had helped Drew, his hand wasn't shaking any longer when he refilled both their glasses.

"I tie the knots and judge the length of rope. The rope is very important, whether you're working with a short or a long drop."

"Long drop?" He stuffed a large chunk of lobster in his mouth, followed by a forkful of baked potato dripping sour cream. He chewed quickly. "What's a long drop?"

Jillian ate thoughtfully before answering. "In Britain, 1872, William Marwood introduced what is called the long drop when Frederick Horry was hanged at Lincoln Prison. He maintained it was a more humane way to kill someone. See, the short drop had been used almost exclusively prior to that year." She took a few more nibbles, watching Drew, who seemed to be studying the pattern along the rim of his dish. "In a long drop, a convict's neck is broken because he falls a certain distance and then is stopped suddenly with a sharp jerk. The scientific principal behind it is that the falling body accelerates with a force of gravity. However, the noose is restricting the head. So when the rope plays out and the body stops, the noose—the knot at the side of the neck—delivers a blow. That blow, in conjunction with the downward momentum, ruptures the spinal cord. Instant unconsciousness results, followed by rapid death because the neck breaks. There's a certain amount of physics involved."

Drew had stopped eating.

"In later years, and I use this method now, a metal eyelet is slipped into the noose knot. It breaks the neck more assuredly. The knot is crucial, you know. Most are simple slip knots. But the traditional noose, which is the one my father favored, has five to thirteen coils, and these slide down the rope. He told me he always tried for a dozen because thirteen was just unlucky for him.

But that many coils . . . you tended to strangle the convict, instead of simply break his neck." She pointed to her own neck, under her left jaw. "I favor the coiled noose detailed in an old US Army manual. The head snaps back so quickly and with so much power that the spinal cord is severed between the superior and the top vertebra, basically slicing the connector to the brain stem."

Jillian finished her lobster tail, then the glass of wine. She felt warm and tingly and happy to have a dinner companion who seemed interested in her work. "In May 2005—oddly on a Friday the thirteenth—Shanmugam Murugesu was hanged by the long drop in Changi Prison in Singapore." She had trouble with the name, the wine making her tongue unwieldy. "I hope to participate in a hanging or two in Singapore while we're in port. But . . . you asked about the long drop and my work."

"Yes." Drew's word sounded more like a croak. Another mouthful of wine helped. "I did ask you about this drop thing."

She beamed. At the far end of the dining room a five-piece ensemble started playing a slow bluesy number. She swayed to the beat. "The long drop, It's the method I prefer, but I yield to whatever is practiced in the country I'm working for. It's all based on a person's weight. Remember that man who brought this bottle? The short one with the love handles? I figure he's two hundred pounds, or fourteen stone. I'd use an eight-foot length for a drop. On the other hand, the little waitress over there? The one that looks like she might have an eating disorder? I'd put her at a hundred pounds, tops, that's a little less than eight stone. She'd need a longer rope, say . . . ten feet. The smaller the person, the longer the rope. You'd need a rope about nine and half feet long for me, one about eight feet, four inches for you. It's all physics. If the rope's too long, you risk decapitating the convict."

"Physics." Drew refilled their glasses and declined selecting something from the desert tray.

"The rope itself makes a lot of difference. I always have a nylon cord with me, just in case. But I like to use a nice manila hemp about an inch in diameter. I ask for it to be boiled, because that takes the elasticity out of it. I try to make sure it's waxed or greased, coated with soap if that's all that's available. Makes the knot slide real easy."

"Easy." Drew gave Jillian the last of the wine. "Soap makes it easy." He swallowed hard and cupped his hands around his goblet. "Physics."

Jillian drank the wine a little too quickly, as she realized she'd revealed a little too much about her profession and feared Drew's lobster was going to make another appearance on his plate. Time to leave.

"I'm sorry, Drew."

"For what?" He carefully sat the glass on the table and fussed with his napkin. "You shouldn't be sorry. I asked."

"And I told you I had places to go and people to kill. Not the best dinner conversation." She pushed away from the table and shakily stood. "I think I'll get a cup of coffee and head back to my cabin, work on my knitting."

He stood too, a little more sturdy on his feet than Jillian. "That ski mask you're making . . . it really isn't a ski mask, is it?"

She shook her head and studied the tips of her leather shoes.

"It's a hood, isn't it? For whoever you're going to hang next."

"Perceptive, Drew the surfer."

"I might be a bum, but I'm not a stupid one."

She took a few steps and wobbled, and he came up to her side. "I'll get you back to your cabin, so you can get that coffee and finish your project. We make port tomorrow and . . ."

"And, yes, I've someone to hang there. I'd like to give him that hood."

The ensemble started an up-tempo jazzy piece as Drew and Jillian wended their way through the dining room, swaying from the wine and the gentle pitch of the deck, and a little bit from the music.

"Maybe I'll see you in port tomorrow," Jillian said.

Drew pulled his lips into a thin line. "Well . . . I . . . Jillian . . . I don't think so."

"I've turned off Mr. Twelve Stone." She let out a great sigh. "Not the first time."

They didn't speak again until she pointed to her cabin door and fumbled for the key. Her fingers awkward, he opened the door for her.

"I'd ask you in for a drink," she said. "But . . ."

"I think I've had too much already." He looked past her and saw the almost-finished hood laid flat on her bed, the coil of nylon cord on top of her nightstand. "A lovely lady you are."

She didn't detect the sarcasm in his voice.

Jillian tipped her face up and he gave her a polite kiss on the cheek. She tottered inside, surprised and pleased that he followed her after a moment and closed the door. "You're interested in that drink after all, Drew?"

He shook his head and pulled her close for another kiss, his hands inching up her arms then circling her neck and squeezing until she fell unconscious. Then Drew slipped on a pair of gloves he'd kept in his pocket and put the partially finished hood over her head. He slid the cord around her neck and coiled it twelve times before tying a slip knot. She was slight enough that he could force her body out the window. And he was strong enough that he could absorb her weight when she dropped nine and a half feet. He thought he would hear her neck pop, but the wind and the water was too loud, and the couple arguing in the next cabin was noisy.

He tied the end of the rope to the window latch, satisfied that it would hold. If he hadn't snapped her neck from the drop, she'd die within minutes of asphyxiation.

He knew a lot about hanging, too.

For the next several minutes he busied himself with wiping away all trace of his fingerprints. No one had seen him in the hall, so he'd get away with this one, too. A serial killer on vacation, Drew hadn't intended to strike at anyone during the trip. Jillian proved too tempting, though.

"I must go on more cruises," he said, as he glided out the door and down the empty corridor toward his own room. "This has been my best vacation ever."

Drew felt a rush of excitement and accomplishment.

He'd just hanged his tenth.

FEALTY

S. Andrew Swann

S. Andrew Swann in a long-time resident of Cleveland, Ohio, who has been writing profession-ally for the past fourteen years. He has published over sixteen novels under various pseudonyms, and this is his fourth short story publication.

THE HALL WAS long, dark, and cold. Stone vaults arched overhead, and windows high on the walls let in no light. A circle of black candles cast an unsteady light around the armored figure of Rossal de Molay. He knelt inside the circle, head down before the pommel of his sword, which he held cruciform before him. His armor creaked as he raised his head from his sword, to face the two men in front of him.

One man was dressed in the rich robes of nobil-ity. Jewels on his doublet glinted in the candlelight, and a smile emerged from a beard that was full, greasy, and black. The other was old and hairless and wore the plain black robes of a monk.

"Exceptional," said the noble. He took a step forward. "And, please tell, what is your name?"

De Molay paused, searching his memory for a response. Smile frozen, the man in the doublet cast a sidelong glance at the monk.

"I am Rossal de Molay, recently returned from Antioch." A strange slowness seemed to infect his mind. Too long in the heat of the desert, too long marching through the mountains, too long without enough food and water. Better men than himself had gone mad on the journey to the Holy Land. . . .

"And do you know who I am?" The noble's question broke the fragile chain of memory. Again de Molay had to pause, to think.

The monk muttered something too softly for de Molay to hear. Almost in response to the utterance, recognition came. "Of course, you are Robert, Duke of Normandy, heir to the Crown of England, my lord and master."

De Molay's lord and master shook his head and turned toward the monk. "You have surpassed my expectations."

The monk smiled as well and his eyes glinted like polished stones. "I am here to serve you. Lord . . . Robert." He turned toward de Molay. "And now that we have called him, so is he."

"Come forward." The noble gestured to de Molay.

De Molay stood, and stepped out of the circle. When his foot crossed the ring of candles, he had the briefest confusion. *How come I to be here? When was it I returned from the siege of Antioch?*

Doubt, however, was overcome by duty when Robert, Duke of Normandy, told him of a heresy brewing in their own lands. Robert, the Pope, and God were calling de Molay to service again.

The night was dark and moonless, the air still and cold. On the path ahead of him lay the town. Home to an evil as vile and godless as the Saracens that had claimed the Holy Land, as dangerous as anything he had fought in Antioch.

The villagers, to a child, held to the Cathar heresy.

To de Molay, Catharism was a novel sin. A doctrine that denied the Trinity, denied the physical presence of Christ on earth, and not only denied the divinity of the God of Moses, but equated Him with the Devil.

The Pope himself had called a new Crusade to wipe this abomination from the earth. And it was de Molay's duty to serve his Lord Robert, the Pope, and God.

He did not question the wisdom of sending one man against a whole village. Nor did he question his ability to do what he was called upon to do. He had seen what God's will could move men to do. He had, with his own eyes, seen a humble monk bear the spear that had pierced the side of Christ, and lead a few dozen starved and starving knights to defeat a fresh force that outnumbered them tenfold.

He had seen that battle, the last one at Antioch.

Anything was possible to someone touched by the hand of God. And after praying with Lord Robert's monk, de Molay knew he was carried in the palm of God, here to wipe the Cathar stain from the land.

He walked the snow-covered road, toward the village. As he walked, his boots melted the snow.

Small wisps of steam rose from his footprints.

De Molay quietly pushed in the door of the first house. Inside, a family slept, a man, a woman, a boy, an infant. He slew the infant first, to keep its cries from waking the others.

Only the woman managed to make a sound, a shocked intake of breath as de Molay's sword pierced her chest. She never exhaled.

De Molay's footprints smoldered as he left the small house. Where he touched the door on the way out, the bloody imprint of his gauntlet began to smoke.

He did not turn as the house erupted into flame.

De Molay could remember Antioch, the glorious awful day when the siege broke the walls, when thousands of Christian men, half-mad from months of heat and hunger, stormed through the streets of the city that had been home to the first Christian church. Knights slew men, women, children. . . .

De Molay had slain, men, women, children. . . .

By dawn, the walls had glistened with the blood of the slain. No one could walk except to step over corpses.

Cathars fell to de Molay's sword, three and five at a time. Buildings burned at his touch. As he passed, livestock fell to the ground, dead. His sword arm glistened with the blood of the wicked. He was all the plagues of Pharaoh, the Wrath of God personified. The population ran from him, and he followed, unhurried.

He laughed when he saw the women and children retreat to their unholy church, as if their false god could protect them from the sword of the righteous.

He laughed . . .

And stopped.

Something was wrong.

The church was the only stone building in the village. It was also the only building not yet burning. De Molay faced the church, a wall of flames at his back, his bloodstained mail steaming in the heat. His shadow danced ahead of him, across the graveyard, to paint the church's doorway with darkness.

The church was like nothing he had seen before. Peaked arches enclosed the doorways, and a circular window of colored glass glowed red above the entrance. Grotesque statues, monsters and skeletons, covered the exterior. Surely, this was a cathedral of hell itself!

But a statue of Christ and his apostles stood above the entrance.

A false Cathar Christ.

De Molay shook his head. When did someone build such a church? He was looking at decades of work. Could it take so long to suppress a heresy?

Yes. It could. The Infidel held Jerusalem for centuries before the Pope called for its liberation. The Pope was not God. The Pope could be fallible.

"No," de Molay whispered in a puff of fog. Such doubts were a direct assault on his faith. It was faith that kept him in motion, allowed him to act God's terrible will. . . .

God's will.

His memory was a fog. He had been in Antioch. How come he to be here, back in Normandy? His last memory before this evening was the miraculous charge from the gates of Antioch, led by the Holy Lance. He was there when the Saracen reinforcements were defeated. They had felt his sword.

He had felt theirs . . .

"How long?"

When did he return from battle?

Wrapped in the smell of smoke and blood, de Molay walked across the graveyard and knelt down at a marker. Heat from the fire had melted the snow from its surface. It was not ornate, the stone barely legible.

De Molay could read the name "Rachel" and the words "Year of our Lord 1205."

No, it was some pagan numbering. He knew he

had charged from the gates of Antioch on June 28, Year of our Lord 1098.

He walked over and brushed the snow from another marker.

1357.

Another.

1419.

He came upon the largest tomb, over which lay the worn stone figure of a knight set to rest in his armor. De Molay knew the arms carved into the petrified knight's shield, but he brushed the snow away enough to read "Rossal de Molay. d. June 28, 1098."

At his bellow, birds fell dead from the sky, the cross fell from the church's steeple, de Molay's tomb cracked in half, and the knight's statue crumbled.

Barred and locked, the doors to the church crumbled with one kick from his boot. The entry disintegrated in a cloud of smoke, brimstone, and falling embers. As he walked toward the altar, frescos of Christ and the stations of the cross turned black, paint and plaster bubbling and releasing the odor of burned hair and rancid oil.

Above the altar was an image of Christ more dire and horrifying than any he had seen before. Emaciated, like his comrades at Antioch, Christ's body was twisted in agony as blood flowed from the wounds. In the agonized face of Christ, de Molay could see the weight of his own sins.

This wasn't the Christ of a sect that did not

believe Our Lord had actually walked the earth as a man.

Crowded at the altar, under the suffering figure of Christ, were two dozen people. A priest stood before the frightened mob, holding a crucifix before him.

De Molay's armor burned and pulled at his body. He glanced at his hand and saw his fingers. They were long, black, and taloned, his mail gauntlet little more than tattered remnants.

"Begone, demon." The priest spoke in Latin. "The power of Christ compels you."

De Molay looked up at the priest. "And what Christ is it you refer to?" he answered, speaking church Latin himself.

The priest stared. Either he was surprised at de Molay's Latin, or surprised he spoke at all.

De Molay reached up and tore free the remnants of armor binding his chest. Underneath, his skin was scaled and black. "Do you speak of Christ, son of man and God? Born of Mary? Or is it the false Christ of the Cathars you implore?"

"Cathars?" the priest looked confused. "No Cathars have walked the earth for a hundred years."

"You acknowledge the Trinity, the God of Moses, and the Pope?"

The priest nodded.

De Molay removed his helmet, revealing a horned, goat-shaped head. "And Robert Curthose, Duke of Normandy?"

The priest shook his head, not understanding.

"Robert, who traveled to free the Holy Land."

"I don't know what you ask." The priest stammered in French and seemed on the verge of tears.

"Do you acknowledge fealty to Robert Duke of Normandy?"

One of the others from the village spoke, "Demon, we pledge allegiance to Phillip the Good, Duke of Burgandy."

"What crown does he serve?"

"Duke Phillip is allied with the English King Henry," the priest said.

"King Henry?" De Molay shook his head. His mind was a confusion of images, one set from a crusading knight whose only purpose was to serve his Lord and his God. The other set came from something much darker.

He could feel enormous leathery wings unfurl from his back and thought again, *how come I to be here?*

A great trickery it was. Even though he thought himself de Molay, even that part of his muddled mind knew it false. De Molay was dust outside the gates of Antioch, and whatever was of him was now in heaven or in hell, remembered only by the wrecked stone cenotaph outside this church. The false shreds of de Molay were falling off his mind just as the remnants of his armor fell from his distorted body.

"We have committed a great sin," he whispered. "Priest, you will hear my confession."

The priest shook his head, backing away, his face white.

The thing that had been de Molay for one long

bloody night, knelt before the priest so its gore-stained shaggy face was even with the priest's own. Its breath stank of an abattoir and its blood-red tongue left a trail of slime across its jagged teeth.

The thing reached and took the crucifix from the priest with a long-taloned hand. "Hear my confession, speak the mass, give communion. Do this because it is your duty as a servant of Christ."

"But—"

"Hurry, I must be shriven," the demon pushed the priest toward the altar. Women screamed, and the villagers scrambled toward the doors. The demon ignored everyone but the priest.

The priest pushed himself up, next to the altar.

"Please," said the demon, "I beseech you in the name of God, while I can still claim de Molay's repentance as my own."

After a moment, the priest approached the altar and, with shaking hands, reached for the host and the wine.

Below the great vaults, the high windows began to show a ruddy light. "Dawn is approaching," spoke the nobleman with the jeweled doublet and the greasy beard.

"Worry not," responded his monk. "It will be compelled to return, just as it was compelled to serve you."

"Is it enough time?"

"For what? To destroy a single Burgundian village? We are talking of a sergeant from the deepest circle of hell. Less than a heartbeat and your traitorous peasants are less than ash."

"Then why hasn't it returned?"

"It walks with the pace of a man now."

The nobleman shook his head and turned to face the circle inscribed on the floor before them. "If I hadn't seen such with my own eyes, I would not credit such a thing."

"You are troubled."

"Would you count me sane if I was not?"

"Do you doubt the rightness of your cause?"

The noble glared at the monk, "Was it not you who first told me that God himself had taken a lowly farm girl and led her to break the English siege of Orlèans?" He shook his head. "When such forces walk the land, how can I but solidify my service to the French crown?"

"You are on the side of God, My Lord."

The noble shook his head, "Our servant was not from God."

"Wasn't he? The demon is but a vessel."

"But how can a centuries-dead knight control such a being?"

"The same way demons have possessed men for millennia."

"But a man possessing a demon?" he looked up at the dawn light in the windows. "What if the spell is broken? What if this sergeant of hell throws off our yoke?"

"Only faith can break such bondage. Whose faith could free such a beast? Whose faith would?"

At the monk's word, the great doors to the hall

blew open with a crash. The candles around the circle blew out. The monk and the nobleman turned to face the doors. Sunlight streamed in, causing both men to squint at the silhouette in the doorway.

"Who's there?"

A deep voice seemed to come from everywhere. "Whose faith indeed?"

The nobleman took a step back, knocking over a candle. "Who are you?"

"You called me Rossal de Molay."

The nobleman shook his head and grabbed his dark-cloaked companion. He pushed the monk out in front of him. "No, take him. It was his doing. He bewitched me."

The old man fell to the ground. As he pushed himself up, he spat. "Bewitched by your own desire for power, more like it."

The silhouette walked into the hall, its wings broad and golden. Its skin emitted a white light that hurt the two men to look at. He reached down and cupped the monk's chin.

"I am not the one you should fear," it said.

The nobleman shook his head and the glowing apparition lifted the monk to his feet.

"I had fallen, turned from God, cast into the lake of fire with my Master." The apparition reached out a glowing hand and caressed the nobleman's cheek. "You gave me enough of a soul that I could truly repent and pledge my fealty to God."

Both men stood in the circle, shaking.

"I offer you the same chance you gave me." The apparition waited, but both men stared, speechless. When no response was forthcoming, the apparition turned to leave.

"How could this happen?" the nobleman whispered, breaking his stunned silence.

"Perhaps a splinter of de Molay's faith touched it," the monk shook his head, "if a demon can lead a man astray . . ."

The nobleman gasped as a ring of fire erupted from the circle. He spun around, patting his clothes, which were beginning to smoke. "What, you said that we had nothing to fear—"

The apparition did not turn around. "You have nothing to fear from me. I might have shriven you, if you had possessed the faith to ask." The men began to scream as the flames began to lap at their flesh. "My former master is the one you pledge fealty to now. And he did not care to lose my service."

The angel, awash with a light white and terrible in its brightness, walked away from the pyre.

BREIA'S DIAMOND

Cat Collins

Cat Collins began writing at the turn of the century. She lives in the beautiful north of New Zealand with her husband and the youngest of their three sons. "Breia's Diamond" is her first short story. Her first novel, *Sleeping Dragons*, was published in November 2005, and two further books in the series await the "right" publisher.

BREIA GROANED and squeezed her eyes shut. Her mouth tasted like the inside of her boots. She rubbed a throbbing temple and groped beside her for the tumbler of water. Her sword slid away from her questing hand, knocked from its always-ready position to clatter to the floorboards. The sound of shattering glass signified the tumbler's fate. She cursed, her tongue thick and clumsy in her dry mouth. A gentle snore beside her had her eyes open in a heartbeat. Squinting in the early light, she turned and focused on her companion.

Tagrin. She sighed in relief. Fellow mercenary and occasional, second-choice bedmate. At least he was clean. She tried to recall the events of last evening but was quite unable. No matter. If the previous occasions were anything to go by, he had been adequate—but not memorable. She leaned across his muscular chest and stole his waterflask. He grunted and opened a dark eye.

"No more. I'm done with you. You turn me inside out."

She scowled and kneed him in the ribs on her way out of the blankets. "I wasn't inviting you. You're hardly Terrano." She drained his flask, then tossed it at him.

"That's harsh, Breia, truly harsh." He rubbed his eyes and yawned. "I admit I am a great disappointment to my mother. The sun doesn't shine out of my arse. Besides, I didn't hear you complaining."

Breia dressed quickly. "In truth, Tag, I don't remember. You may have been magnificent." Buckling her sword belt, she glanced through the dingy window and cursed. "I'm late."

"For what?" Tagrin pulled up the coarse blankets and folded his arms over his chest. His bottom jaw jutted, and his close-set eyes gave him the appearance of a powerful ape that Breia had once seen in a merchant's caravan.

"Terrano. I'm riding with him today. We drew targets in adjoining towns."

Tagrin rubbed his stubbled jaw. "Lucky you. Be sure to wear your eye-shields. If he bends over, you'll go blind."

Breia snorted. "It's business, Tag, don't be bitter. You know how it goes—places to be, people to kill." She picked up her mantle and stood before the door. "Where're you headed today?"

"Crevice Pass." Tagrin sat up and scratched his chest, grimacing at the light that fell across his face. "After breakfast. By Carrannah's Tits, my gut needs food."

Oily nausea in her own stomach had Breia nodding in agreement. She pulled her fingers through her hair and wove it into its usual short braid. "See you on our return, then. Give my love to the rest of the lads."

"I thought you already had," Tagrin muttered.

"Not all of them, Tag," she said sweetly. "Only you, because you don't keep me awake too long." She blew him a smacking kiss and dodged the pillow he threw at her. Chuckling, she descended the narrow staircase and followed her nose to the inn's breakfast table.

Hot ham and egg scramble packed into a rye trencher seemed the perfect antidote to her hangover. She tossed two coppers to the pimply serving girl. Exiting the shabby inn, she blinked at the glare of winter sun on the whitewashed walls that lined the street. Her head still ached, and probably would all morning. She sighed, bit into her breakfast, and turned west, heading uptown.

The sun warmed her back as she strode toward

her rendezvous with Terrano. She smiled around a mouthful of buttery eggs, recalling Tagrin's scornful remark. That the sun shone from Terrano's arse was not true. She knew that for fact, having bedded him on many occasions.

The squat shabbiness of their current quarters glowered at her from the shadow of the tall tower it hunkered beneath. Two horses stood tethered outside the structure. Breia's cheeks heated. Both mounts were ready, bedrolls and bags attached behind the saddles, their breath misting in the cool air.

"Damn," she muttered, patting Ashen's warm rump in passing. The gray whickered and rolled an eye at her. Terrano leaned in the doorway holding a steaming mug in one hand and his gauntlets in the other. He sipped the hot brew, his brows raised over eyes the color of a deep lake in summer.

"Glad you could make it." He tapped the leather gloves against his thigh, his gaze steady and appraising. Breia chewed her cheek and turned toward the gray gelding, checking the animal's girth straps. Cinched and ready. She dropped the saddle flap and rubbed the animal's neck.

"Thanks," she said diffidently. "I, uh . . . sorry I'm late."

Terrano drained the mug in long swallows and tossed the dregs at his feet. He wiped his mouth and shrugged. "We should go." His eyes glinted.

Devilry, or irritation? The man was so damned hard to read. "So. Did you have fun?" He set the mug down and pulled on his gauntlets, his steady blue gaze now intent on his preparations.

"I did, thanks. You?" Memory of the previous evening filtered back. Breia's skin goose-bumped. Tagrin's blighted Jem-Jem Juice. The fiery orange liquor had fogged her brain, leadened her limbs, and lent seduction to her tongue. Terrano had declined her advances. He always did when she was drunk. Angry, she had stalked away, arm in arm with Tagrin, wearing her tattered dignity as a shield against Terrano's rejection.

He grinned suddenly, the usual lopsided grin that brought a sunrise to his face. "It was a quiet evening, Bree. Always is when you take yourself somewhere else." She watched his hands while he fastened his travel cloak. Her head ached in dull throbs. Terrano mounted his tall roan and sat waiting. She hauled herself aboard Ashen, still not meeting Terrano's eyes.

Terrano clicked his tongue. The roan sidled past Breia and broke into a canter. She sighed and kicked Ashen to a disgruntled trot, watching Terrano's straight back. She caught up with him just before he reached the Necromancer's tower. He glanced up at the tall structure, then at her. His horse snorted when he pulled it to a stop.

"Do you know what it is?" His gaze rested atop the tower. One hand shaded his eyes.

Breia reined in and shook her head. "He's taking his time to build it, whatever he means to use it for. The foundations alone seemed to take forever to put down."

A faint furrow appeared between Terrano's brows. "Strange. There's nothing inside, you know. No floors, no stairs, nothing."

Breia stared at the odd tower. Two doors, one at the bottom, one at the very top. Between the two doors, one massive window the height of several men, crisscrossed with iron bars. She shrugged. "Mages are strange men, and Necromancers the strangest of them. Pays well, though, eh?" She grinned. "He can be as odd as he likes if he keeps the coin coming."

"And makes good on his promises," Terrano added, kneeing his roan to a trot. Breia kept pace.

"There's seven of us to answer to should he try a double-cross. Tag'd rip the man's arms off and beat him with them, and I don't think Hex or Del would let him off too lightly either." Breia frowned. "D'you think he's planning to cheat us?"

"He'll owe us all a fortune when the list's done. It's likely he'll try to stiff us for the rest."

Breia chewed her cheek. The list was two thirds complete. Only one more page of targets remained. Carefully allocated to each of them by the Necromancer himself, each "target" had proved to be a ne'er-do-well: a drunk, a bum, a down-and-outer with no hope and no light in the eyes. "What about his tower? Why build it if he's planning to disappear once we've done the job? Besides, he's already paid us a third of the coin."

A sudden thought sent a shiver down her back. "What's to stop him hiring another band to get rid of *us*?"

Terrano's eyes flashed azure in the brightening light. He grinned another sunrise and tapped his left ear. "Simple, Bree. The Diamond Dogs are the best. That's why he sought us out, and that's why another band would think no more than twice before turning down such a dangerous assignment." He winked at her. The five kiffs in his earlobe winked also, reflecting the pale sun. Four studs of metal, and the fifth, a brilliant white diamond. Of the seven in their band, only Breia did not yet wear the high kiff. She fingered her own earlobe. Four kiffs: copper, bronze, silver, and gold. The last piercing still stung. She had come to the gold only last month, but Terrano spoke true. She smiled wryly.

"The best," she agreed, kicking Ashen to a canter. Leaving doubt and the mysterious tower behind, they rode on.

By the time they reached Riverton, Breia's stomach howled with hunger and her rear felt like a slab of stone. "Carannah's Tits," she muttered, standing in her stirrups and rubbing her saddle-numbed backside.

Terrano chuckled, turning his horse toward a public ostlery. "A beautiful round arse like yours, and it's not a good cushion?"

Breia bared her teeth at him. Ashen's iron-shod hooves clanged on the stone of the yard. She slid from her saddle with a groan of relief, and handed the reins to the ostler's lad. A tossed silver piece brought a grin to his clear-skinned face. "A good rubdown, mind." Breia arched a brow at the boy. "And the *best* grain, not the leavings."

Terrano leaned forward, resting his forearms on the pommel of his saddle. The roan shifted beneath him and snorted. The fading sunset sent a last wash of golden light over his face, then died, casting his features into shadow. "Until we meet again, Princess." He touched a finger to his forehead and kneed the horse from the yard.

"The road home?" Breia called after him.

His teeth showed white in the gloom. "The road home," he said over his shoulder, his voice and image fading into the dusk.

"Take care," she whispered, then turned her thoughts to her night's work.

Later, slouching beside a midden heap up to her ankles in foul-smelling, freezing mud, Breia cursed the unpredictable nature of these assignments. She shifted her position, hoping she needn't wait much longer. Her fingers warmed in her armpits and her breath steamed in misty whorls before her face. The Necromancer's scrying told him where the target would be—*when* the target would arrive was not so easily predicted. This night, she knew that a man dressed in russet would pass this way: a man bearing a pauper's candle-lantern and wearing a distinctive hat of red hessian.

A night bird called. Breia held her breath at a sudden rustle behind her. A small rodent sprang from the midden heap and scurried past her. A large shadowy form swooped from a rooftop and flew after the movement, ghosting on silent wings. She was only distracted for a moment, but long enough for the approaching man to notice her, to check his hurried progress through the moonlit lane. She cursed, tightened her fingers on the knife she held, and stepped from the shadows.

It happened quickly. Moving with practiced ease, Breia stepped into the man's path. His breath steamed in long streams, his eyes wary. He raised his candle-lantern and opened his mouth to speak, but Breia laid a finger to her lips and shook her head. A small frown crossed the man's face. One step, one thrust. Breia's longknife entered the man's belly, tore up through his gut, and found his heart. She held the knife firm. He grunted. The frown melted into surprise, then faded. Breia saw death-knowledge in her victim's eyes even as blood ran from his mouth. A last choking breath sprayed her face with wet warmth.

"Tits!" She spat and wiped her mouth against her shoulder. Heat flowed over her hand, warmed her fingers. When the man sagged against her and life faded from his eyes, she let the body fall. Still allowing no feeling, no reaction, she listened to the night. No sound other than the light wind. One last task. She bared the man's neck. With quick strokes of her knife point, she scratched a symbol into the skin beneath his hair. Blood oozed, dark and slow, from the death-mark. Number eight. Two to go, and the list would be complete. The band would collect their promised payment from the Necromancer and move on.

Breia slunk away from the midden heap, keeping her thoughts from the stink of blood and the sound of flesh riven by steel. Her penance would be paid in the long hours before dawn. Dead men's fingers crawled along her spine at the prospect. Damn Terrano. She could have used his solid presence in her bed this night. Even Tagrin, bless his dark heart, kept the specters at bay. Touching cold fingertips to the burn of the golden kiff in her earlobe, she entered the empty lane behind the ostlery and slipped through the tackroom door.

Ashen's whiskery muzzle probed Breia's neck with warm and moist insistence. The horse lipped at her ear. Opening gritty eyes, she pushed him away and yawned. He blew gently and stamped a hoof in the packed straw. Breia pulled her blankets closer beneath her chin.

"By the Divine Witch, I hate cold." She extended a reluctant arm from her bedroll, clutched her mantle, and drew it beneath the blankets, only succeeding in entangling herself in the fine-woven garment. "Tits!" She stood and wrapped the mantle around her shoulders, shivering and goosebumped in the chill morning. Blasted alchemists. Couldn't they have worked a little heat magic into the robe? Her "Mantle of Exclusion," gifted to her by a Sister of the Flame of Fianna in return for services rendered, had yet to be put to the test for any of its purported protections. Still, she wore it in the hope that it *would* deflect weapons and magic. And besides, its ability to conform to the wearer's shape and size made it a damnably flattering garment to wear. It also hid armor plates and weapons alike beneath its clever folds.

The night had taken its toll, as usual. Fatigued and irritable, Breia saddled Ashen and made a clandestine exit in the dawn's peach glow. Breakfast could wait until she reached the first town on the road home. As well to be away before the frozen russet mound was discovered beneath the dusting of snow that had fallen overnight. A layer of innocence over a dark deed, she reflected. *Carrannah forgive me. These killings lay like stones on my soul.* She heaved a sigh. Two more. Then she would return to good, honest mercenary hire-outs. No more knifing desperates in the dark. No more nights of relived killings, of eyes leaking life and light.

And yet, the Necromancer's coin had been too good to refuse. A small fortune, in fact. Enough to ensure a comfortable future. After all, a bluff woman such as herself was unlikely ever to know the comforts of the marriage bed. As if she had need of a man. She had always provided for herself, and among her fellow mercenaries she had found acceptance, although it had been hard-won. A few cracked heads had convinced them she was a worthy fighter and not an easy mark. She grimaced and tightened numb fingers on the reins.

Except for Terrano. He had observed her struggle for acceptance, for respect and a place in his small band. Observed with his usual amused indifference and kept his distance.

Kicking Ashen to a canter, she shook her head. Terrano was not averse to sharing her bed, but he never sought her out. It was always she, drawn like a moth to a bright flame, who instigated their trysts. She sighed, her breath misting only a little in the warming air. She knew his reputation. Tagrin had delighted in passing it on. *He used to hire out to the Temple Tribunes in Tamisia, until they found him humping a priestess or two. Tribs didn't take too kindly to that. Ran Terrano out of the last five northern regions he tried to work in.* Similar stories abounded. *Don't be getting fond of him, Bree,* Tagrin had warned her.

Breia put all thoughts of Terrano aside. That he was under her skin was an unfortunate fact, but she would dwell on it no longer. Carannah's Tits! Was she not a fine mercenary? Self-made and already wearing the golden kiff? She shortened rein and dug her heels into Ashen's ribs, sending the gelding into a full gallop. The road was straight and even, and her irritation was soon lost in the exhilaration of speed.

By midday, Breia's rump numbed once more. "Well, Ashen my friend," she murmured, rubbing the gelding's neck beneath the slate-gray mane. "My backside tells me it's time for a stop." Deciding to seek a hot tavern meal and perhaps an ale,

Breia turned Ashen away from the main route that would bypass the next village.

Before they had reached the village way-stone, the sound of a fast rider made Breia's spine crawl. Always, after these missions, she feared discovery. Hunching into her mantle, she drew up the hood. Ashen plodded on, his head bobbing in a steady cadence with each step. Breia stared straight ahead, her pulse loud in her ears. Within the mantle, her hand crept to the hilt of her shortsword. Ashen rolled an eye at the newcomer and whickered in greeting. Breia glanced sideways. The red-speckled muzzle of Terrano's roan set her fears to rest.

"Good hunting, Princess?" Terrano's familiar grin seemed a little strained, and fatigue shadowed his lake-blue eyes.

"Of course," she said airily, then frowned. "What happened? You look like shit."

The grin faded. He ran a hand through his hair. "I'll be glad when the list's done, is all." He kicked the roan to a trot. "Come on. It's festival day in these parts. Hare pie and venison steaks, and any pastries you care to name. Hungry?" The grin reappeared, but did not touch his eyes. Heartened at the prospect, Breia followed.

A short time later, they sat outside a busy tavern, claiming a corner of a long table. Breia ate a hearty stew of mutton and vegetables. Terrano dipped coarse bread into the pink juices that ran from a generous portion of roasted deer haunch. "Today is the Eve of the Rising Flesh," Terrano murmured, and winked at a girl whose coy glances had not escaped Breia's notice. The maiden dimpled at him, licking her fingers clean of grease.

Breia snorted. *"That's* the festival?"

Terrano shrugged. "It's only a name. Same function as May Day serves in the north."

"Fertility rites and associated trysting?" Breia raised her brows.

"We should stick around." Terrano spoke around a mouthful of venison. "There's no hurry to get back, and festival night's always entertaining."

Breia stared. "For who?"

Terrano nudged her gently. "Ah, Bree. I could use a little diversion this night." He raised his tankard and took a long swallow of ale, his eyes roaming the growing crowd in the village square.

"You want me to leave you here?" She scooped up the last of the stew with a crust of bread. He considered her. She washed the bread down with cool ale. "You're staring," she muttered, licking her fingers before wiping them on her breeches. A faint line appeared between his brows. He looked away.

"Go if you want." His diamond kiff glinted in the wintry sun. His eyes rested on the girl who had caught his attention earlier. Following his gaze, Breia sighed.

"Festival sounds like fun, Tee, but I don't want to . . . get in your way." She drained her tankard and rose from her seat, wanting to kick his licentious backside.

He frowned. "Stay, Bree. Have a little fun." He waved a hand at the crowd of young people heaving a gaudy pole upright in the square. Blessed Carannah! Breia gawked, then chuckled. The wooden pole, painted and beribboned, was crudely carved at its tip. Still grinning, Breia watched while several young men secured the pole. Maybe she *would* stay and ingest enough liquor to ensure an untroubled night's sleep.

A spell-hawker approached, selling charms and potions to the tavern's patrons. "A philter to ensure your potency tonight," he proclaimed, thrusting a packet at Terrano. The small man winked at Breia. "Perhaps he won't need it with a lusty woman like yourself in his bed, eh, my dear? But if he does, it's only four coppers—three to a beauty such as yourself."

Irritated by the hawker's misplaced flattery, Breia pushed away the offered philter. "I have no need of your spells, good fellow, and my friend here can answer for himself."

Terrano chuckled and declined the packet with a wave of his hand. "As you so rightly pointed out, spell-maker, my lady's beauty is all the potion I need." He pushed himself to his feet and tossed the man a few coppers. "Take yourself to the lass over there by the well. The one in green. Give her my regards and your prettiest ribbons." He turned to Breia, his expression suddenly unreadable.

"And my apologies. I won't be seeing her to-night." His mouth firmed. The spell-hawker grinned and left them with a sly wink at Breia.

"My *lady?*" Breia arched her brows at Terrano and folded her arms over her chest. Terrano's eyes hardened. He grasped her elbow, steered her away from the table and shoved her against the tavern wall.

"You know, Breia, for a moment I forgot who I was talking to." His voice was low and hard. "I saw a beautiful woman, forgetting that beneath that elegant mantle lies a breastplate of hardened leather and a sword that could take off my head." His eyes glittered like blue gemstones. "For a moment, I saw a lady, not a killer."

Breia stiffened. She shook off his hand and stabbed a finger at his chest. "I don't need your pity, nor your pretty lies."

He blinked. "I've never lied to you." His brows drew into a frown. "For all your miscreant ways and unusual life path, you *are* beautiful." He stepped away from her.

Breia stared at him, daring him to laugh, to admit the jest, the tease. He only tilted his head a little and returned her stare. Beautiful? She threw the mantle back from her shoulders, baring the scarred leather armor, the glint of knives and the comforting presence of her shortsword. "Let's not fool ourselves, eh?" she whispered.

The shadow returned to Terrano's eyes. Before he could answer, a collective cheer rose from the burgeoning crowd behind them. It was late afternoon, and much ale had flowed. Several youths hoisted lasses onto their shoulders. The girls shrieked, skirts askew and pale limbs wrapped around their mount's shoulders. A race ensued. The crowd whooped encouragement while the sturdy lads strove to outdo each other, flushed and panting beneath their giggling burdens.

Breia leaned against the tavern wall and folded her arms. The hardened leather pinched her armpits and flattened her breasts, but it was a familiar discomfort. The breastplate did not accommodate the female form. Beautiful? She had hair and eyes the color of mud and a mouth that grimaced more readily than it smiled. She snorted under her breath and scuffed a booted heel into the packed earth. Either Terrano had questionable judgment, or he was muddle-sighted.

He stood with his back to her, his arms crossed over his chest. His longsword glinted in the late sunlight, its hilt resting between his shoulder blades. Wanting to restore their usual, easy peace, she reached out one foot and poked him in the back of the knee. "Hey." He didn't turn. The race ended amid much cheering and applause. The winners were liberally doused with ale, and the girls dismounted from their steeds with as much decorum as they had managed to retain. "Come on, O complimentary one. I'll buy you a drink. May as well catch up with the rest of them, hm?" Breia elbowed him in the ribs on her way into the tavern.

*　　*　　*

Much later, the horses attended to, Breia and Terrano had indeed caught up with the villagers. Twilight settled over the village. Lively music played, and old and young swung partners in dance. The phallic pole stood resplendent among the revelers, its paper ribbons fluttering in the heat of bonfires lit around the square.

Breia lounged against the tavern wall, having lost her place at the long table. She sipped warmed wine and closed one eye to focus on Terrano. Challenged to an arm-wrestling match, he had assessed the risk and made a substantial bet. The raw youth who had challenged raised coin from his friends and matched Terrano's stake. Others had joined in the betting, and now a noisy crowd surrounded the table where the combatants had claimed space.

Breia knew his technique. Had laid a bet of her own. Terrano's lean form belied his strength. If he put coin on the line, it was fairly certain he'd win. Two years of riding with the Diamond Dogs had taught her much. His face contorted in a fierce grimace, and his biceps bulged. She grinned and took another swallow of spiced wine. Terrano's opponent gave a mighty roar. Terrano twitched, a slight release of his shoulder. Breia closed her eyes and counted to three. Groans and cheers erupted from the watchers. She grinned and looked again. The massive youth rubbed his arm and shook his head ruefully. Terrano collected his winnings and tossed the defeated man a silver coin, to the loud approval of the crowd. With only a slight weave, he made his way to Breia.

"Yours, I believe." He dropped two gold coins into her palm. "I thank you for your faith in me." She inclined her head in gracious acknowledgment. Before she could suggest utilizing the winnings on a night in the comfort of an inn, the music stopped playing. In the sudden quiet, a rhythmic drumming began. A slight shift in the direction of the breeze blew smoke across the square. In the haze, a group of young women gathered. All wore mantles of bright-dyed wool, and slow-stepped around the pole in time to the drums.

A gradual hush fell over the square. Terrano took the goblet from Breia and drank, watching the ritual. The drumming stopped. A lone piper began a high, sweet melody. The girls formed a circle, moved to the edges of the crowd and began a weaving dance in and out of the line of young men who stood at the front. A fiddle and a flute joined the piper, and before long the drums began again. At the full crescendo of the music, the girls unfastened their mantles and each singled out a lad. The music stopped abruptly. Mantles flew. As each gay mantle settled around the shoulders of a young man, the girls stepped away, hands clasped behind their backs and eyes downcast.

The lads glanced around the crowd. Some grinned, some looked uncomfortable. One tall lad pulled the mantle from his shoulders and handed it back to the girl beside him, grinning awkwardly and shaking his head. Disappointment filled her round face, but she shrugged and smiled. Several others were similarly rebuffed, and the crowd groaned in sympathy with each returned mantle. When the youth closest to the tavern reached up with deliberate slowness and fastened the yellow mantle across his chest, the girl beside him threw her arms around his neck and kissed him with great exuberance. The remaining youths also accepted their mantling, and the musicians began a lively dance.

Terrano rolled his eyes. "Fools! Going so meekly to the mantle. Hardly more than boys, yet committing themselves to support a wife—and a babe before the year's out." He shook his head. "No experience of life, nor their options. Blind fools."

Breia pursed her lips and glanced at him sideways. "What of the warm bed and the home, to say nothing of the care and affection? Mantling is good for a man, especially these village lads. Most of them will live here all their lives."

Terrano snorted. "Or run away to sea when the squalling of babes and an acid tongue greet them each evening. I'll settle for an occasional warm bed." The beginnings of a smile curved his mouth at the corners. He leaned closer, tickling Breia's ear with his breath. "Your bedroll or mine, Princess?" His hair brushed her cheek. He smelled of leather and wood smoke, and she leaned into him, already responding to his invitation. Jingling the gold coins in her pocket, she took his arm and tugged him toward the inn beside the tavern. "No bedrolls tonight," she breathed in his ear. "Let's get *really* comfortable."

He grinned and followed her into the welcoming pool of lamplight that spilled from the inn's doorway.

Two weeks after Breia and Terrano's joint sojourn, all of the band except Keenan had completed their lists. Breia's last kill still haunted her. A ragged and pathetic young whore, dying from her disease, a dead infant lying in filth at her side. Wrestling with her conscience, Breia had taken several days to complete the mission. Eventually, she smothered the girl with her own greasy pillow and vomited outside the shack until her eyes watered and bile dripped from her nose. Memories of the thin body twitching beneath her hands filled her nights with shame.

But it was over. The list was done, her future secured. Breia ran her fingers down the blade of her sword. She poured a dipper of water onto her whetstone and began the careful process of honing the weapon.

"Keenan's back."

Lost in her thoughts and the scrape of metal on stone, she started at the voice behind her. Terrano dropped to the bench beside her and leaned his elbows on the scarred table behind him. "We can be gone from here in the morning." He scanned the worker's quarters where they had lived for the past few months. Breia followed his gaze. The low building had been an adequate shelter in which to pass the winter—more of a bunkhouse than a home, but they had seen worse. A wide hearth set into the back wall was seldom without a blaze, and a cook pot hung close to the fire, bubbling with the evening's offering. Rabbit with onions, according to the aroma that filled the quarters. She tested her blade with her thumb.

"So where to next? Any ideas?"

Terrano grunted and stretched out his legs. "Tag's making noises about the northern lands."

"And you?" Breia kept her eyes on her sword. "I heard tell you were run out of the north. Something to do with the Temple Tribunes, I believe."

He narrowed his eyes. "So Tag talks in his sleep, does he?" She squinted down the length of her blade and frowned. Terrano chuckled. "The Tribs don't last long. The Temple is a hard master. I doubt I'd be recognized now."

"And the priestesses?" Breia sheathed her sword and tucked the whetstone into her pack.

He sighed. "Gentle does, with the curves of the Divine Witch herself."

"And Divine Carrannah's lusty appetite for pleasure, I hear." Tagrin's rumble announced his arrival. "Keenan scored. We're to gather tonight at the tower." He pulled a chunk of rabbit from the simmering pot and blew on it. "Did you see the latest development?" The meaty chunk waved in the direction of the tower, then disappeared into Tagrin's mouth.

"The slide? Hm. Who would have thought that the old corpse-waker was building a helter-skelter?" Terrano barked a short laugh. "A desperate attempt to shore up his reputation—gain the approval of the townsfolk."

"By providing a costly toy for their children," Breia said thoughtfully. "The metal alone is worth much coin, not to mention the work that's gone into bending it around that tower." The chute had arrived in sections, and workers had this day assembled it, fastening and smoothing each length of the slide with the help of a metallurgist's spells. The curved slide spiraled its way from the top door of the tower to the bottom, encircling it several times like a giant silver serpent.

Horses clattered into the small yard before the mercenaries' quarters. Terrano turned, peering through the doorway. "Here's Hex and Del. Where's Donell?"

Tagrin thumped his chest and belched. "Gone to buy bread to soak up the stew." He stirred the cook pot with a massive ladle, shielding his fingers with his thick sleeve. He grinned at Breia. "And Jem-Jem Juice, if you'd care to join me . . ."

Breia grimaced and shook her head. "No thanks, Tag. That stuff's dangerous. A girl could wake up *anywhere*." Tagrin clutched his heart and staggered, his broad face contorting into a grieved expression. Breia grinned and ignored him.

Terrano's jaw twitched. He pushed himself to his feet and left the bunkhouse without another word. Tagrin pursed his lips and raised his eyebrows. "Was it something I said?"

"Shut up, Tag," Breia muttered, suddenly aware of how things had changed between the three of them.

The Diamond Dogs ate, drank, and swapped dreams and plans for their extravagant futures. Hex and Del, dark-skinned brothers from the south coast, cleaned up after the meal. When the sun sank below the town's western skyline, it was time to meet with their employer.

Before they left the quarters, Terrano addressed them all. "No more drinking." His serious gaze swept the band. Tagrin belched. Hex chuckled and elbowed his brother. Terrano frowned. "There will be much gold to watch over this night, and I would have you clearheaded enough to do so. We will sleep in shifts—three to stay awake at all times. Agreed? Come on, then. Let's go get rich." He stood aside, and the band hustled into the yard.

The helter-skelter loomed tall and silent over the quiet street. Early twilight gleamed pale pink on the metallic chute that embraced the tower. The Diamond Dogs approached the open door at its base. Stacked against the outside wall were sections of the giant spiral staircase that would take would-be sliders to the small door at the top of the chute. Lamplight glowed within the tower, and the sound of voices came from within. Terrano stepped up to the doorway and knocked.

"Come in, all of you," called the familiar rasp of the Necromancer. Peering around Terrano's shoulder, Breia saw the mage standing alone on the circular stone floor. Beside him sat a large wooden chest. Terrano scanned the inside of the tower.

"Who were you talking to?" He leaned a shoulder against the doorframe.

The Necromancer blinked. "Myself. And my . . . guide, of course."

"Your guide." Terrano straightened.

"Not of this world, my dear Terrano, and not something that need concern you."

Breia's skin goose-bumped. The mage's indigo robes swished when he bent to the chest and opened the lid. Breia's eyes widened. Gold coin filled the chest to the brim, and a soft yellow glow haloed the fortune. The Necromancer's features smoothed. He tucked his hands into his sleeves. "You distrust me, I see." He sighed. "My art is one feared by many. I do not hold your suspicions against you." He indicated the gold with a pale hand. "Here is what I promised you, and more besides. I have been well pleased with you." He smiled, a mere stretching of lips over teeth. "You have helped me achieve a vast work. Take your reward."

Terrano sought Tagrin over his shoulder. His brows lifted. "There's no one about," Tagrin said in answer to the unspoken question.

Terrano nodded. "Be quick, all of you." The band filed into the tower. Tagrin closed the lid of the chest and grasped one of its rope handles, testing its weight. It barely moved. Terrano gestured to Hex and Keenan. Del and Donell took the third side, and Terrano and Breia, the fourth. They heaved together, but the chest did not move. The movement of the door caught Breia's eye too late.

"Tee!" Her eyes met his just as the door closed with a solid whump. Tagrin ran for the exit, his massive shoulder connecting with the wood in an impact that should have shattered the planking.

Terrano whirled toward the Necromancer, but the mage no longer stood on the stone circle. He floated the height of two men above them, and continued to rise toward the topmost door, his features set in a serene smile.

Keenan gazed up at the escaping mage. "The slide! He's running out on us!"

"But the gold . . ." Breia stooped and opened the chest. Empty. Shock pierced her gut. "Illusion," she breathed, and drew her throwing knives. Terrano's knives already hissed through the air, and Breia's followed. Before the wicked blades could reach the Necromancer's flesh, he made a brushing gesture with his hands. The knives fell away, clattering harmlessly at their feet.

"What have you done, you stinking corpsewaker?" Tagrin's raw bellow drew the mage's eye. And Breia's. He clutched his shoulder, and his arm hung at an odd angle. The door remained undamaged. Terrano reached behind his head and drew the longsword from the sheath at his back. He strode to the door and took a mighty swing at the wood. The strident ring of metal on metal filled the tower. A long diagonal slash in the wood revealed the truth. A thin skin of wood over a metal plate. Tagrin and Keenan drew swords and attacked the walls, only to discover more metal plating.

The Necromancer's thin laughter floated down from the exit to the chute. He stood braced in the upper doorway, his face a pale moon in the cowl of his robe. "Did you think you would escape judgment for your deeds, Terrano? You and your band have sent seventy souls to the realm of the dead. Seventy! Does that number hold any significance for you, Diamond Dogs?" He paused, resting his gaze on each of them in turn. Breia's breath came in gasps, and her heart threatened to escape her chest, so frantic was its pounding. The slight mage rubbed his chin. "Then perhaps seventy-*seven* will hold more meaning for you." His tone chilled Breia's gut.

Terrano's face drained of color. "The arcane key," he muttered, nursing his sword arm. Breia saw a dreadful understanding in his eyes. "*We* are the seven," he grated. "He means to dispose of us here." The whisper of drawn steel sounded around the tower. Terrano's longknives appeared in his hands. Breia's mouth dried. She slid her sword from its sheath and stood, shifting her weight from side to side, her gaze darting around the band.

High above them, the Necromancer muttered in a constant burble of sound, his hands outstretched. The tower's foundations shifted beneath Breia's feet. She backed toward the curved wall, Hex at her left and Donell at her right. Keenan and Del remained in the center, staring at the stone which writhed as stone should not. The mage's mutterings grew louder. The foundations heaved, and a massive grinding rumble began far beneath their feet.

Opposite Breia, Terrano's eyes widened, flew to meet hers. "The death-mark," he called above the groaning stone. He extended an index finger, moved it in a wide pattern over the floor. "It's here, marked into the stone!"

Oh, Carannah, save us! A dusky red line she had not noticed before curved in a sinuous design, simple yet awfully familiar. The mark they had all inscribed into their victims' flesh. A violent crack resounded in the small space. The stone floor rent from Terrano's side straight across to Breia.

The Necromancer's voice rose to a thin screech. "Come, Avatar! Rise, Golem God!"

Avatar Golem! The mage had worked a summoning. Breia swallowed, gripped her sword hilt in sweating palms and stared into the riven stone. Keenan and Del stepped back, separated by the widening fissure, their swords held before them. With a sound like the first crack of overhead thunder, the floor beneath Del opened. He fell straight down. His sword skittered away when he gripped the edge of the stone, scrabbling and heaving, his face contorted with fear.

Hex leaped toward his brother. Before he could reach him, a massive hand the color of a stagnant pond reached from the rift and gripped Del around the neck. Hex swung his sword down on the green-scummed forearm. The blade impacted with a wet, sucking sound. Del's eyes bulged. His mouth worked soundlessly. His fingers slipped, leaving trails of blood. Hex roared and struck again. Tagrin charged toward them, but Del had gone. Keenan raised his sword against a second arm that hooked over the edge of the fissure. Before he could swing the blade down, the stone opened beneath him. He disappeared without a sound. Tagrin and Hex hacked at the emerging back and shoulders, their blows causing no obvious damage. When the hunched creature lifted its head from the depths of the stone, its mouth opened in a gurgling hiss.

Breia's knees turned to water. She stumbled back against the wall. The Golem's eyes, deep holes of darkness in a ridged, bony face, stared straight at her. She panted, ashamed to hear a sob at the end of each breath.

"Breia!" Terrano shouted, but she could only stare into the soulless eyes, seeing in their depths the deaths of each victim. The Golem's face rippled. In quick succession, she saw the features of those she had killed. The last, the young whore she had smothered, stared at her in mute appeal.

"Breia! Look away!" Suddenly beside her, Terrano gripped her chin, forced her face from the Golem. Cringing and trembling, she stared into his eyes, blue and alive, his brows drawn in fierce intensity.

Tagrin leaped at the Golem's back. His long-knife flashed at the corded neck. Terrano pushed Breia behind him. "Tag, no! Get clear . . ." Before he could complete the warning, the Golem reached behind its head with both huge fists. It grasped Tagrin by the head and pulled him over one shoulder. Tagrin roared and struggled, slashing wildly with his knife. Wherever the blade cut, the gray-green flesh melded together, leaving no evidence of harm. The Golem raised its head, looked straight at Terrano and snapped Tagrin's neck like a dry stick.

"Tag . . ." Breia choked on the word. Tagrin's limp body fell from the Golem's grasp and disappeared beneath the foundations. Hex staggered toward them, his mouth twisted with grief and rage. Terrano pulled Hex beside him. "Don't look at its eyes," he rasped. "It'll paralyze you until it can reach you. Hex!" He shook the dark man. "Grieve for Del later."

Hex stared at Terrano. Without warning, he launched himself at the still-emerging Golem. Terrano cursed. Hex's guttural battle cry was cut short. His sword fell, knocked away by a fist the size of a man's head. The Golem's other hand crushed Hex's throat, lifted his body, and threw it at the wall above Breia's head. She didn't turn when it landed in a sickening thud behind her.

The Golem braced its hands on each side of the yard-wide rift. Its shoulders bulged and hunched. The stone groaned. The gap widened.

"It needs all of us to free itself entirely," Terrano murmured urgently. "Seven, each with the blood of ten on their hands. Seventy and seven: the arcane key." He glared up at their left. Breia looked. The mage appeared to be in a trance.

"How could *you* know that?" Terror thickened her voice.

Terrano threw her a sideways glance. "A little priestess told me."

The Golem heaved one huge knee from the rift, but its hips remained wedged. The rotting-meat stench of its breath blasted Breia with each frustrated roar.

"Donell, are you hurt?" Terrano leaned past Breia. Donell's ragged breathing belied his calm expression.

"No. What do you have in mind?" He drew his brows over coal-dark eyes. Terrano gazed up above their heads. Sweat trickled from his temple. The Golem bellowed.

"The window we saw from outside. It must be above us, but boarded up."

Donell edged along the wall to where the fake treasure chest rested. Free now of illusion, its weight had returned to normal. He pulled it back to them and climbed atop it. Terrano mounted beside him, pulled two short daggers from his belt and handed them to Breia. "It's up to you, Princess." He and Donell clasped each other's wrists

and held their makeshift step ready for her foot.
Misery rose in her throat. She could only nod
dumbly and tuck the knives into her own belt.
Behind her, the Golem thumped a mighty arm on
the floor, trembling the walls. It heaved and
reached, its fingers only inches from Donell's legs.

"Carannah's Tits, Bree! Go now!" Terrano's
chest heaved, his eyes darted toward the stagnant
fingers that strained toward them. She set a foot
in their hands and felt them heave her up. Donell
fell. Breia shrieked and toppled sideways. Terrano
grabbed at her, steadied them both against the
wall.

"Don't look," he breathed, but she did. Twisting
and screaming, Donell clawed at the stone. The
Golem gripped his lower leg and drew him
toward the fissure.

Breia closed her eyes and fumbled with the
clasp of her mantle. Pulling it free, she laid it
around Terrano's shoulders and clipped it across
his chest.

The fabric swirled and settled around his body,
adjusting to his shape. He blinked and frowned,
but held his hands ready for her. She set one foot
in his palms and pressed her mouth to his. He
boosted her high. She stepped onto his shoulders.
He braced himself against the wall and raised his
hands, and when she stepped onto them, pushed
her higher. She wobbled and stabbed at the wood
above her with one dagger. Below, the Golem
roared a foul-breathed blast. The stone cracked
loudly. Her blade struck metal. Weeping with

frustration, she stabbed again, but higher. The wood splintered. The knife sank to the hilt into bark-thin veneer, then tore down and lodged on a metal bar with a dull clunk.

Terrano gasped a curse. She felt him twist beneath her. Not daring to look, she tore through the wooden fascia with the second dagger and heaved herself up. Dropping the first knife, she drove her fist through the shattered wood and gripped the bar behind it. She swung one leg up and kicked in a toehold, pulled the remaining dagger free, and stabbed it higher. Within moments, she clung to the iron-barred window with both hands, and both feet stood firmly on the metal rungs.

She looked up. The Necromancer stood, trance-like, still braced in the exit to the slide. She looked down. Terrano flattened his back into the wall and flinched away from the Golem's reaching fingers. His face ran with sweat. He fumbled at the mantle's clasp with one hand.

"Tee, no!" she screamed at him. "Forget the mantling! It's a Flame Guard's cape—a Mantle of Exclusion." Seeing the dawning understanding in his eyes, she continued her heaving climb, gasping for breath, her shoulders burning with effort. Reaching the top of the window, she balanced carefully, then inched her hands up the wall toward the struts that supported the step to the tower's exit.

Contact. Her raw fingertips closed over the strut. She closed her eyes and swallowed. A loud curse from below and the tremble of the walls powered her tired arms into a prodigious heave. Inch by inch, she hauled herself up until her chin reached the step. At the end of her strength, she hooked an elbow over the small platform, colliding with the Necromancer's feet. Horrified, she clung to the step. A fall would mean certain death.

His lips moved in a continual mutter, but he did not register her presence. She glanced down and saw the pallor of Terrano's upturned face. And the Golem, one thigh remaining in the rift, one giant knee now braced on the stone floor. Fresh panic fueled her. *By the Divine Witch, let the Mantle's power be true, and not just myth.* Her toes scrabbled against the rough wood paneling, providing just enough propulsion for her to drag herself up in front of the mage's feet. The tower shook. Breia wormed past the Necromancer and thrust herself through the exit. Holding on to each side of the doorway, she drew her knees to her chest, screamed a foul curse, and shot her legs out.

Her boots caught the mage behind his thighs. His arms flew up. He crumpled forward and fell in a billow of indigo robes. Breia spun and pushed herself out into the chute, desperate to reach Terrano before the Golem could. Night air rushed past her cheeks and whined in her ears. Faster she slid, and faster still. Her eyes watered; fear for Terrano trembled her whole body. The dizzying spiral ride ended in a tumble headlong into cold mud.

Rolling to her feet, she sprinted around the

tower to the door. There was no sound. All evidence of their dreadful ordeal lay sealed inside the tower, no doubt concealed by the Necromancer's art. Reaching the door, she pulled on the heavy latch. The screech of metal on metal set her teeth on edge. Heaving her whole weight against the lever, she groaned in relief when it lifted with a sullen clank. The door itself was solid. Bracing a foot against the outer wall, she strained to pull it open. It swung slowly outward.

Shoulder muscles on fire, Breia slipped through the opening. The Golem turned its eyes on her. She did not look at it, nor at the crumpled indigo heap beside it. Terrano lay still beside the empty chest.

"Tee!" The scream hurt her throat. He opened his eyes and lifted his head. Blood ran from his temple, but he managed a crooked smile. Relief weakened her limbs. "Can you move?" He bared his teeth and sat up, swiping blood from his eyes with his sleeve. The Golem growled, a sound between a belch and a drain. Wrapping the mantle tightly about him, Terrano braced his back against the wall and pushed himself to his feet. The Golem's hand extended toward him, brushed the mantle. Terrano turned his shoulder, and the enormous fingers slid from his back. Astonished, Breia heard a faint hiss, smelled the stench of burning flesh.

The Golem howled, snatched its hand back, and lowered its repulsive head. Terrano half-slid, half-stumbled along the wall toward Breia. Just before he reached her, a gobbet of green expectorate jetted from the Golem's mouth, coating Terrano from shoulders to hips. In the same instant that Breia grabbed Terrano's wrist, the Golem's hand closed around the slimed mantle.

Terrano choked. A phlegmy chuckle gurgled in the Golem's throat. It pulled Terrano toward the fissure. Terrano tried to prize Breia's fingers from his wrist, but she would not let him go. His face darkened. The Golem's grip squeezed the breath from him, and Breia was drawn along with him, her boots sliding on the stone. In sudden inspiration, she leaped forward and released the clasp of the mantle.

The garment slid from Terrano like a shed snakeskin. He heaved in a great breath and tumbled forward. Confused for a moment, the Golem stared at the smoking mantle in its hand. Long enough for Breia to drag Terrano the last few feet to the door. She pushed him through the gap and threw herself out, landing on top of him in an inelegant tumble of arms and legs. He groaned and lay still, apart from the heaving of his chest. Gray-green fingers scrabbled at the doorway.

Breia rolled off and lay beside him, regaining her own breath. She turned her head and looked at him. His eyes were closed, his face bloodied and bruised. "It can't get any farther out without killing one of us, right?"

"Not one inch," he breathed. "Without us, it'll be long gone before morning. Returned to the depths it came from."

Breia nodded. She rolled over and stood. Setting her shoulder to the door, she pushed it closed and latched it. "And now?" she asked, dropping to her knees in the mud beside him.

He opened his eyes and licked blood from a split lip. "You *mantled* me." His tone was incredulous.

"And I *released* you from it." She shrugged and looked away, out toward the peaceful village. "Think nothing of it, Tee. It protected you. That's enough." His attitude stung her. Delayed reaction to the evening's events rose in her chest. Tagrin and four comrades, lost to the Golem. Tears prickled her eyes.

Mud squelched beside her. Terrano sat up with a soft gasp of pain. His shoulder rested warm against hers. "I owe you, Princess. A new mantle, among other things." He turned her face toward him, his fingers gentle beneath her chin. "And if you should choose to employ it as you did your last, that's well enough with me." His arm came around her shoulders.

Exhausted and sad, kneeling in cold mud beneath the stars of early spring, Breia turned and embraced the man who called her beautiful.

WHILE HORSE AND HERO FELL

Sarah A. Hoyt

Sarah A. Hoyt lives in Colorado with her husband,
two sons, and a multitude of cats. She's the author of a Shakespearean fantasy trilogy (*Ill Met
By Moonlight, All Night Awake, Any Man So Daring*). She's currently working on a couple of projects. Her mystery series featuring the Three
Musketeers (written as Sarah D'Almeida) will
debut November 2006 with *Death Of A Muske-
teer.*

I WAS A COMPUTER nerd, and she was the
world's most beautiful witch. She was in bad
trouble, and I had to save her.

Which did not really explain why I was crawling on my belly along the second floor of the
headquarters of the Magical Legion. Nor did it
explain the mackarov in my hands, the Glock in

my underarm holster, and the two tempered blades on ankle holders.

I was not a man of action. All right, I was— through a series of mistakes—a member of the Magical Legion. But my job was to sort, file, and enter into the computer four hundred years' worth of records on legionaries, on operations, and on supernatural outbreaks combatted without ever disturbing the normal world.

I did not go out into battle, I did not throw hexes, I would not know how to weave a spell, and I had absolutely no power with which to power a jinx.

What I did have was the gun butt growing warm in my hands and an intimate knowledge of the layout of headquarters. It wasn't as easy as it might seem, since the thaumaturgically expanded space connected the sixteenth floor of a high-rise in Denver, the attic of a townhouse in Vienna, a warehouse in Madrid, the backroom of a restaurant in France, and who knew how many other forgotten, lost, or invisible spaces.

I was crawling on my belly because I knew— from diagrams and records I'd entered—that the magical sensors started at knee level and went all the way to the ceiling. They would give an alarm at my unauthorized entry. And then they would activate spells to make me into a pile of steaming cinders. But the floor couldn't be activated because that would make the joined spaces fall apart.

I wriggled down the hallway connecting to the

Madrid space and felt the tiny magical jolt—like a low-wattage shock—as I made it over the partition and each half of my body was, for a moment, in different continents. And then I was over it and crawling along a smooth cement floor.

The Madrid warehouse had been divided with the sort of partition used to make multiple cubes out of vast offices. The only light came from above, from skylights set into what looked like a corrugated tin ceiling. In the middle was an empty area, which was set up exactly the same as the hallway back in Denver. Sensors at ankle level and above. I crept on my belly and counted the doors set into the openings of the cube.

Three, four, five. The sixth belonged to Lyon Zaragoza, the greatest invoker in the Legion. The man I needed. The man who—whether he knew it or not, was going to help me.

I took a deep breath. There would be no sensors on the door or the wall opposite. Just in case a magician woke up, sleep befogged and forgot to turn on his own personal protection before opening the door. If he were so crazy as to take a step down the hallway like that, then he would die. But there was no reason to thin the personnel more than the operations already did.

The narrow space in front of the door being safe, I pulled all of myself into it, till I was kneeling in front of the door. Most mages were paranoid enough that they had their own personal alarms in this area—ethereal eyes roving above and watching for intruders, ears that amplified every sound, or simply a floor hex that rang of intrusion.

So it had to be done quickly. I'd dressed carefully, for quick movements, in loose black sweat pants and a black T-shirt. The elastic fabric molded to me as I jumped and, in a smooth movement, kicked the door open. I didn't hear any alarms, but then I wouldn't. The alarm would be tuned for Lyon Zaragoza's ears only.

I don't know if that's what woke him or the sound I made as I slammed the door open. But he sat up in bed, with a springlike motion, as I entered his room. And I had my gun out and pointed at him.

He'd made his room cozy by moving it to another time and another continent. Once through the door, I was in an all-stone cell, from which the rounded window of a medieval building opened onto endless fields and vineyards in gently rolling hills. I glanced at it and had a hard time not staring at the pastoral scene in the moonlight. There was no way in hell that was anywhere in the world in the twenty-first century. Damn it, they weren't supposed to do that. I'd read—and archived—the regulations about time travel. Strictly forbidden. Almost as forbidden as making your fellow legionaries practice their magic at gunpoint.

A trickle of sweat formed somewhere at my hairline and drifted down my forehead. I held my gun in front of me, the arms just slack enough to accommodate the kick if I had to fire it. My father, who was a wiser man than I'd ever been, had told me when I was little more than a boy never to point a gun at a man unless I intended to use it.

I didn't want to have to use it. Dead, Lyon wouldn't actually do me any good. But if I had to—if I absolutely must—I'd splash the brains in that handsome Spanish gentleman blinking confusedly at me, against the stylish stone walls of his dormitory. And if that left me stranded in the Middle Ages, so be it. I couldn't live in the twenty-first century and let Gwen be killed.

"Who are you?" Lyon asked, more in puzzled tiredness than in shock. "What are you doing in my room?" His dark eyes beneath the straight black eyebrows were staring above and to the side of me. Trying to see my magical aura with his second sight. More the fool he, as I had none.

"I'm George Martin," I said. "Legionary third class."

He frowned harder, bristling his luxuriant black mustache and glared down at my gun. "Why can't I see your magic, boy? And why are you pointing that toy at me?"

"You can't see my magic because I don't have any," I said. "I'm the archiver." It all had to do with my foolishly answering an ad for a computer wizard, and their being so desperate for someone who actually would archive that they hadn't checked my pattern. They assumed I was powerful enough to hide it. But I wasn't about to explain it to Lyon, if he didn't know it.

He made a sound of disgust. "The paper

pusher?" he asked. "Bah. And you dare wake me?"

He had some reason for his outrage, as he was a captain of the Legion. Which meant that, since the commander had died last week in the Hell gate closing, he was one of the three leaders of the Legion. And I was as low a rank as one could be and still be called a legionary.

But I was long past paying attention to rank or propriety. You have to understand, Gwen Arcana, the world's most beautiful witch, wasn't my girl-friend. She wasn't even a friend. Friendly acquaintance, perhaps, as she smiled at me as she walked past my vast, paper-choked office. And she would never expect me to rescue her. But she was . . . wondrous, with her thick red hair that fell to the middle of her back, her sparkling green eyes, her quick intelligence, her musical laughter. At twenty years old, she didn't deserve to be left to the lack of mercy of a drunken centaur band. To be honest, no one did. But if it weren't Gwen, I might not have summoned the courage to act.

"I need you," I told Lyon's irate expression. "I need information from you, and your help."

He waved his hand. Like that—without warning, my gun vanished from my hand. Damn. Of course I anticipated that and before he could move again, I'd reached into my shoulder holster and brought out the Glock. Small and deadly like a viper, it fit into my hand, filled with a sense of viciousness. I'd gotten it from the archives where it rested as evidence of a magical crime. It was spelled to stay with the person who said certain words over it.

Lyon must have seen the spell, because he didn't even try. Instead he said, very slowly, as though speaking to a small child, "What will you get if you shoot? Do you think I don't have life protection and healing spells."

"Silver bullets," I said. "And I know enough anatomy to know where your heart is."

"But you know then you'll be lost in eleventh-century Saxony."

"Indeed. And isn't that forbidden?"

"I'm one of the three principals. Who'll punish me?"

And this was exactly what was wrong since the commander had bought his peace everlasting. "I will," I said, between clenched teeth. "I will, right now, unless you agree to do what you must to help me find Gwen Arcana and get her back."

He got out of bed, revealing that he was wearing an ankle-length nightshirt which billowed around hairy ankles and large feet. "But, my dear man, Gwen Arcana was taken by centaurs. We didn't count on them when there was that supernatural outbreak in Italy. We counted on a dragon or an out of control saint. Instead, it was the damn centaurs and their ancient magic. Only the commander knew that type of magic. He's dead. We haven't recruited a replacement classical magician. Until we do—"

"Stop," I yelled. He'd been edging toward me as he spoke in a soothing tone. "Stop, or I will shoot off your right hand."

"How do you know I'm right-handed?"

I laughed. I couldn't help myself. "How not? I'm the archiver." I made my voice slow and thoughtful. "I know all about you, Captain Zaragoza." I saw his minimal flinch, as he realized that I knew the reason he was in the Legion. He'd been tracked down and brought to ground by the magical authorities after a streak of animating recently deceased people who were then forced to make wills in his favor. I wondered how he'd feel about having other people know about it. "And you're going to help me bring Commander Lars Oktober back, so we can figure out how to get Gwen."

He looked at me, his dark eyes so wide open they appeared to be bulging. "You want to reanimate the commander?"

"No," I said. "I'd do quite well with calling his shade."

He grumbled something under his breath, then said, "And if we manage that, what do you think you can do? A ghost cannot wage magical war. And the girl was captured by centaurs, not ghosts."

"And you'd just leave her behind . . ." I said. I'd heard the discussion between Lyon Zaragoza, Maria Alsas, and Pierre Grenoir, the three highest ranking captains in the Legion, and equally sharing command since the commander had died. I'd hate to say it, but though it was rumored the three of them couldn't agree that the sun rose in the East, there had been no complaints about leaving Gwen behind after the lost skirmish against the centaurs.

Lyon shrugged, and in that moment I almost let fly with the Glock. Except being left behind in medieval Europe wouldn't help her. "You do what you have to do. Should we have risked the life of other legionaries to save her when she was as good as lost?"

"And yet," I said. "When I enter the records of past raids and past battles, time after time the Legion doesn't leave one of its own behind, when it can save them. We don't. There was the journey of a detachment across the parched deserts of Africa where the natural magic of the land didn't allow the opening of magical portals. One by one they fell unconscious, victims to thirst, and had been dragged or carried by other legionaries scarcely less stricken than themselves, till they'd come upon a secret oasis and all been saved. And we're not afraid of dying. In 1643, in the battle against the forces of hell, the Dutch detachment died, one by one and man by man, until the last one of them directed his power outward to kill all of the enemy and died from it."

Lyon looked at me with the look a sane man might give a fool or a child. "Those are very pretty stories," he said. "But the truth is, no one joins the Legion because he wants to. We are all rogues; we all have a past."

He looked at me with the sort of look that meant surely I, also, had one. I wasn't buying. I'd joined the Legion because I'd been determined to get a job during the computer job bust a few years ago. Somehow, in a way no one could explain, this had caused me to see the invisible sixteenth floor in the building. It hadn't occurred anyone I wasn't a magician until I'd had the job for two weeks.

So I stared at Lyon and said, simply, "We're not going to leave Gwen with the centaurs."

He sat back on his bed and looked at me. "It's been two hours," he said. "Since she was taken. She might be dead."

"Or she might not," I said. "We don't leave her."

He blinked. "Why won't a spell take on you, Martin?" he asked.

"What are you talking about?"

"I've tried to cast a spell on you three times now. Oblivion spell, aversion spell, and even a disappearance spell. And yet there you are, holding your little gun and telling me we won't leave Gwen Arcana behind. How? You have no magic."

I shrugged. "We won't leave Gwen behind," I said.

He opened his hands. "So be it," he said.

Ten minutes later, he was walking ahead of me—far enough ahead that I judged he couldn't just turn around and take my gun. He'd deactivated the spells in the hallway and walked me down it, till the floor changed to dark red tile, the far-off roof of the warehouse to a rounded brick tunnel. "Tuscany," Lyon told me. "Maria lives here."

I must have looked blank because he added, "Sangre Dios. Are you stupid? Even if we wake the commander and he tells us the hexes needed to immobilize the centaurs long enough to get Gwen we won't be able to translate it on our own. Maria will understand the language, at least, even if ancient magic is not one of her specialties."

"And will she cooperate?"

He gave me an exasperated look. "If she can't spell you," he said. "And if I can't, I don't see why she should be able to."

But Maria couldn't. Or at least I'll assume so from the fact that she fell in, next to Lyon. Her incongruous pink robe was only slightly less strange than her pink, fluffy slippers. Not exactly what one expected the most powerful witch in the world to wear at night. She shuffled along, her small, peaked face showing above the pink robe with an expression like an angry bantam hen. She muttered things—mostly, I think, curses at Lyon, who gave back as good as he got. The source of her anger seemed to lie in the fact that he couldn't spell me. "Well, why can't you?" she said, at one point and, to his shrug, "All Spanish men are impotent."

"You can't either," he said and I realized part of the reason he'd insisted on her presence was that he hoped she would be able to spell me.

"I'm a woman," she said darkly—as if that explained everything.

"We must get the commander to speak," I said. "And tell us how to get Gwen. Until you do, I'll be holding both of you at gunpoint."

This started another round of bickering, but in the middle of it several rational facts emerged: we didn't have the commander's body, so spelling near his body or ashes, or even thinking of reanimating him was pointless. However, we did have his portrait in the grand gallery. And Lyon said the portrait would help his concentration. "Candles," he said. "We need candles. There will be some in the larder."

A few minutes later, after what seemed like much too long a trudge through bits of headquarters located in several other countries, we found ourselves in the gallery, the candles lit in a complex pattern on the floor.

For a minute or so, I was accidentally in the middle of the central pattern of candles, but when Lyon started muttering incantations, I stepped out. He looked a little surprised, making me wonder whether he'd been trying something magical again. I really had no idea why it wasn't working, if he was.

And then I started worrying that the same raid in which Gwen had been lost had, somehow, damaged Lyon's powers and that he wouldn't be able to summon Lars Oktober.

I shouldn't have worried. After a few words

and half a dozen incantations, the commander appeared. He was, or rather he'd been, a tall man, spare and blond, with the sort of features that speak of fjords and ships departing through ice-choked waters.

He wore his hair very short and he always dressed in black. I knew, because I had access to his file, that he'd come to the Legion after his youthful enthusiasms had made him the right-hand man to the dark Lord that controlled most of the magical world of Europe for seventy years—and, incidentally, by the principle of sympathetic reflection, made the Soviet Union possible. However, as I'd known him, he'd seemed like a totally different person, one always ready to fight for justice and proper treatment for his legionaries—one who'd managed to keep even the smoldering rivalry between Lyon and Maria in check.

Even now, as his form spiraled out of thin air, seeming to assemble pale hair, long face and square shoulders from the shadows and the scant light of candles, Maria and Lyon stopped their bickering.

"You dared summon me," Commander Oktober spoke. It wasn't so much a voice, as a normal thing, made of sounds. It was a whisper of dark, and intimation of shadows, the sound light would make rubbing on dark, if either of those could be heard. And yet it was his voice, down to the Eastern German accent. His pale blue eyes—not really there but looking as substantial as a reflection in a clear mirror—stared at Maria and Lyon.

I cleared my throat. "I made him summon you," I said.

He turned to me. Did I imagine that a smile creased his lips? We'd always gotten along. He'd told me I could stay in the Legion even if I wasn't a true wizard. He'd told me I fitted in better than I thought. I hadn't understood him, but I appreciated his acceptance.

"Ah, George," he said. "And why would you interrupt my well-deserved rest?"

"Gwen Arcana was left behind in a raid on centaurs," I said.

"It was just a magical eruption," Lyon said. "We didn't know what it was."

"In Italy, it's more likely to be an out-of-control saint these days," Maria put in.

"And we didn't have the knowledge to deal with centaurs," Lyon said.

"We were retreating," Maria said. "Well, not us personally, of course, but the small raiding party that we'd sent."

"And they grabbed Gwen and galloped away with her."

"And it wasn't worth it to try to rescue her," Maria said. "The whole party could have died. And if we'd sent people after her, they could have died."

Lars looked toward me, "And yet you woke me?" he asked gravely.

"A legionary doesn't leave a legionary behind,"

I said. "We're all rogues or orphans." In my case an orphan since my mother had died when I was a child and my father just before I joined the Legion. "Or both. We're all the other one has. We have to stand up for each other, because no one else will."

"Well, Lyon," Commander Oktober asked.

"The young man is clearly a romantic," Lyon said.

"An armed romantic," Commander Oktober said and again the not quite a smile crossed his ghostly lips. "And I'd say you'd best do as he wishes, or he will not let any of us rest. What you need," he said, "is the Apollo invocation, Maria. Done properly, to break through their magical defenses. I can't give you anything to bring them down physically, though. They are almost pure magical creatures, and amazingly strong ones, to have survived these last two millennia and still be able to manifest in the flesh. So they will fight. I can give you the spells to pull down the magic around their hideout. The rest will have to be fought out by you with your hands and brains and wits. And you will need more people." He looked at me. "George, I would advise you to keep the gun on Lyon and threaten to kill him, and get an assault party ready." Waving aside Lyon's protest, he added "I don't know how much they care about him, but it will give them an excuse to obey you. I will guess the men and women in the ranks won't be too happy about leaving one of them behind. And Maria, take it two hours back in time. Get her just as they pull her into their hideout. Or it will be too late."

"We can't use time travel," she said virtuously.

"Oh, really?" Commander Oktober asked and looked first at her and then at him. I knew his room was in violation of that statute, but I wouldn't even guess at what she had done. "Right," he said. And then he started talking in what was, in effect, a foreign language, giving Maria instructions on how to deal with centaur magic.

The raiding party was much larger than we'd expected. Almost a hundred people had claimed a great concern for the life of Captain Zaragoza— whom I was still holding at gun point—and offered to go rescue Gwen.

Most of them opened their own portals from the bland and utilitarian inside of the part of headquarters that was located in Denver and which looked like a beige-carpet-and-blonde-wood office of the twenty-first century.

I crossed through the one Maria opened, with Lyon just ahead of me.

On the other side of the portal it was night in some rural part of Italy. It was summer—the sky above velvety blue shot through with stars, the air warm and carrying with it a smell of flowers and ripening fruits.

The place where we'd come through was at the base of a small hillock. At the top of the hillock stood what looked like Roman ruins. Bits of columns and remnants of wall covered in ivy seemed incongruously animated. Light shone from the middle of them, and song in an ancient language burst forth.

We were so far from civilization that those songs, and the distant barking of a dog, were the only sounds we heard. But I could see far in the horizon, the lighted ribbon of a highway stretching. From this distance it looked like a flickering strand of light crossing the darkness. Humans. Who might very well fall prey to these centaurs, since the centaurs were so strong as to manifest even now, millennia after anyone had last believed in them.

And they had Gwen, I thought, and shuddered.

I shoved the gun in the middle of Lyon's back. I'd taken the precaution of binding his hands, particularly the right one. "Forward," I said.

In fact, I could sense, more than I saw, the whole group of people—who had crossed over in a big circle ringing the hillock—start to move forward, like a noose closing on the ruins.

Behind us, Maria was chanting in Latin so old that no historian or priest would recognize it. She had an instrument made from animal horns and played it with a plaintive effect, while calling on Apollo. The smell of strange herbs emanated from her general vicinity.

Stumbling on rocks, but moving ever forward, we slowly, slowly approached the hill.

We were halfway up the hill when the singing stopped at the top.

"They know we're here," Lyon said, and tried to throw himself back against me and push us both over down the hill.

"Good," I said, and pressed the Glock against the middle of his back. "We know they're there, too. Your point is? Gwen is still up there, and we're going to get her."

He made a sound of terror. "You don't know what they're like."

"Then it's just as well they don't know what I'm like," I said, and pushed him forward. Truth was I was scared. But if I was scared, what would Gwen be feeling? After all, the centaurs' reputation with women was still well known in my time.

We had moved forward another ten steps when out of the skies, in a noise like sheets unfolding, a fury of pegasi descended. For those of you out there so little acquainted with arcane art that a pegasus reminds you of cute and cuddly plush toys favored by little girls, let me assure you these pegasi were quite different.

For one, they smelled. It was a smell of fresh kills, a smell of spilled blood and ravaged flesh. And then they dove out of the sky, in a flurry, aiming at our men, with teeth bared and hooves kicking. They looked like large horses with black, glossy wings which, in the dark night looked like barely glimpsed phantoms.

I had a second to think. Maria was far back behind us. And Lyon was in front of me. I didn't know if there was anything we could do to physically banish the pegasi or if the pegasi were material or not. But I knew that no one was actually in command of this mission and that was a bad thing. Commander Oktober would be disappointed in me if I let any other legionaries be hurt or captured.

Before the thought had fully run through my mind, I yelled, "Everyone duck."

There was the sound of several bodies hitting the turfed ground just in time for the pegasi to fly over them and miss them. And then a scream, from my right.

I turned. It was Helen, a young legionary from Ireland. A pegasus had grabbed her by the back of her jacket and was lifting her up in the air, feet kicking, blonde hair gleaming in the moonlight.

I didn't think. I aimed and fired. The pegasus shrieked. Helen fell—fortunately only about five feet—and landed with the grace of someone who'd been through the Legion's boot camp. And then the pegasi gave a sort of cry.

I thought that meant they would attack us again, but instead, they fell on their stricken brother. I didn't look. The sounds were as of a several hungry mouths tearing at prey. "Move," I yelled out. "Move forward, all of you."

They did. Legionaries were well trained. Legionaries obeyed.

We went twenty steps and then the rain of arrows started. The one thing I can say for the centaurs was that they were lousy shots, though perhaps that had something to do with their being drunk. The smell, even that far, was unbelievable.

It stank of overheated horse slathered in liquor—that's the best way I can explain it. It was clear they'd found some wine reserve to raid.

They ran at us, firing their bows, then retreated, then ran again. From the crowd, I started hearing weapons fire. Every legionary was armed with a gun, of course, a gun loaded with silver bullets. Silver, for whatever reason, was immune to magic and could kill even the most magical of creatures.

Centaurs started falling, left and right. Some ran back into the building, though.

And then a centaur emerged. He was holding Gwen in front of him. She looked like she was in a trance. "You will let us go," he shouted. To be honest, he looked like an Italian peasant, even if he were an Italian peasant built on two and a half times the normal scale. "And you will not follow us. Or the girl will die."

He wore only a loose red vest on his bare trunk, so it was easy enough to see his huge, muscular arm holding Gwen around the waist, while his right hand held a knife to her throat.

Our entire group stopped its advance. "He'll kill her," Lyon said. "He'll kill her."

"I don't think so," I said. My dad had taught me several things. One of them was accurate shooting. The other was that a gun could be far quicker than a knife. Of course, I'd never risked so much.

Gwen looked lovely, even then. Her eyes were wide open, unseeing, but it seemed to me that she

was looking straight at me, hoping . . . I didn't
know what she was hoping.

I let out a quick prayer to whichever local saint
might be listening. To believe the others, in Italy
there was always a saint listening. And then I
raised the Glock quickly and fired.

The centaur looked surprised. The knife clattered to the ground. And Gwen snapped awake
and ran. Toward us. Toward me.

The rest of the rescuers took aim and fired at
the centaurs.

Gwen hit me mid body, her lips touched my
skin. "Thank you," she said.

I didn't even notice Lyon's sound of disgust.

Of course, when Gwen thanked me, it was just
for her immediate rescue, not for having assembled the rescue party and forcing them to go back
for her. That she found out about two weeks later,
through office gossip. Which is when she asked
me out for the first time.

That was six months ago and since then we've
received a note from higher up—the Council of
Magic, a group of wise magicians that governs us
as well as the thaumaturgic police and all the
other branches of supernatural authority—
dictating that I was to become commander in
place of Commander Oktober. It seems that my
inability to perform magic was outweighed by my
organizational aptitude and by the fact that I was
so stubborn that hexes and spells slid off me. And

perhaps, the note said, stubbornness of that order was almost magical.

So, next week I'll be putting an advertisement out. Looking for a computer wizard with good administrative skills.

DEADHAND

John Helfers

John Helfers is an author and editor currently living in Green Bay, Wisconsin. He has published more than thirty-five short stories in anthologies such as *The Sorcerer's Academy*, *Faerie Tales*, *Alien Pets*, and *Apprentice Fantastic*. His novels include *Tom Clancy's Net Force Explorers: Cloak and Dagger*, *Twilight Zone: Deep in the Dark*, *Siege of Night and Fire*. Recent books include *Shadowrun: Aftershocks*, co-authored by Jean Rabe, and the illustrated young adult novels *ThundeRiders* and *Nightmare Expeditions*.

DIM MOONLIGHT GLEAMS off the alleyboys' blades as they step out to accost me in the narrow, filthy lane. Their flashing dirks are matched by the feral glint in their eyes, three among both of them. The would-be thieves are dressed in a ragbag collection of leather and fur castoffs, with scraps of cloth wrapped around their feet. Their hunched shoulders and shaking hands tell me they're either nervous or hoping I might resist. Plumes of white breath congeal from their mouths as the winter night air wraps dozens of chill fingers around us. Although the cool metal of my twin *real'gais* lies against my forearm, I know I won't need it.

"Pay and pass," the taller one says.

"Or fight and die," his partner chimes in, a wicked grin creasing his seamed and dirty features.

Time dilates for me in that instant, seconds stretching out like tortured minutes on the rack. The Master's presence stirs in the back of my skull, and I know that what is to come is his doing.

The silver moonlight shifts, turning pale shades of gray, and I now see the bonds holding the two gutterkin together, shackles of fear and greed and desire, invisible to most, but writhing and glow-bright as the sun around this pair. The dark red-and-black strands bind them in an uneasy alliance, one the taller thief will soon end, much to the permanent disadvantage of the shorter. My knowledge of this won't help, however, as he is unlikely to listen to any warning from me.

Another second slides by, and—as if I was watching a japes play at the crude pit theater on the other side of town—I see how I will kill both of them.

I watch my left hand snake out and grab the taller one's wrist, yanking him off balance, dragging him to me along with his blade, my true target. I see the iron glint disappear, buried in the belly of the shorter man, his own crude dagger dropping from his fingers, forgotten as he tries to draw enough breath to scream. That blade falls, handle first, into my right hand, and I jerk the taller one's arm back up, folding it across his throat, while my right arm comes up to the other side of his neck.

Just as the first alleyboy comprehends the end of his short life, I draw both blades through skin and muscle, almost severing his head from his body. I watch it all, the crimson jet of blood, gleaming black in the moonlight, as his body collapses beside the other one, which tries to suck in one last breath, clinging to the little life left in him. I step over and finish it with one precise stab. It would all be over in three blinks of an eye. . . .

With a roar like an earthen dam breaking, my reverie is halted, and I am jerked back to the present. I know that no time has passed, that these two still wait for my purse to fall into their greedy hands.

My traitorous body desires their death, aches with the need of it. The Master stirs again, a dull, hot weight just above the top of my spine. If he does nothing, I very well may spill their blood tonight. My own hands tremble at the thought, every nerve inflamed with the desire to kill them and be done with it.

No. I block the impulse with every fiber of my being, and my quivering fingers still again. With a grimace, I reach up and sweep matted black hair away from my forehead.

The two thugs pale when they see what is there, fear blanching their ruddy faces. They exchange uneasy glances, understanding the mistake they've made in choosing me for their night's work. The shorter one still looks like he's ready to swing iron, though, no doubt spurred by *thal*-induced visions of killing one such as I, perhaps becoming so notorious as to have his name strike fear into whomever hears it, much like my Master's does. I decide to forestall the possibility of anything more from these two.

"Leave. Now." My voice rasps like a rusted hinge. At this, the two back away, blades held out in front of them; as if that would stop me. Reaching the relative safety of the alley's far end, they're off like coneys tearing through the woods, invisible hounds nipping at their heels, though the only predator they'll see tonight is my face in their dreams.

"That was almost a lovely repast, don't you think?" the Master's voice is a silken hiss in my mind. *"And here I thought you were actually going to end them, too."*

"Can't have blood on my leathers when I step into the tavern," I mutter. I try to speak out loud whenever I must answer to the Master. It is a small victory, given his power over me, but one I savor whenever I can.

"Surely you've killed enough now to be able to avoid that." The Master's grin is evident in his words. *"No? Perhaps you need more practice. That hut on the outskirts of town, the family there—"*

"No," I growl this time, my blood-rage rising even further. "I will follow the trail you have commanded, no other."

"I would belie that tone of voice when speaking to me, pawn," the Master replies. *"Look down."*

Doing as he bids, I spot the faint blue-white line leading out of the alley and turning right down the street. I feel the slight tug of the strand that connects me, however tenuously, with my target. That is where my fate lies, intertwined with the death of another. That is why the Master chose me for this task, because my tie to him is the strongest.

I walk to the end of the alley, looking up and down the street. At night, in this part of town, the only things roaming are gutterkin like the ones I chased off and victims who don't know it yet.

The tavern I am supposed to wait in is at the far end of the block. I head toward it, my battered leather boots making no noise on the rough cobblestones. Pulling up my dirt-crusted hood, I reach for the door handle, worn smooth by thousands of thirsty hands.

Judging by the interior, the name of the tavern, the Maid's Fount, is a beggar's joke. If I still cared about such things, the stench alone—a palpable combination of sour wine, cheap beer, stale smoke-sweat, and fresh vomit—would drive me right back out again. But this feels almost comfortable after what I've been through.

Scarred and battered tables and benches line three of the walls and are scattered throughout the room, all filled with motley men of varying shapes and sizes. A bar that looks like it's being held up by the pug-faced bald man behind it rather than the other way around stretches the length of the fourth wall. Although the place is crowded, it being the end of the trading season even for freeblades and pursefingers, no one spares me a glance. Everyone here is too busy drowning their various existences in tankards of watered-down drink.

I scan among dozens of feet for the blue-white line, spotting it after a few seconds, and follow it back out the door. It pulses a little brighter to my eyes, indicating that my target is coming closer. No reason not to be comfortable while I wait. Spotting an open small table near the guttering fire, I make for it, ignoring the muttered oaths and glares tossed my way as I elbow my way through the crowd.

I feel a small hand dart for a nonexistent purse that should be on my hip. Without breaking stride, I grab the questing fingers and twist, breaking three of them. Above the general din I hear a strangled yelp, and the hand whips out of my grasp so fast I might have imagined the whole thing if I didn't have bits of the pursefinger's skin under my nails. I force myself to keep walking, resisting my hands' insistent pull to find the thief and finish the job. The Master, his presence still coiled in the back, is silent now, apparently not wanting to waste time with a pickpocket when larger prey is approaching.

Reaching the table, I sit down and wait for a barmaid. I attract a few stares, but I make a point of meeting each one from the depths of my hood, and the message is received soon enough. For my part, I am busy enjoying the feeble warmth of the fire. Although ill weather does not bother me anymore, I am always cold.

At length, a sallow woman with a underfed waif's body but a face decades older pauses at my table. My hand snaps out again, grabbing her wrist and drawing her down to my face. With my other hand, I push back the hood enough to reveal my face, my muddy eyes pinning her underneath their dead gaze. I don't need to show her my forehead, as her own blue eyes widen in sudden recognition.

"Ale, no water," I whisper. She draws back as if my words have just slapped her across the face. Even though she knows she won't be paid for the drink, she'll do what I ask, and make up for it out of her own meager wages. A fair price, considering she will still draw breath at the end of this evening.

The Master stirs, restless in the confines of my mind. *"Hmm, do you fancy her, pawn? All it would take is a simple look, and she can be yours."* I feel my eyes burn with his shared power. When she returns, all I would have to do is force her to meet my gaze for a moment, and she would be my own slave. . . .

"Of course, there are other . . . pleasures you could extract from her . . . much like you did with the last one—" the Master says, always insinuating, always teasing, his glass-smooth tones chipping away at what little self-control I have left. It is only one of the ways he extracts pleasure from my joyless existence, making me kill and rend and destroy at his whim.

"I said no," I mutter, dropping my gaze to the table. The thought is already there, however, and I feel my hands react, curling into clawed talons, desperate to rend, to crush, to destroy anything they can get a hold of. I could fill this common room with the blood of everyone in it, enough to wade in, and that still wouldn't be enough for my killing hands. Whatever the Master has done to me, he has filled my hands with a different kind of unholy life, one that exists only to destroy. They never attack me—I am too important to his plans—and are under my command for the most part, but now and again, I wonder just how much control I can exert on them if I must.

The barmaid returns with my drink, serving me before the other customers. Derisive hoots and cat-calls cross the tavern floor. The trembling woman almost throws the tankard of ale onto the table, she's so anxious to get away. I keep my eyes averted until her back is to me, fearful that the Master might make me use his power on her any-way. He has before, when he wishes to punish me. At times like those, he likes to control my hands himself, making them even more terrible instruments of destruction.

I hoist and drain the tankard, the pale amber liquid sliding down my dry throat. I could drink a river of it and not feel a thing. Setting down the empty flagon, I lean over and check the line again. It glows even brighter, the pulsations indicating that my prey is very near now.

The Master claims I am distantly related to the one I have been sent to kill, which is why he is using me tonight. *"Most likely the bastard offspring of his father's dalliance with a pox-ridden whore,"* he had told me when he first gave me the assignment, his presence filling my mind with a palpable darkness, blacker than the grave he had torn me out of several months earlier. My target and I are bound to each other by what would seem to be the strongest of bonds, that of blood. I know, however, the fragile strength of that tie; and how it means nothing to me now, save as the way to find and kill my foe, bringing me one step closer to freedom.

I don't often have time to think about things, and if a spare moment like this one comes, I usually choose not to. Past memories contain nothing but pain. The Master made me kill everyone I'd ever held dear, and whenever I had one of them within my reach, he always made me use my hands. I expect that tonight will be no different, even though I've never met this kinsman before.

For that is my power, that is why the Master

holds me so dear, above all the rest. When I was first awakened, he told me that he had been looking for one such as I for years. There had been others, and he had reached out with his skills and magic to find them. But they had always died before his legions could get to them, either in the streets or discovered and destroyed by the other side. All before me.

I do not know how this person opposes the Master's plans; indeed, he has never seen fit to share his unholy designs with me. The visions he sends when he has a new task for me, sometimes carry other images along with them, pictures of war and ruin and terror; of vast armies clashing on blood-soaked fields, and the Master's crimson-and-black standard—a scaled hand with claw-tipped fingers clutching a sword—rising above the battlefield, or over a large city. Whether this is happening now, or is just a fevered dream of the thing that controls my every move, I do not know.

Nor do I care. To him, I am just a tool, albeit a vital one this evening, but one of many that he has created for this purpose. All of that means nothing to me now, for even if he were to accomplish whatever madness he schemes at, he would still have need of me, to track and kill more men, or anyone who would dare to resist him. But for now, my singular purpose is to end the life of the man at the other end of the trembling, blue-white line that snakes from my feet through the room and out the door.

There is a commotion at the door as a half

dozen more men crowd into the packed room. The blue-white line flares with sudden brilliance, and I know he is in here at last.

"You had to pick the table farthest from the door, didn't you?" the Master mocks.

"They would expect an attempt right away," I reply. "Better to let them get in, surrounded by the crowd, before attacking. Harder to escape."

"You have been planning this, haven't you?" the Master says. *"Perhaps I should let you kill him yourself. After all, I have so many other matters to attend to."*

He doesn't fool me with his seeming nonchalance; I know a trap when I hear one. The Master is very powerful, able to command undead like myself across vast distances, carrying out his desires while staying safe in his keep far, far away. However, his power over me is lessened when he is not in contact, and there exists the small possibility that my target might escape. If that occurred, the punishment would be worse than anything I could imagine. "I know how you like to watch." Rare enough that I am able to tease him, but the lure works.

"Mmm, you are correct, my pawn. Ah, they approach."

The group will pass close to my table on their way toward the door of a back room. I crane my neck, fingers digging into the tabletop, trying to see which one is connected to the other end of my line.

They approach in a tight cluster, a ring of out-thrust hands to ward off the tavern's denizens. Although I should be able to feel my target this near, they are all so close together that I cannot fix on the one I need. The wise thing would be to go for the one in the middle and so . . .

They pass by, their eyes looking everywhere but down. Picking up my empty tankard, I stick out my foot, tripping the nearest, a blond-haired, callow-looking boy in his late teens. He staggers over my leg and falls against the table next to mine. The three men at that table, judging by the empty tankards littering it, have been there for a long time with nothing to do but drink. As a match set to a keg of ballpowder, they are up and spoiling for a fight.

Which leaves me with all the time I need. Still holding the flagon, I stand up and come around the table. Half of the group is trying to pacify the troublemakers at the next table, the other half is moving toward the entrance to the back room. The presence in my head tenses in anticipation. *"Now!"*

A boot moves forward, and I see the blue-white leading to a solid, well-built man of about thirty. His stained travel cloak shifts for a moment, and I see the royal crest beneath. It's him.

Time blurs and stretches yet again, only this time I am moving like lightning in the space between each second. I tap the nearest man, who is looking away from me, on the shoulder. The instant his head turns, I bring the heavy pewter tankard up and catch him square across the face, a spray of blood squirting from his crushed nose. He doesn't feel it, his eyes rolling back as he drops like a poleaxed steer.

With the boy being held by one of the other ruffians and this one out of the way, I have a clear shot at the man they're guarding.

Flexing my wrist, I feel my *real'gais* slip down and lock into place. Before anyone can react, I take one step and drive the twin blades up through the bottom of his chin, deep into his brain.

"Guh—" is all he has time to say before the cold iron pins his tongue to the roof of his mouth. Death is instant, and so should be the severing of the fate line that binds us together. Pulling my blades out of his head, I glance down, expecting to see it dissipate, the way it always has whenever I have killed a member of my own family.

Instead, it flares again and twists on the bar-room floor, still leading away from me to my brother. Something is very wrong.

"You imbecilic fool! You killed their decoy! Destroy them all!" the Master shrieks in my mind. That pause, however, is enough for one of the guards to sound the alarm.

"Deadhand!" he yells, and the tavern erupts in panic. Half the patrons and all of the staff scramble for the nearest exit, be it door, window, or even the narrow chimney. The rest produce weapons of various makes and purposes, from coshes to daggers to one swarthy Easterner who ratchets out a *real'gais* of his own and advances toward me, along with a half dozen newfound allies.

When one of my kind is found, all rivalries and grudges are forgotten until I am destroyed. It is the one law all obey Aboveground.

My bloodthirsty hands would love to oblige each one of them, but I only have eyes for my prey, who is still somewhere among the herd of men crowding into the back room. I choose the easy way to get to him.

My own *real'gais* flicks out, and one of the noble's bodyguards staggers back, clutching his gaping crimson throat. Two others, seeing this, rush me from both sides, thinking numbers can make up for experience. A stab and a slash later, neither of them will ever think anything again.

I have just reached the doorway to the back room when hands grab my shoulder, my cloak, my tattered tunic. I spin around, slashing fingers off with a vicious upswing. The others fall away, and the rest of the crowd draws back for a moment, working up their nerve.

Knowing where the noble's party is headed, I leap onto the table once occupied by the thugs that had provided my distraction, and dive through a small window near the chimney, slamming open the crude shutters and just scraping through.

Falling out, I land with boneless grace on the muddy ground. The rest of the noble's group are mounting their horses, the reins of which are being held by one man; a woodswalker, by his dark leathers and broadsword.

"By the Gods!" he exclaims as I stand up, uncaring of my dislocated shoulder and cut face, and step forward. He brings up a heavy crossbow and looses a barbed quarrel into my gut, a wound that would drop any other man in shrieking agony. I keep walking, the fearful neighing of the horses an unwanted balm to my ears. The woodsman shouts at the others to get the lordling out of there as he swings up onto his own mount. They herd him away, surrounding the white-faced youth in a tight pack, while the hunter faces me. I keep walking forward, but the man is ready, goading his wild-eyed horse straight into me. The animal's withers strike my chest, bowling me over. It is a minor distraction, but the forester has done his job, buying time for the noble to escape.

Wheeling his mount around, he claps heels to hide and gallops down the alley, racing to rejoin his comrades. Rising, I try to follow, but am suddenly paralyzed, unable to lift even my evil fingers. With my left leg out, I lose my balance and topple over, sinking into the chill mire of mud, horse droppings, piss and vomit. The stench is almost unbearable, even to me.

Cold, hard fury invades my mind like a physical blow, and I know exactly what is coming next. *"You pitiful wretch, I send you to do one simple task, and you fail at that. He was right next to you, and you could not even reach out and take his life, a task you have demonstrated you are capable of time and time again.*

The Master is so furious he can barely get the words out. *"You will lie there until I fetch you again, thrall. Think about your failure, and of the punishment that will be your world when I bring you to me.''*

With that he is gone—not completely, but away from my mind, going to another of his vassals to pick up my half brother's trail. It is a good thing, too, as he will not know the grim smile of satisfaction frozen on my face as I lie limp and motionless in the slime.

Several of the other tavern patrons come outside now and encircle my inert form. I hear muttering as the various criminals and vagabonds decide what to do with me. The general consensus is to burn my body. They carefully reach for my *real'gais* and try to remove it. The weapon is a part of me now and doesn't budge. The motion causes my arms to twitch, making everyone leap away. They confer again and decide to burn me right there.

Brush is brought and piled around me, but before a torch can be applied, pounding hoofbeats are heard, and a group of the local constables thunder into the back square, scattering the mob to the shadows and trampling me farther into the mud and filth. It is ironic that those who were doing right would be punished for it if the law catches up with them.

My arms and legs, now bent and twisted, still refuse to function. I know I must leave, but the Master will not let me. I know he won't sacrifice me because I am too valuable to him. He is trying to scare me, as if that is even possible after all I've been through. Even his threat of punishment strikes no chord in me now. The one thing that remains is the smile frozen on my face. All has gone as I had first planned when the Master gave me this task.

At first, when he had ripped me from my final rest and bound my struggling, confused soul back into my lifeless body, he had total control over me—every movement, every impulse. He sought to break my mind and spirit by sending me to my home to slaughter my own family. If he had gotten to me when I had just died, it might have worked. But he was too late, and by the time he raised me, the other side had worked its own designs on me as well, protecting some of my thoughts from his constant prying mind. Now, years later, he has grown complacent, distracted, and that has worked to my advantage.

It was I who attacked too early, I who went after the wrong person. While my hands are no longer a full part of me, true, they are still weapons that I can wield, pointing them in the right direction. It is difficult but worthwhile, especially at times like this.

If my Master wanted this prince dead, that alone was an excellent reason to make sure he survived my ambush. The fact that he is a blood relative is a lesser reason, for I bear as little resemblance to him now as a mouse does to a hawk. But in time, perhaps, someone will defeat the Master, and make sure that I am freed from this unholy condition, this constant unlife. If this man can help that happen faster, then I will do everything I can to help from the other side.

Perhaps, someday, that will happen. But that thought is little comfort to me as I lie in the cold, stinking mud, water and dung filling my eyes and mouth, trying with all my might to make my hands move.

ALL IN THE EXECUTION

Tim Waggoner

Tim Waggoner's most recent novels include the *Godfire* duology, *Thieves of Blood*, *Pandora Drive*, and *Like Death*. He's published close to eighty short stories, some of them collected in *All Too Surreal*. His articles on writing have appeared in *Writer's Digest*, *Writers' Journal*, and other publications. He teaches creative writing at Sinclair Community College in Dayton, Ohio. Visit him on the web at www.timwaggoner.com.

"SO . . . HOW WOULD you like to die?"
     Sarsour often began with this question. He found it an effective way to put prisoners—especially the sort he dealt with—off-balance. But it didn't work this time. The man sitting cross-legged on the straw pallet simply smiled and continued looking at Sarsour with ice-chip blue eyes.

Sarsour found the mage's gaze disconcerting, and he fought to keep the unease he felt from showing on his face.

You are Sarsour Burhan, he told himself. *Lord High Executioner of the Citadel of Tabari. And regardless of who this mage might have been on the outside, he's merely another prisoner now.*

But Sarsour couldn't bring himself to believe that last part. Kardel Duvessa was one of the most powerful mages in the kingdom of Qadira, and a necromancer in his own right. But even a mage as skilled as Kardel couldn't escape from the confinement ring surrounding his straw pallet, nor could he cast spells while inside it. The ring was a complex enchantment created by the Master Warder herself, an array of mystic gems, arcane symbols, and intricately woven energy lattices, that when activated, could imprison an arch-demon, let alone a human mage.

Still, this *was* Kardel Duvessa—a powerful, dangerous, cold-blooded killer. Less than a month ago, Kardel had destroyed a monastery far to the north by calling down a rain of fiery sky-rock upon the structure. None of the forty-eight monks inside at the time survived. At his trial, when asked why he had committed such a horrendous crime, Kardel simply said, *I never did like monks*.

The man was in his late forties, wolfishly thin, and completely bereft of body hair. Not only was he bald, but he had no eyebrows, no eyelashes, no hair on his hands, fingers, or knuckles. The absence of hair gave Kardel an otherworldly look, which Sarsour supposed was the point. The man wore the same clothes he'd had on when the Citadel's Enforcers had finally caught up with him: an expensive doublet fashioned of crimson silk, cerulean leggings, and highly polished black boots with gold buckles. The Duvessa family were well known for their rarified tastes.

Sarsour decided to try another tack. He sat down on the stone floor opposite Kardel so as to address the mage on an equal level. Mages of Kardel's stature never responded well when looked down upon, whether literally or figuratively. Sarsour wasn't worried that he might be putting himself at a disadvantage. Though there were no bars on Kardel's room—and thus no barriers between the two mages—none were necessary. Not as long as Kardel remained within the Circle of Confinement and Sarsour remained outside it.

Not that Sarsour was especially intimidating either standing *or* sitting. He was a short, chubby man with greasy black hair and an overlong droopy black mustache. He was garbed in the black robe of his office, the silver fur trimming his collar, sleeves, and hem a symbol of his rank as a master of necromancy.

"So you are to be my murderer." It was the first time Kardel had spoken since being captured, and Sarsour was surprised by how calm the man sounded, considering the topic under discussion.

"Executioner," Sarsour corrected. "Yes, I am. It is my responsibility to carry out the sentence handed down by the Council of Hierarchs. And unfortunately for you, that sentence is death." Sarsour always said *unfortunately* to be polite. The truth of the matter was he thought the prisoners he dealt with got precisely what they deserved, but he knew it wouldn't be very professional to say so. "However, the Council—out of respect for your family name—has granted you the courtesy of a private death, so that your family can avoid the spectacle of a public execution. Also, in appreciation of all that your family has done for Quadira throughout the centuries, the Council has also given you the freedom to choose your specific means of death. I have a quite a variety to offer, everything from a simple Twilight Sleep spell to the Ecstatic Demise of Ten Thousand Blisses. Do you have any preferences or would you like me to make some suggestions?"

"It doesn't matter," Kardel said in a bored voice. "You won't be able to kill me."

Sarsour clenched his jaw in irritation, but he managed to keep his tone even as he replied. "Many others before you have said similar words to me. And let me assure you, those words were among the last they ever spoke."

A mocking smile played about Kardel's lips. "You misunderstand. I do not mean that you lack the skill to execute me, either by physical means or mystical. I'm saying that in my case, you will be unable to slay me. No one can."

Sarsour let his irritation get the better of him then. "I suppose you're telling me that you ascended to godhood when no one was looking?"

Kardel laughed, but it was a laugh without mirth. "Not quite."

"You'll forgive me if I don't take your word for it." Every mage that had been found guilty of a crime by the Council of Hierarchs pled innocent, and every one sentenced to death presented him or herself as too powerful to be destroyed. But in the end, they all took the final passage across the Bridge of Unspoken Sorrows, and entered the shadowy realm of Gadaran, land of the dead.

Sarsour decided to call Kardel's bluff right away. "Since you say you cannot be slain, you won't mind if I cast a spell of Swift Passage upon you." This was one of the most powerful death-spells in existence, and few mages could counter it.

Kardel shrugged. "Do as you will."

Sarsour concentrated and whispered words in the ancient thaumaturgic language of magekind. His spirit reached out to a dark dimension filled with necromantic energies and drew a portion of the fell power into himself. He then flung his hands toward Kardel, sending twin bursts of crackling ebon lightning toward the condemned mage. The shadow-energy coruscated across Kardel's body for a moment before finally dissipating, leaving the man unharmed. He didn't blink an eye, let alone keel over dead.

With increasing frustration, Sarsour tried several other deadly enchantments—Fire-Blood, Ice-Hold, and even Astral Severance—but none worked. Exasperated, he eventually summoned one of the Citadel's guards and ordered the man to drew his sword and slay Kardel. The guard tried, but though his steel was sharp and penetrated Kardel's body with ease, the wound produced no blood and healed the moment the blade was withdrawn. Kardel grinned, as if the piercing blow caused him no pain, and Sarsour dismissed the bemused guard.

Sarsour struggled to keep the frustration he felt out of his voice as he spoke. "It seems that you were telling the truth when you claimed you cannot be killed."

Kardel's only response was to grin wider.

"Powerful as you may be, you couldn't have managed this on your own. The power necessary to accomplish what you've done is almost beyond imagining."

Kardel's smile remained in place, but his voice took on a cold, hard edge. "Perhaps beyond your limited mental capacity to imagine. But then, the members of your family have never been known for their intellectual gifts, have they?"

Sarsour ignored the gibe. He was used to prisoners taunting him with false bravado. The problem here was that Sarsour feared Kardel's bravado was real.

"Now I understand. However you managed it, you've made yourself immune to death in order to disgrace me and stain my family's reputation."

"Think of what you're suggesting. In order for it to be true, I would've had to find a way to do what no other mage before me has been able to accomplish—defy death—and then destroy that monastery so the Council would sentence me to be executed. Why would I want to go to all that trouble just to embarrass you, Sarsour? Surely you don't think you're *that* important."

"As an individual, no. But as a member of the family Burhan and the current High Executioner, yes. Your family, the Duvessas, served as High Executioners for fifteen generations until my great-great-grandfather took over the post, and it has remained in my family ever since."

"Why should something like that bother me?" Kardel said. He was no longer smiling. "Just because after your great-great-grandfather's betrayal, the Duvessas have had to bear the burden of having been bested by a clan of inferior mages? Because from virtually the day I was born, I've watched you live a life that is rightfully mine? How could any of these piddling trifles possibly goad me into taking such extraordinary measure to embarrass and humble you?"

"Because if there's one thing the Duvessas value more than power or wealth, it's pride," Sarsour said. "So now I know *why* you did it. The question is *how* you managed such a feat and what I need to do in order to counter the enchantment."

Kardel laughed. "Don't waste your time. There's nothing you can do. Except fail, that is. Fail, disgrace your ancestors, and lose the position of High Executioner, not only for yourself, but for your descendants as well."

Sarsour had no direct descendants to worry

about at the moment, but he saw no reason to point this out to Kardel. The disgrace to his ancestors would be bad enough.

"Even if I do fail, Kardel, you shall never leave the dungeon. You shall remain here, bound within the Master Warder's confinement spell for all time."

Kardel shrugged. "Perhaps. But that will be a small price to pay to see my ancestors avenged. Now if you'll be so kind as to go away and begin your life as a failure, I'd appreciate it. I'd like to get some sleep." Kardel then lay down, curled up on his pallet, and closed his eyes.

Sarsour watched him for several moments, trying to think of a witty rejoinder. But none came. Before long, Kardel's breathing deepened as sleep came to him, and the High Executioner turned and walked away.

"It's not as if you haven't had to deal with difficult situations before."

Sarsour nodded and took a sip of his thorn tea. Adila had made it tepid and bitter, just the way he liked it.

"But this is the first time I've ever had to execute a mage of Kardel's caliber before." Sarsour sighed. "I'm not sure I'm up to the task."

Sarsour sat at the head of a long mahogany table in the dining hall of his home. As Lord High Executioner for the Citadel of Tabari, he was granted a small manor home to the south of the Citadel itself. It wasn't the best location in the city:

that would be directly east or west of the Citadel. The view these locations offered of the Citadel's crystalline structure at sunrise and sunset was magnificent. Still, his home was pleasant enough, and members of the Burhan family had occupied it for several generations. Though that might well change if Sarsour couldn't find a way to execute Kardel.

Adila sat on Sarsour's right, though her proper place was at the other end of the table. But the damn thing was so long that if she sat that far away from him, they couldn't hear each other unless they shouted. So when it was just the two of them—and it almost always was—they dispensed with protocol.

"You managed to kill Berra, Queen of Blood, didn't you?" Adila pointed out. "And she had the ability to regenerate organs and missing limbs."

"True." That had been a tricky case. It had taken Sarsour almost three months to devise a spell that transformed Berra into a sentient pool of water. He then had her poured into a rain barrel and placed outside during the dry season. She evaporated over the course of a week and had never been seen again.

"And what about Jarkar the Spiritwalker?" Adila asked.

Jarkar had possessed the power to make his body completely intangible so that nothing could harm him. The Master Warder had been able to create a confinement ring that held his ethereal form, but for the first time Sarsour—despite his best efforts—had been unable to carry out the sentence of execution. He tried withholding the evil mage's food and water but soon realized Jarkar didn't require either as long as he remained wraithlike. Eventually, Sarsour developed an intangible blade matched to the specific density of Jarkar's ghostly form. The executioner set the blade into a very tangible handle and was able to use the newly created weapon to fulfill his duty.

"If you could figure out a way to kill those two, then you should be able to do the same with Kardel," Adila said. She was a slim, petite woman with curly brown hair tinged gray in spots. Neither she nor Sarsour were especially old, but they weren't exactly young either. Though the spouse of a master mage usually wore clothing that resembled her husband's (or his wife's), Adila wasn't overly fond of black. She favored bright colors, and this afternoon she had on a yellow dress with billowy sleeves that her arms seemed lost in.

Adila taught youth preservation and restoration at the university, popular specialties to be sure, given the demand for such services, especially among the rich and powerful of Qadira. Such magic could do little more than postpone the inevitable, of course, but that was more than enough for most people. Adila's colleagues at the university often made the observation that it was ironic that she should marry Sarsour, considering that she specialized in spells to extend life and he was a necromancer who specialized in magical executions. But where others saw irony, Adila saw balance.

We complement each other, she'd once said to Sarsour. *Male and female, life and death . . . What could be more perfect?*

What indeed?

Sarsour smiled and reached out to pat his wife's hand. "I appreciate your faith in me, my love. But I'm afraid the situation is different this time. Somehow, Kardel has managed to find a way to make himself immune to death."

Adila's eyes widened in surprise. "Is such a thing possible?"

"Apparently. I fear Kardel may be the first prisoner a member of my family has failed to slay since the Buhrans took over the office of High Executioner."

"Even if that does occur—and I'm not saying it will—would that be so awful? The Council of Hierarchs would just commute Kardel's sentence to life imprisonment without the chance for parole, yes?"

"That's right. Kardel will still be punished for his crimes, no matter what. Nevertheless, I will be disgraced in the eyes of the Council, and they may well decide to replace me." And if that happened, it would mean the end of the Buhran family's tradition of service to the Council. Sarsour's replacement—whoever it might be—would become the founder of a new line of High

Executioners—and Sarsour's family name would eventually be little more than a footnote in the history books.

Adila didn't say anything for a time. And when she finally broke the silence, she looked down at the tabletop instead of meeting her husband's gaze.

"There might be advantages to your leaving office," she said softly.

Sarsour couldn't believe he had heard her correctly. "You can't be serious!"

Adila continued to avert her eyes as she went on. "It would give you more time to research our . . . problem. And perhaps finally find a solution for it."

Now Sarsour understood. He reached out and clasped her hand, and when he spoke, his tone was gentle and loving. "I've been trying, you know. For years now, I've spent every extra moment researching fertility spells and counterspells to remove curses."

Before marrying Sarsour, Adila had been betrothed to a mage named Xorat, another professor at the university. When she caught him cheating on her with not one but several of his students—at the same time—she broke off their engagement. Xorat was a vain man, and angered by what he perceived as the damage to his reputation for Adila's "jilting" him, he cast an infertility curse on her. Adila had attempted to remove the enchantment herself, but it was beyond her capabilities.

She consulted other mages, but none could help her.

She and Sarsour had met not long after that, when the university invited him to give a lecture on developing counterspells—something of a sub-specialty in his family as they often were forced to discover ways to remove mystical impediments to carrying out prisoners' death sentences. To Sarsour's great surprise and good fortune, Adila for some unaccountable reason had been attracted to him, and they eventually married. Ever since, Sarsour had been searching for a counterspell to remove Xorat's curse, but so far he'd met with little success, and Adila and he had been unable to conceive the child that she so desperately wanted.

Adila looked up and he saw her eyes were brimming with tears. "But if you were able to devote all your time to your research . . . I know it would mean giving up your station, and we'd have to vacate the manor, but I don't care about that." She reached out and touched his cheek. "I love you, and I want to have your child."

Sarsour leaned forward and kissed his wife. "I love you, too. But I have to do everything I can to fulfill the duties of my office. Both for my family's honor and for mine. Please try to understand."

Adila put on a brave smile, choked back tears, and nodded. "Of course. It was silly of me to suggest otherwise. I just want to be a mother so badly."

Then the tears came, and Sarsour held his wife close and gently stroked her hair while she cried.

After speaking with his wife, Sarsour went to his study. Books, scrolls, and loose sheets of vellum were crammed into numerous bookcases that lined the room. Most of the texts had been written by one ancestor of Sarsour's or another. Scattered about the study were other accouterments of the necromancer's art—skeletons, skulls, finger bones, vials, and jars labeled *Dead Man's Breath*, *Essence of Putrefaction*, and the like. Sarsour hardly ever had any use for these materials, but a certain amount of morbid atmosphere was expected of a necromancer's lair, even more so when said necromancer also served as High Executioner. And so Sarour tolerated the bones and vials of bizarre substances, though privately he felt they were rather childish.

He sat cross-legged on the stone floor, half-closed his eyes, and began chanting the first of the Seven Exhortations to Summon the Dead. By the time Sarsour reached the Fourth Exhortation, a softly glowing mist began to coalesce in the air before him.

"That's good enough." The voice sounded like a cold autumn wind blowing dried leaves across cobblestones.

Sarsour stopped chanting and opened his eyes to behold the translucent form of a stout bearded old man. The apparition resembled Sarsour a great deal, though he was shorter and had a full white beard.

Sarsour smiled. "You never were one to stand on formalities, Father."

The ghostly figure shrugged. "Such foolishness doesn't seem all that important once one has crossed the Bridge of Unspoken Sorrows for the final time."

Ferran Buhran had been High Executioner before Sarsour, and now that he was truly dead, he acted as if being deceased was far superior to being alive.

"Before we begin, give me some good news," Ferran said. "Tell me I finally have a grandchild on the way."

"I'm afraid not, Father. I've made no new progress on lifting the curse of infertility on Adila since last we spoke."

Ferran sniffed. "And you call yourself a mage! If you do not produce an heir, how will our family continue to hold onto the position of High Executioner?"

Sarsour sighed. Ferran had nagged him about this often enough while alive, but he'd become absolutely insufferable about the matter since he'd joined the ranks of the dead.

"I don't want to speak of such things now, Father. I've summoned you for a more important reason."

"Well, of course you did. I didn't think you'd brought me all the way from Gadaran just to chat. What do you want?"

Now that Ferran was here, Sarsour found himself reluctant to tell his father precisely why he needed his help. The mage didn't want to give his father another reason to berate him. But if he were to have any hope of solving his current problem, it would be through Ferran. So Sarsour took a deep breath and told the shade of his father about Kardel.

When Sarsour finished, he expected Ferran to chastise him for being so thick-headed. Instead, the mage's spirit looked thoughtful.

"So Kardel claims he cannot be killed. Presumably by anyone or anything."

"My most powerful spells failed to slay him, as did the sharp edge of a steel blade. Did you ever encounter anything like this during your tenure as executioner?"

Ferran thought for several moments, his ethereal body blurring in and out of focus as he did. Finally he shook his head.

"I've never heard of anyone possessing the ability to so completely defy death. It's almost as if . . ." He frowned as he trailed off.

"Almost as if what, Father?"

In response, a slow smile spread across the lower half of Ferran's face, and his ghostly eyes gleamed with unearthly light.

"I think it's time for you to pay *me* a visit, son."

"You can't be serious!" Adila sounded angry, but Sarsour knew that she was only attempting to conceal her worry.

They were in their bedchamber. Sarsour lay atop the silken sheets covering the large round mattress, hands clasped over his belly. Adila stood next to the bed, gazing down at her husband with concern.

"Father believes that this is the only way for me to discover Kardel's secret," Sarsour said. "And once I know how he's made himself immune to death, I'll be able to counter the enchantment and fulfill my duty." *And preserve the family honor*, he added mentally. But he didn't say so aloud. Adilia wasn't much on honor; she was far too practical a woman. He reached up and took his wife's hand. "Please try to understand, my love. This is something I must do."

"Of course it is, and I do understand." She squeezed his hand, and though her eyes glistened with tears, she did not cry. "Do what you have to do. I will remain by your side the entire time and make certain your body is safe until you return."

Sarsour gave his wife a last smile and removed his hand from hers. "It will be fine, Adila. I promise."

She nodded, though she didn't look convinced. Sarsour closed his eyes.

He had traveled astrally before—no mage could attain master rank without gaining some facility at out-of-body movement. But though he'd trained in necromancy since childhood and had served as High Executioner since he was a young man, he'd never before attempted to travel to Gadaran. He knew the way, theoretically at least, but the journey held many risks.

But he couldn't afford to dwell on such things now. He relaxed and allowed himself to slip slowly into a trance. The sensation was pleasant, not unlike immersing one's self in warm bathwater. The warmth enveloped him, and then he felt himself begin to grow lighter, less substantial, as if he were floating and at the same time losing mass. Soon, he could no longer feel any physical sensations whatsoever, and the warmth gave way to a vague suggestion of coolness, though this was more sensed than felt.

Sarsour was free of his body.

Though he had no physical eyes, he could nevertheless see, and a swirling ocean of darkness filled his vision. He concentrated on moving toward the darkness, pictured the image of the place he wanted to go, a place he had never seen but only read about. The darkness cleared then, parting as if it were little more than ebon fog blown apart by a strong wind, and Sarsour found himself standing at the edge of a cliff beneath an empty black sky. He appeared to have physical form once more, but he knew this to be an illusion. He was still very much a spirit in this place.

A rope bridge was attached to the edge of the cliff—the lines weathered and fraying, wooden slats warped and cracked. The bridge stretched across a vast gulf of space, and though Sarsour could not see the other side, he knew that the opposite end of the bridge was attached to another cliff much like this one. This was the Bridge of Unspoken Sorrows, the entrance to Gadaran.

"Are you going to stand there staring for all eternity or are you going to cross?"

Sarsour turned and saw his father standing next to him. In this realm, Farren appeared not as a translucent shade but rather a flesh-and-blood man. But Sarsour knew that appearances could be deceiving, especially in this place.

He gave his father's spirit a smile. "Nice of you to join me."

"I wasn't about to let my son and heir enter Gadaran without a proper escort. What would our ancestors say?"

"What, indeed?" Sarsour responded, amused. Farren was just as gruff in death as he had been in life, but Sarsour was grateful for his presence. Though the mage technically had no lungs here, he inhaled deeply as he stepped forward, took hold of the bridge's guide ropes, and began crossing.

The air was cold and dank, and smelled of rot and grave mold. Strong crosswinds blew through the canyon, making the bridge sway. Though he knew it wasn't a good idea, Sarsour looked down and saw nothing but darkness between the wooden slats. According to legend, the abyss below stretched on forever without end. It was one legend that he had no intention of confirming, however. Sarsour looked forward again, gripped the guide ropes tightly, and kept his gaze fixed on the bridge ahead of him so that he wouldn't get dizzy.

The wind picked up speed, whistling and howling as it surged through the canyon. It sounded almost like voices—mournful, lost, despairing. It had to be his imagination, though. Legend made no mention of any spirits guarding the bridge. But the wailing sounds grew louder the farther Sarsour walked, and by the time the opposite end of the bridge finally came into view—the shade of his father following silently behind—the voices had taken on an edge of anger, and specific words became clear. Or rather, *one* specific word: they were shouting Sarsour's name, over and over. Strands of etheric mist became visible, darting and swirling, over, around, and under the rope bridge. Faces coalesced out of the mist, disembodied ghostly heads that glared at Sarsour as they flew by, crying out his name as if it were some sort of epithet. At first Sarsour didn't recognize any of the faces, then their features gradually became more defined, and he realized that he was looking at the spirits of all the men and women he'd executed over the years.

He recognized Renlak, originator of the Great Pestilence, and Paraselcis, also known as She Who Walked in Darkness. And there were so many more, all of them mages, all of them men and woman who'd chosen to use their mystical abilities and training for their own selfish—if not outright diabolical—purposes. Hundreds of them, and all had met their ends thanks to the necromantic spells of Sarsour Buhran.

Without taking his gaze from the swirling storm

of angry spirits, Sarsour shouted back to his father. "What is this?"

"A welcoming committee!" Ferran shouted back. "When you're Lord High Executioner for the Council of Hierarchs, you tend to make a lot of enemies—*especially* over here!"

"Wonderful," Sarsour muttered. He'd already dispatched these villains once before. Now it seemed he would have to do so one more time. Making sure his feet were firmly planted on the wooden planks beneath him, Sarsour raised both of his hands high and began chanting a rite to repel angry spirits. It was a simple exorcism spell, but it might serve well enough. Though these spirits had all been powerful mages while alive, they didn't appear to be anything more than angry ghosts. But even as he began the rite, he knew something was wrong. He could not feel necromantic energy flowing into his body, and the words that passed his lips sounded like nothing more than nonsense syllables, with none of the sinister sonorous overtones they took on as magic began to activate. The spirits showed no reaction either. Instead of turning away and fleeing back into the eternal blackness that had birthed them, they continued flying through the air, glaring at him and shouting his name. If anything, they flew faster and shouted more loudly than before.

"You're wasting your time!" the spirit of his father shouted. "This is the *land* of the dead. Death-magic holds no power here!"

Sarsour halted his chanting and lowered his arms. "You might have told me that before I got started!"

"I thought you would figure it out on your own."

The heads continued swirling around the bridge, so many that they formed a solid column of etheric energy. The noise of their wailing became deafening, and Sarsour had to clap his hands to his ears to try to muffle the sound, but it didn't help much. While the heads continued circling, ghostly, disembodied hands appeared in the air above the guide ropes on both side of the bridge and began violently shaking it. The spirits obviously hoped to knock Sarsour off and send him tumbling into the dark abyss below to fall forever and ever, without either hope of rescue or death.

Sarsour yelped and grabbed hold of the guide ropes, but a large pair of phantom hands—so big they could only have belong to Arthis the Strangler—grabbed Sarsour's wrists and forced him to release his hold on the ropes. The ghost hands then began to tug Sarsour toward the edge of the narrow bridge and the vast yawning emptiness that waited below. Sarsour knew he would be lost if he didn't do something soon. So he did what any grown man might do in a similar situation: turned to his father for help.

"You're supposed to be my spirit guide in this realm. *Do* something!"

"Guide, yes. Rescuer, no. It's against the laws that govern Gadaran for me to interfere so directly." Ferran considered for a moment. "I suppose this *is* an extraordinary situation, though." He reached into his robe pocket and brought out a miniature ram's horn carved out of bone. He placed the horn to his lips and blew. A high-pitched tone rang forth from the horn, seeming to grow louder and stronger until it filled the entire dimension of Gadaran, echoing from one end of the land of the dead to the other.

The ghostly shades of Sarsour's enemies stopped and hovered in midair, eyes darting nervously back and forth. When the last echo of the horn blast died away, everything was silent for a moment. But the silence was soon broken by a loud battlecry as a stream of new spirits poured onto the bridge and came toward Sarsour like a flood of mist. Sarsour saw no faces in the mist, but he sensed numerous presences within it.

As the mist drew near, it separated into individual streams that arced into the air toward the hovering spirits of Sarsour's enemies. The mist-streams slammed into the disembodied heads, creating small masses of roiling white that thrashed about violently.

"What's happening?" Sarsour asked his father.

"Family reunion," Ferran said, grinning. "I summoned our ancestors to come help. Now quickly—while they have the others busy—hurry across. Once you're in Gadaran proper, the spirits will bother you no longer.

Why this should be, Sarsour had no idea, but he assumed it had something to do with the laws of Gadaran his father had mentioned before. Keeping a loose hold on the guide ropes with both hands, Sarsour began hurrying to the other side.

When they saw Sarsour escaping, the spirits of his enemies howled their fury and fought to free themselves from his ancestors. But the spirits of the Buhran family line managed to keep hold of the vengeful ghosts until Sarsour had set foot on the rocky soil of Gadaran. The spirits of the mages Sarsour had executed let out one last frustrated howl before dissipating into nothingness. An instant later, the misty forms of his ancestors did the same, and all was quiet once more at the Bridge of Unspoken Sorrows.

Sarsour sighed with relief, then turned to his father, who'd followed him off the bridge and now stood beside his son.

"Thanks," Sarsour said.

"Don't thank me just yet, boy. You've still got a ways to go. Ferran gestured past Sarsour, and the necromancer turned to behold a huge desert of black sand stretching toward the gray horizon.

"I don't suppose I can just will my astral body to soar across that," Sarsour said.

Ferran shook his head. "The laws of Gadaran—"

"—forbid it. I was afraid of that."

He started walking, Ferran following close behind.

Sarsour knew, academically anyway, that time passed very differently in Gadaran than it did in the realm of the living. But actually experiencing this phenomenon was an entirely different matter. Sarsour had no idea how long they had walked. Indeed, he had no real sensation they had made any progress at all. The sky above remained so unchanging that Sarsour wouldn't have been at all surprised to learn that he had been merely lifting his feet and putting them down in exactly the same spot for hour after hour. But eventually a black spire appeared in the distance, slowly growing larger as Sarsour and the spirit of his dead father approached.

Sarsour had read descriptions of Tenebron, the Obsidian Palace, in various sources, but while most had gotten the basic details right, none had been able to communicate the immense majesty of the dark tower. Seemingly miles high in length, it stretched toward Gadaran's empty sky as if it were a pillar holding up the great void above. The pinnacle of Tenebron—if indeed there was one—blended with the dark sky-shroud, making it impossible to tell where one began and the other ended.

Father and son continued on until they reached the tower and stood before its main gate. It rose fifty feet into the air and at first glance appeared to have been wrought from black iron. But as Sarsour looked closer, he saw that what he'd taken to be bars of metal were instead long lengths of bone—femurs, to be precise. But these were the leg bones of giants, and colored black instead of ivory. Sarsour knew of no such creatures in

Qadira—at least, none humanoid—that were huge enough to have femurs like this. But this wasn't Qadira; it was Gadaran. The sight of the gigantic leg bones, and the thought of what they'd might have once belonged to, sent a shiver through Sarsour. He hoped his father hadn't noticed.

"This is Tenebron, the Obsidian Palace," Ferran said, speaking loudly and formally, as if he were a tour guide or perhaps one of the palace staff greeting a newcomer. "Home to her most dread majesty, Lady Sumehra, Queen of the Oblivion." Ferran lowered his voice and added, "Be careful, my son. Though you yet live, that condition can be remedied easily enough should Sumehra wish it."

Though his physical body was an illusion in this place, Sarsour nevertheless swallowed nervously. "I understand." He started to reach for the gate, but it swung open of its own accord, as if the tower had been expecting him. Who knows? Perhaps it had.

Sarsour passed through the open gateway and underneath the black stone arch that formed the tower's entrance. He expected the atmosphere inside to be cold and frigid as midnight in winter, but he was surprised to find the temperature most comfortable. Beyond the arch was a long corridor—the floor, walls, and ceiling of which were made entirely from blocks of highly polished black stone. Though no source of light was visible, Sarsour had no trouble seeing. More of Sumehra's magic, no doubt. The corridor had no door or open entryways—at least, none that Sarsour could detect—so he began walking. His sandals made soft slapping sounds that echoed up and down the corridor, seeming to grow louder and harsher with each echo. Ferran's feet made no noise; he *was* dead after all.

The corridor seemed to stretch on and on, far longer than it should have given what Sarsour had seen of the tower's apparent circumference from outside. But he didn't question this and, in fact, really didn't care how and why this could be so. He'd come here in search of only one piece of knowledge: how Kardel had made himself immune to death. After a time, the corridor began to widen, and finally it opened onto a grand chamber that Sarsour guessed lay at the center of the Obsidian Tower. A large gleaming black throne rose from the middle of a round stone dais. Atop this throne sat a woman so beautiful that for a moment Sarsour couldn't think, couldn't breathe, wasn't even aware that he wasn't breathing. The woman had smooth skin as white as porcelain, and long alabaster hair that hung down on either side of her finely sculpted face. Her lips were black instead of red, and her eyes were open and completely white, like those of a statue. She wore a dark-blue gown cut low in the bodice, along with a great deal of jewelry. Earrings, necklaces, rings, bracelets, all of them made form the same highly polished white substance. With a sick roil of his stomach, Sarsour realized he wasn't looking at *real* jewelry. Sumehra's accessories had been made from human bones, ligaments, and teeth.

Though Sarsour had studied every text that had ever been written on Gadaran and its queen, none of them had ever attempted to describe Sumehra's appearance. Many scholars believed this was because the Dark Lady was too hideous for mortal comprehension, but now Sarsour knew otherwise. It was because she was too beautiful.

The floor in front of Sumehra's throne wasn't empty, though. It was filled with dark figures that appeared roughly human-shaped, but which seemed to have been fashioned from living shadow. These creatures knelt before their mistress, row upon row of them. Incoherent whispering filled the chamber like the susurration of ocean waves as the shadow-things prayed to their goddess-queen.

Sumehra turned toward Sarsour and Ferran as they approached, and she smiled. Her ivory teeth were so white—*Like polished bone*, he thought— that they seemed to glow with a bright light. So intensely did they gleam that Sarsour had to squint, and even then he couldn't look directly at Sumehra. He'd read numerous accounts written by men and women who'd nearly died but managed to hold onto life and revive. They all spoke of moving through a dark tunnel at the end of which waited a dazzlingly bright light. Sarsour now understood just what that light truly was: the smile of the Queen of the Dead as she greeted her new subjects.

"Welcome, Sarsour, Lord High Executioner of the Citadel of Tabari, and one of my most loyal and faithful servants."

Sumehra's voice seemed to emanate from the very air, issuing forth from everywhere at once. Her tone was warm and smooth as honey, but there was a jarring undertone that sounded like the buzzing of angry bees.

Out of the corner of his eye, Sarsour saw his father kneel to the Dark Lady, and he began to do the same.

"Hold, Sarsour," Sumehra commanded. "In Gadaran, only the dead owe me obeisance. You, however, are still alive . . . for the moment at least." Her smile widened slightly, and though still bright, Sarsour no longer had to avert his eyes from the glare.

Having no wish to offend the Queen of the Dead, Sarsour straightened and inclined his head in thanks.

Sumehra stepped down from her dais and came toward Sarsour, the hem of her long dark-blue gown hissing softly across the stone floor as it trailed behind her. Sarsour could hear no footsteps as she approached, nor could he detect any movement of her legs. He had the impression that the Dark Lady was gliding toward him, her feet— assuming she had any, that is—hovering inches above the floor. When she was within five feet of Sarsour, she stopped. He could feel the other- worldly strength of her presence pressing against him like a crashing ebon wave. He wanted to step back away from her, wanted to avert his gaze. But he stood his ground and forced himself to look her in the eyes.

Sumehra gave a slight nod, as if she were pleased.

"You summoned your father's shade to guide your astral form to me and now you are here. State your business."

Sarsour took a deep breath, and when he spoke, his voice was strong and firm. "The Council of Hierarchs has tasked me with executing Kardel Duressa for crimes he committed against the people of Qadira. But I am . . . having trouble performing that duty." Sarsour went on to tell her of his attempts to slay Kardel, and how all of them had failed. When he was finished, he added, "It is my belief that the only way Kardel could've made himself immune to death is if he entered into some sort of pact with you."

Sumehra looked at him for several long moments, during which time Sarsour noticed the Dark Lady never blinked or breathed. But then, she wouldn't need to do either, would she? For though she looked like a human woman—and an unimaginably beautiful one at that—she was the embodiment of Death itself. What need would Death have to blink or draw breath?

"You are right, of course," Sumehra said at last. "Kardel was so resentful of your family taking over the position of High Executioner that he came before me in spirit form—as you are doing now—and asked me to grant him a boon. If I would make him immune to death by all means other than natural aging, the spirits of his ancestors would serve as my personal attendants for all eternity." The Dark Lady turned and gestured at the shadow creatures still kneeling before her throne. None of them had moved since Sarsour's arrival.

Sarsour's eyes widened in amazement. "There are hundreds of those creatures."

"Thousands, actually," Sumehra said. "Those you see here are but the shades of the highest-ranked mages of the Duressa line. The remaining ancestors are elsewhere in the tower, waiting until I have need of them."

Sarsour was both impressed and appalled. "I can't believe that Kardel would go to such lengths to embarrass me."

"Not just you, Sarsour," Sumehra pointed out. "But your entire family. If he succeeds, not only will you undoubtedly be relieved of your duties as Lord High Executioner, but no member of the Buhran line will ever be permitted to hold the office again."

"But what good will that do?" Sarsour said. "After the crimes Kardel was committed, no member of his family will ever be able to serve as Executioner either!"

"True," Sumehra admitted. "But he doesn't care about that. All that matters to him is avenging his family and damaging the reputation of yours."

In Qadira, family honor was everything, especially among the higher classes. But even so, Sarsour still couldn't comprehend paying such a high price for vengeance. He looked upon the hundreds of shadowy spirits kneeling before Sumehra's throne. All of them had willingly entered into the Dark Lady's eternal service—all in the name of revenge.

"I wish to avoid allowing such disgrace to fall upon my own family name," Sarsour said. "And more than that, I have a sworn duty to perform. Will you allow me to slay Kardel?"

Sumehra looked thoughtful for a moment before answering. "I'm sorry. I made a pact with Kardel, and I cannot break it."

Sarsour sighed. "That's it, then." No matter how skilled a necromancer he was, his power was nothing compared to that of Sumehra. Kardel would spend the rest of his life in prison, where he would eventually die of old age. But Kardel would have succeeded in revenging his family against Sarsour's.

"Of course, there *might* be a way that you could still perform your duty," Sumehra said. "For a price."

Sarsour swallowed. He feared to learn what price the Queen of the Dead would ask of him, but whatever it was, he knew he would pay it. But before he could say anything, his father's spirit stood and stepped between Sarsour and Sumehra.

"My Lady," Ferran said. "I stand ready to pay whatever price you might set for your assistance."

"Father!" Sarsour protested. "You have no right to make that offer!"

Ferran turned to glare at his son. "I have *every* right. I was High Executioner before you, and I, too, am a Buhran. My honor is on the line as much as yours." Ferran's expression softened and he laid a hand on Sarsour's shoulder. Sarsour couldn't feel his father's touch, but that didn't matter. The gesture spoke for itself.

"Please, son. You still live and have a wife that loves you very much. And, the gods willing, the two of you may yet have a child one day. Let me do this for you."

Sarsour hesitated, but he saw the pleading in his father's eyes and finally nodded. Ferran smiled gratefully, then turned once more to face the Queen of the Dead. "It is settled. Whatever your price, I shall pay it."

Sumehra looked from father to son then back again. "Very well." She gestured with her left hand and Ferran's form grew dark, his features indistinct. Within seconds, he had become a shadow creature just like the others that still knelt before Sumehra's throne. Once the transformation was complete, the shadow-thing that had been Ferran Buhran walked over to join the others and knelt with them

"One can never have too many personal servants," Sumehra said.

Sarsour knew the only reason he didn't cry was because his astral form didn't possess true tear ducts.

"Now listen closely," Sumehra said. "As I told you, I will not go back on my agreement with Kardel. Only natural aging will kill him. But you are defining your duty too narrowly, Sarsour. You may be incapable of destroying Kardel's body, but what of the man himself?"

Sarsour frowned. "I don't understand."

"When you return home, tell your wife what I said. She'll know what to do."

Sumehra gestured with her right hand and the throne chamber began to blur around Sarsour. He realized that the Dark Lady had dismissed him, and his astral form was preparing to return to his physical body. But just as Sarsour's vision began to grow too hazy for him to see Sumehra, he understood what the Queen of the Dead had suggested to him, and the necromancer laughed.

Sarsour and Adila stood looking down at the squirming, cooing, gurgling, pink-faced creature swaddled in soft, warm blankets within the newly purchased crib. The room—which until recently had served as Sarsour's study—had been refurbished, entirely under Adila's direction of course, into a child's nursery, complete with colorful murals of cute woodland animals on the walls and mounds of toys wherever one looked.

"Thank you for helping me, my love," Sarsour said.

"My pleasure. After all, what are spouses for? Besides, I benefited, too." Adila gazed down lovingly at the recent addition to their family.

Kardel's body might still live, but the man—his identity, his memories—had been wiped away thanks to Adila's youthening magic. An enchantment this strong could only be used once on a particular person, Adila had warned, but that was all right. Once was enough. For all intents and purposes, the man known as Kardel Duressa was dead. The Council of Hierarchs, while pronouncing Sarsour's solution unorthodox at best, was nevertheless satisfied that justice had been served. What's more, they had granted Sarsour and Adila permission to adopt the baby.

"Isn't he the most precious thing?" Adila said. "What shall we name him?"

"I thought we might name him after my father," Sarsour said.

Adila looked down at their son, considered for a moment, then smiled. "I'd like that. How about you, Ferran? What do you think?"

The baby gazed up at them with eyes that were wide, blue and—most of all—innocent.

MONEY'S WORTH

Bradley H. Sinor

Bradley H. Sinor has seen many of his short stories published in the last few years in numerous anthologies, such as *Knight Fantastic, Dracula in London, Bubbas of The Apocalypse, Merlin, Men Writing SF As Women, Haunted Holidays, On Crusade: More Tales of The Knights Templar, International House of Bubbas, Gateways*, and *All Hell Breaking Loose*. Three collections of his short fiction are available: *Dark and Stormy Nights, In The Shadows*, and *Playing With Secrets* (which also features two stories by his wife, Susan Sinor). His nonfiction appeared in a variety of magazines. His latest essays can be found in *Stepping Through The Stargate* and *The Cherryh Odessey*. His Web site is located at www.zettesworld.com/Sinor/index.htm.

I HAD MY hand on the dagger before I was fully awake. Sleeping with a knife under your pillow isn't the most comfortable thing to do, though you can get used to it. I'd rather be uncomfortable than wake to a sword at my throat.

When I had leased the villa last month, the caretaker had apologized profusely about the number of things that needed fixing; after all, the place had been empty for nearly two years.

One of the problems he had mentioned was the hinges on the master bedroom door; they squeaked and needed replacing. He had sworn by any number of local gods that he would have it fixed quickly.

It hadn't been. Right then, I didn't have a problem with those squeaky hinges. They had been enough to awaken me.

There were two intruders, small hunkered forms clinging far too closely together as they came across the floor. When they sprang, I threw my blanket over them as I rolled over the other side of the bed.

"So what enemies have tried to ambush me?" I demanded, my voice as melodramatic as possible, since I already knew the identities of these intruders. I threw the blanket aside and fought hard to suppress a grin at the scene in front of me, a jumble of legs, arms, and tangled hair, mixed in with gasps and giggling. "Is it some demon or perhaps an advance scout for the Kelmigie Horde? Whatever foul creature it is I will crush it under my heel and serve the remnants to the dogs!"

"No!" The bundle of arms and legs separated into two forms and scrambled madly toward the far side of the bed.

Kellian was eight; his sister Jayce was two years younger, but nearly as tall. Their red hair came from my side of the family. Their chaotic nature was a legacy from both their father and myself.

"It's us, Mother," Kellian yelled.

"Really it is," his sister added.

"I don't know! Those could be very good disguises. You could be dwarfs from the deep mines. I'd best beat you severely, just in case."

Jayce turned to her brother. "I told you this was a bad idea, that Mommy would be mad and punish us."

I wasn't mad; I was actually quite pleased with the two of them. They had been at each other's throats for the last several days, over some incident that they had both forgotten by now. That they had made peace and decided to attack *me* was a good sign.

"Mother, we were just playing! We thought it would be fun to play Kyber assassins!" Kellian proclaimed.

Kyber assassins? It didn't surprise me the least bit.

There were half a hundred tall tales about the Guild, told by children and adults to frighten each other, most all of them far, far from the truth.

Nothing in my possession had the Guild name on it; only a seal, hidden away in a compartment in one of my trunks even bore the emblem.

"All right! I believe you aren't dwarves wearing a disguise spell to make me think you are my children. I will let you off, this time, young Kybers." I picked up a piece of fruit from the table next to my bed, and broke it into several smaller sections. "But only if you help me eat this. Do you agree to my terms?"

"Yes!"

Six weeks ago I had announced that I was taking an extended holiday, officially to escape the seasonal heat in the capital, as were as many others who could afford to move to the mountains or the sea for a few months. Actually, I just I needed some time away from not just the Kyber Guild but the various businesses I ran as a part of my "everyday" identity.

I had chosen Yallon's Bay because it was several days' travel from the capital, far enough away for some privacy but close enough not to be completely out of touch.

Of course, this was not the first time I had come to Yallon's Bay; that had been a decade and a half before with my beloved Micah.

Here, he was remembered as one of the five thousand men lost in the Battle of Summer Falls. I had no intention of disillusioning anyone about that tale; besides, who would want to know that he had died in an attempt to assassinate General Zyon, one of our officers who had defected to the other side. I preferred to let our "friends" think of Micah as a dead war hero and myself as a rich, respectable widow.

The down side of Yallon's Bay was a number of social obligations that I would cheerfully have ignored; however, attending them was part of my public persona.

"Lady Danya, it is most gratifying to see you again," Lord Junius had said as I arrived at his home for what had been billed as a small gathering. Conservatively, I estimated that, excluding servants, there were well over fifty other guests: human, dwarves, and elves, along with a smattering of other races.

"Danya, are you all right?"

I turned to look at Cyma Tamu, her thin face furrowed as if she was uncertain of what she wanted to hear me answer. She was an inquisitive sort, but Cyma did have the good sense to know there were some questions that were best left unasked.

I realized that I had been staring out at the bay, studying the ships. There were three new ones that had arrived on the morning tide. They were small, compared to the large merchant ships more common near the capital. But Yallon's Bay was off the major trade routes and too shallow to take the really large vessels.

"Oh, it's nothing, Cyma," I said. "It was just

seeing the bay right now, something about the way the light is falling on it reminded me of the first time that Micah and I came here."

I let a long sigh write a look of nostalgia on my face. Let Cyma take whatever interpretations of it that came to her mind; she was very good at that. Truth be told, Micah and I had first come here seeking a hideout. A mission for the Guild had gone wrong, and we needed to be someplace where no one knew us.

That had been a good time. For a moment I let myself miss Micah more than I had in a long time.

"Now, Danya, you must accept the fact that Micah is gone. Remember always, he died a hero of the Empire; that is something that you and the children can be proud of. While I didn't know him, I have the feeling that he wouldn't want you to lose yourself mourning for him forever. You are still young and very beautiful."

I smiled. "Beautiful, hardly; but thank you, Cyma."

"You are definitely beautiful, don't deny it," she laughed. "In case you haven't noticed, someone can't take his eyes off you."

"Indeed?" I asked, searching my memory for any recent arrivals that I was not aware of.

"Oh, yes." Cyma gestured toward a tall man, dressed in silken finery, at the far end of the room. Even at this distance I could see the marks of elven blood in him—silver-streaked hair, long fingers, and a narrow face.

"Interesting" I said.

"He's been asking about you," Cyma said, a slight purr in her words.

"Does he not have the courage to come and face me himself?"

"Who knows what will happen. This gathering has at least several more hours of life in it. Then there is the rest of the night." The suggestive purr was back in Cyma's voice.

"Indeed." I admit I was a bit intrigued. I looked back to where he was standing, but the man was nowhere in sight.

An hour later I found myself back at the balcony, having made a half transit of the room, speaking with a number of my neighbors, letting them see the "me" that I wanted known around the town. It would be a bit longer before I could withdraw and return home without committing a social faux pas.

I caught sight of the stranger only twice, always at a distance. It seemed an odd little dance the two of us were doing.

The sun had begun to disappear over the horizon, letting dusk streak itself across the waters of the bay as the three-quarter moon appeared in the sky. The full moon would come in a day or so.

"Is the wind from the south, Lady Sable?" It was my admirer stepping up beside me. His words were pitched low, intended for me alone.

"Pardon me, m'lord?"

"Is the wind from the south, Lady Sable?"

I was a little taken aback. No one should have known my Guild name, let alone *that* phrase, in Yallon's Bay.

"Ask about the weather and it will change in a blink."

Sign, countersign.

"How do you know me?" I demanded.

"The Widow told me," he said. "After the proper payments, of course. I hope I get my money's worth."

I wanted to turn and walk away. This man knew far too much about me for my liking.

"Very well, but this is not the place to talk. There are too many ears attached to wagging tongues," I said.

It wasn't that I really wanted to hear what he had to say, or, frankly, gave a damn. I just didn't want anyone else hearing it.

Besides, I was not happy at his being here at all, I had been very specific about my wishes. Of course, knowing The Widow, enough money would make her forget my degree. She knew I could say no; that's an option all of us have, and the Guild would still have the money, since the introduction fee was nonrefundable.

"Fear not, I've laid a minor glamour around us. All anyone will hear will be whispers that no one can quite make out and none will approach, thinking it a near romantic tryst." He reached up and took my hand. He didn't lean forward and kiss it, just did a slight bow.

"You are prepared."

"I try."

"I need you to kill someone, and it must be soon."

No big surprise there. "First, there are some niceties to be observed, m'lord," I told him. "The courtesy of your name would be a good start, though I suspect I could find it out easily from any one of a dozen people around us."

"My name is not necessary. The only name you need is that of she who I want you to kill."

"On the contrary, it is very necessary. You have sought me out, at some great expense if I know The Widow. Obviously you know who and what I am."

"A killer," he said with a certainty in his voice. "As are all the Kyber Guild."

"Understand this," I said. "I know of five ways to kill you, where you stand, without even breaking a sweat or staining my clothing with blood. Three of them would look like you had just died a natural death. So shall we start again?"

I could see him thinking, wondering just how far to take my challenge to him, wondering perhaps just how far I would go right now.

"Very well. I am Rathbin of the House of de Costa." I vaguely knew the family name, one of the lesser elven houses, too much human blood for the High Houses to give them more than the briefest acknowledgment, too much elf blood to "fit in" as more than a token among the higher born human clans.

"See, that didn't hurt at all," I said.

De Costa scanned the garden just below us. He gestured toward the far end where I could see a woman, dressed in a fur-edged cape.

"That is her, your target. Her name is Layra. She is my sister."

On more than one occasion I had heard my children threaten to kill each other, but the next moment they would be laughing and playing together. De Costa was taking sibling rivalry a good ways further along the track than normal.

"I must decline your offer."

De Costa's face went paler than it had been, then ran red with anger. 'What! You can't! She must die by your hand!"

"Not by my hand. Do it yourself if you are that adamant. I decline. I'm on holiday; there is no argument that will persuade me otherwise"

He grabbed me, his face a grim mask of hate, long finger tightening around my arm. "It must be you!"

With my free hand, I slapped him hard and then drove my knee into his groin. That was more than enough to get him to let go of me. I stepped away and saw him draw back, my unexpected attack being quite effective.

In spite of the glamour that de Costa had cast, that little exchange caught more than a few people's attention.

Cyma came running up. "Are you all right?"

"Lord de Costa just needs to learn that when I say no, I mean no."

I left Cyma doing what she did so well, drawing the wrong conclusion.

Over the next two days I saw de Costa a half dozen times, always silently staring with the same grim face. I didn't give a rat's ass if he wanted his sister dead; I just couldn't figure out why he insisted that I had to be the one to do it.

That was why, two hours after sunset, on the third night since the party, I was sitting concealed in the branches of a tree just outside of his house.

I had plumbed certain local sources to find out what I could about the man. It turned out not to be much. He had come from the south, but no one knew exactly where, arriving in Yallon's Bay a month before, having purchased the house through an agent earlier in the year. That proved he had money, but I knew that since even a chat with The Widow can cost an arm and a leg, not to mention your firstborn.

What bothered me was that there was even less to discover about his sister than about de Costa, save that she lived only a mile from her brother. There was endless speculation, but no hard facts.

I had taken to my bed early in the afternoon, complaining of a sour stomach, leaving instructions that I was not to be disturbed. If anyone looked into my bedroom, they would see a figure enshrouded in heavy blankets.

De Costa had spent most of the evening in the house's library, studying a number of documents and books that looked very old. Just before midnight he finally blew out the last candle and left the room. I remained on my perch for a slow count of a thousand before dropping onto the balcony outside his window.

Once inside, I lit a small candle and put it into the metal holder I had brought; the shutters could be opened one at a time to direct the light where I wanted and to keep it to a minimum.

I sat down and began to study what he had left behind. The books were old and had the smell of ages on them. One of them left the palm of my hand tingling after I touched it. I could make out only a single word embossed on the cover, *Aubic*.

There were also loose papers, written in a clear concise hand, spread over the desktop; most were business dealings, nothing personal.

"I think you might find something interesting in the lower right-hand drawer, Lady Sable." A section of the bookcase on the far side of the room had swung open. De Costa stood there, a much too satisfied look on his face.

Damn it! I would have read the riot act to any first-year apprentice who didn't check for hidden doors when they invaded a room.

"Good evening, Lord de Costa. I get the feeling that you were expecting me. I presume that you've got a spell on the chair to keep me from getting up."

"Actually, no," he said leaning against the bookcase frame. "But before you decide to bolt or to use any number of those skills that I know you possess, I think you really should look at what is in the drawer."

I rose up slightly, just to test his words and could feel no restraints, sorcerous or otherwise. It would only be the matter of a few seconds to get me out of the window. Opening the drawer, I found a wooden casket. The wood was smooth, almost silky, to the touch. The hinge and latches were almost impossible to find; whoever had made it had been a master craftsman. I doubted that there would be any sort of contact poison. That seemed to be a far cry from what de Costa had in mind.

Inside was a silver blade laying on a red silk piece of cloth. Two glyphs were emblazed on the blade; I recognized one of them as a Dakarian Moon, the other I did not know but even the sight of it sent a shiver down my spine.

"A Moon Dagger?"

Moon Daggers were few and far between; no more than a dozen were even rumored to exist. They were said to have been forged from sky metal by a dwarven smith nearly a hundred years ago for an order of sorcerers that had been destroyed in the Three Sabers War.

I personally knew where six of them were; safely buried under several tons of rock in the ruins of the Fulgrham Temple. If this happened to be one of those, then there was a lot more to de Costa than I thought.

"I searched for more than a decade after I first learned of them," he said. "Then one day I saw it lying on a fishmonger's table. He accepted a rather large payment and never knew what he had."

"Some people have all the luck."

"I want you to use it this very night."

"On you perhaps?"

"I'm sure that would please you to no end. Before you try, I would suggest that you look at what else is inside that casket." He moved over to a bookcase and picked up a small statuette, running one hand across its surface.

I lifted the cloth and found a pair of small hand mirrors. De Costa nodded, indicating that this was what I was looking for. Hefting one of them I stared deep into it and felt my heart drop out from me.

Instead of my own reflection I saw my daughter. She was asleep. In the other one I saw my son. Both children were seemingly undisturbed. A small dark spot hovered over each, gradually shifting form into that of a dagger, identical to the one lying in front of me.

"Those are echoes of the Moon Dagger. I assure you that neither of those fine young people will come to any harm; they will simply sleep the night away," said de Costa. "Provided you do as I have requested. The spell that I am weaving will require the heart blood of the house of de Costa. You have two hours to plunge that blade into my sister's heart. If you don't, those blades in the mirror will plunge into your children's hearts."

"You slimy bastard." It took all my concentration to control myself. Losing my temper would not save my children. "I should use this on you."

"I wouldn't. I crafted the spell so that should anything happen to me, then the knives do their work," he said casually. "As for my sister, with her defenses, I can't enter her sanctum, nor she mine, without an invitation. Trust me; neither of us is going to be issuing the other one of those. Now, be on your way, the moon is full. I need her blood spilled with the dagger while the moon is full."

He picked up the two mirrors and looked into their surfaces, smiling.

Given the minimal amount of time involved, there was no way to plan a quiet way into the house of de Costa's sister, so I opted for something simple and straightforward—I went in the front door.

It wasn't barred and there was no sign of any guards. Given the siblings' magical interests, that didn't surprise me, any more than the distinct feeling that I was being watched from the moment I crossed the threshold.

If I believed de Costa, then his sister would be asleep in the master bedroom, toward the rear of the house. He seemed to think that I should be able to waltz right in, carve her like a goose and wander away at my leisure. I, on the other hand, had my doubts about that plan.

"Why don't we have a drink and talk about it?" I had barely stepped into her bedroom when

Layra de Costa spoke. Like her brother, she seemed able to turn up when no one expected her.

It took a moment for me to locate her, sitting in a large thronelike chair just to the right of the bed.

"I'm not going to insult you by assuming that you don't know why I'm here." I said.

"Lady Sable, you're quite direct. I like that." That she knew my Guild name made me wonder just how many people had paid The Widow for information about me.

I suppose I expected Layra de Costa to make some sort of magical gesture and conjure up a globe of light or some such thing like that. Instead, I heard the very distinctive sound of flint being struck, followed by sparks and a shard of wood glowing as its tip burst into flame.

She held it out to the wicks of several candles nearby; the light was enough for me to see her face. Layra de Costa wore green, so dark it was almost black. Her silver-streaked hair spilled loosely over her shoulders. I could see the resemblance to her brother.

"Half brother, actually; our father, shall we say, got around a bit and had a taste for human women. In our cases, two different human women," she said.

"Interesting, you can read minds." That would be all I'd need in someone I had come to kill.

"Not actually; it just seemed a logical thing that you might wonder," she said.

Simple and straightforward, I liked that. I reminded myself that no matter how much I might like her; there was the matter of those two ghostly daggers hanging over my children.

"Did he at least provide you with a reason that he wants me dead?" Layra said, pouring two glasses of wine and passing one to me.

I waited until she had taken a sip before lifting my own, not that I drank from it, but there are ways of appearing to.

"Nothing specific, something about tapping the power of your late father, though he did give me some damn good motivation to follow through on his wishes." I held my hand on the pommel of the Moon Dagger, its metal now ice cold to the touch, letting her see the weapon.

"Did you see a very old book, with the word *Aubic* on the cover?"

I nodded and mentioned the fact that touching it had left my hand tingling.

"Our father's grimoire; then it is obvious that my dear brother has broken the seal and found the spells that were the source of our late father's power. From what our parent said, it *would* require the blood of our family to do such a casting," she said.

"Wouldn't your father have had to have a Moon Dagger to do it in the first place?"

Layra reached down to the side of her chair and brought out a blade identical to the one I held.

"He had one," she said.

"It figures," I muttered, then I let fly with the Moon Dagger.

* * *

I probably should have been a lot more discreet, given the large bag I was carrying, when I went back to de Costa's villa. I wasn't in the mood for subtlety; I just wanted to make sure my children were not within reach of his slimy fingers one minute more than they had to be.

De Costa was behind his desk when I entered. "Welcome, Lady Sable, welcome," he said. "I trust all went well and as I requested."

"It did, and I have brought you proof of my deed." I laid the bag down on the floor, near the bookcase with the sliding panel. Very carefully I untied the ropes at the top and pulled it open. In the dim light Layra's face was pale as her head rolled lifelessly to one side.

"Unnecessary; her blood on the Moon Dagger would have been sufficient. If you felt you had to bring proof, I would have been happy with just her head," he said. "Oh, sweet sister, I've never been more pleased to see you." For a moment it was as if the two of them were alone in the room.

De Costa came around the desk and toward the body. I stepped in between him and his goal.

"Hold it right there. You get her, and I frankly don't care what you do with her," I said. "But only when you fulfill your end of the bargain by taking those ghost daggers from my children's throats!"

I watched his jaw tighten as he stared at me, unblinking. I already knew that he wasn't used to people telling him what to do, and didn't like it when it happened, but I didn't care. I was prepared to do some serious damage to him if that was what was necessary to keep the children safe.

"Very well, Lady Sable," he said at last, his voice as casual as if talking about the time of day rather than children's lives. "You did as I asked and my word is my bond."

De Costa went back to the desk and picked up the casket that the Moon dagger had been in. I could see the two mirrors from where I stood and I felt a tug at my heart seeing the vague forms in them that were my son and daughter.

Holding the mirrors in one hand, he smashed them down against the corner of the desk. Shards of glass flew everywhere. For a moment I felt like I could see the forms of the blades over the pieces of glass, then they dissipated.

I wanted that to be the end of it. But what you want and what happens are often two different things.

"As promised, both of your little darlings are safe," he announced.

"One thing," I said.

"Our bargain is completed. Your Guild will have its fee, and you have your children. What more is there to say?"

"There *is* more," I continued, ignoring his attitude. "Why me when there are any numbers of street thugs, mercenaries, even other Kybers you could have hired? Why did you insist on me?"

De Costa laughed: it was a sickening cackle. "The night I acquired the Moon Dagger I had a vision: my sister, dead, the hand that had wielded the blade was yours. You were a key pivot point to achieving my destiny," he said. "Does that satisfy your curiosity?"

I nodded and stepped to one side. I've dealt with any number of magic users over the years. The necromancers like him left me repulsed. Kneeling beside her, the man moved the cloth farther away from her head, and then gently ran his fingers along her hair.

"Not that you weren't planning to do this to me, Layra. You shall bring our father's power to his rightful heir, me."

De Costa grabbed the bag and began to rip it down the center, revealing Layra's blood-stained blouse right over her heart. I caught myself wondering if the man knew where that was; he certainly didn't seem to have one.

Even with his back to me I could tell when he realized that something was wrong.

"The dagger, where is it?" He screeched in a voice that was almost feminine. "I will need it to finish this night's work."

"Oh, is this what you want?" I asked innocently, holding the blade up.

"I think not, brother," said Layra. Her eyes were open, a look of pure hatred on her face. Since she couldn't enter the house without an invitation, I gave her one. It wasn't that I didn't trust de Costa fully to keep his side of the bargain, but it pays to have a backup plan.

Layra brought out the other Moon Dagger. Her

aim was good; as close as she was to her brother, it would have been hard to miss. The blade drove easily through cloth, flesh, and bone and into de Costa's heart.

I could tell when the shock passed and pain swallowed Rathbin de Costa. Blood began to run around the edges of the blade, spewing out after a few moments to strike Layra, the furniture and even me. He trembled and then collapsed backward.

Layra struggled out of the bag and to her feet. She stared at her brother for a time and then began to chant. I couldn't understand the words; there are more dialects of elfish than there are grains of sand in the desert.

Any possibility that it might be a mourning chant passed quickly. I could feel the magic stirring in the air around me. I realized she was doing exactly what her brother had planned. I had the feeling that this was not a good thing. Apparently, she had known more than she had let on.

Vague images formed in the air above the body, most of them things that I did not want to even put a name to. But when I saw Killian and Jayce there, I knew what I had to do.

I stepped up behind Layra, threw my arm around her neck and brought the Moon Dagger around. This time it did not strike into the chair to one side of her, as it had earlier, but drove directly up under her rib cage and into her heart.

"I could ha . . ."

That was all she got out before the light faded

from her eyes. I let go of her, and she fell down into the arms of her brother.

"I guess you got your money's worth," I told the dead sorcerer.

SUBSTITUTIONS

Kristine Kathryn Rusch

Kristine Kathryn Rusch is a best-selling award-winning writer. Her work has won awards in a variety of languages. Most recently, her novella, "Diving into the Wreck" won the prestigious UPC award given in Spain. Her latest novel is *Paloma: A Retrieval Artist Novel.*

SILAS SAT AT the blackjack table, a plastic glass of whiskey in his left hand, and a small pile of hundred dollar chips in his right. His banjo rested against his boot, the embroidered strap wrapped around his calf. He had a pair of aces to the dealer's six, so he split them—a thousand dollars riding on each—and watched as she covered them with the expected tens.

He couldn't lose. He'd been trying to all night.

The casino was empty except for five gambling addicts hunkered over the blackjack table, one old woman playing slots with the rhythm of an assembly worker, and one young man in black leather who was getting drunk at the casino's sorry excuse for a bar. The employees showed no sign of holiday cheer: no happy holiday pins, no little Santa hats, only the stark black and white of their uniforms against the casino's fading glitter.

He had chosen the Paradise because it was one of the few remaining fifties-style casinos in Nevada, still thick with flocked wallpaper and cigarette smoke, craps tables worn by dice and elbows, and the roulette wheel creaking with age. It was also only a few hours from Reno, and in thirty hours, he would have to make the tortuous drive up there. Along the way, he would visit an old man who had a bad heart; a young girl who would cross the road at the wrong time and meet an oncoming semi; and a baby boy who was born with his lungs not yet fully formed. Silas also suspected a few surprises along the way; nothing was ever as it seemed any longer. Life was moving too fast, even for him.

But he had Christmas Eve and Christmas Day off, the two days he had chosen when he had been picked to work Nevada 150 years before. In those days, he would go home for Christmas, see his friends, spend time with his family. His parents welcomed him, even though they didn't see him for most of the year. He felt like a boy again, like someone cherished and loved, instead of the drifter he had become.

All of that stopped in 1878. December 26, 1878. He wasn't yet sophisticated enough to know that the day was a holiday in England. Boxing Day. Not quite appropriate, but close.

He had to take his father that day. The old man had looked pale and tired throughout the holiday, but no one thought it serious. When he took to his bed Christmas night, everyone had simply thought him tired from the festivities.

It was only after midnight, when Silas got his orders, that he knew what was coming next. He begged off—something he had never tried before (he wasn't even sure who he had been begging with)—but had received the feeling (that was all he ever got: a firm feeling, so strong he couldn't avoid it) that if he didn't do it, death would come another way—from Idaho or California or New Mexico. It would come another way, his father would be in agony for days, and the end, when it came, would be uglier than it had to be.

Silas had taken his banjo to the old man's room. His mother slept on her side, like she always had, her back to his father. His father's eyes had opened, and he knew. Somehow he knew.

They always did.

Silas couldn't remember what he said. Something—a bit of an apology, maybe, or just an explanation: *You always wanted to know what I did.* And then, the moment. First he touched his father's forehead, clammy with the illness that would claim him, and then Silas said, "You wanted to know why I carry the banjo," and strummed.

But the sound did not soothe his father like it had so many before him. As his spirit rose, his body struggled to hold it, and he looked at Silas with such a mix of fear and betrayal that Silas still saw it whenever he thought of his father.

The old man died, but not quickly and not easily, and Silas tried to resign, only to get sent to the place that passed for headquarters, a small shack that resembled an out-of-the-way railroad terminal. There, a man who looked no more than thirty but who had to be three hundred or more, told him that the more he complained, the longer his service would last.

Silas never complained again, and he had been on the job for 150 years. Almost 55,000 days spent in the service of Death, with only Christmas Eve and Christmas off, tainted holidays for a man in a tainted position.

He scooped up his winnings, piled them on his already-high stack of chips, and then placed his next bet. The dealer had just given him a queen and a jack when a boy sat down beside him.

"Boy" wasn't entirely accurate. He was old enough to get into the casino. But he had rain on his cheap jacket, and hair that hadn't been cut in a long time. IPod headphones stuck out of his breast pocket, and he had a cell phone against his hip the way that old sheriffs used to wear their guns.

His hands were callused and the nails had dirt beneath them. He looked tired, and a little frightened.

He watched as the dealer busted, then set chips in front of Silas and the four remaining players. Silas swept the chips into his stack, grabbed five of the hundred dollar chips, and placed the bet.

The dealer swept her hand along the semicircle, silently asking the players to place their bets.

"You Silas?" the boy asked. He hadn't put any money on the table or placed any chips before him.

Silas sighed. Only once before had someone interrupted his Christmas festivities—if festivities was what the last century plus could be called.

The dealer peered at the boy. "You gonna play?"

The boy looked at her, startled. He didn't seem to know what to say.

"I got it." Silas put twenty dollars in chips in front of the boy.

"I don't know . . ."

"Just do what I tell you," Silas said.

The woman dealt, face-up. Silas got an ace. The boy, an eight. The woman dealt herself a ten. Then she went around again. Silas got his twenty-one—his weird holiday luck holding—but the boy got another eight.

"Split them," Silas said.

The boy looked at him, his fear almost palpable.

Silas sighed again, then grabbed another twenty in chips, and placed it next to the boy's first twenty.

"Jeez, mister, that's a lot of money," the boy whispered.

"Splitting," Silas said to the dealer.

She separated the cards and placed the bets behind them. Then she dealt the boy two cards—a ten and another eight.

The boy looked at Silas. Looked like the boy had peculiar luck as well.

"Split again," Silas said, more to the dealer than to the boy. He added the bet, let her separate the cards, and watched as she dealt the boy two more tens. Three eighteens. Not quite as good as Silas' twenties to twenty-ones, but just as statistically uncomfortable.

The dealer finished her round, then dealt herself a three, then a nine, busting again. She paid in order. When she reached the boy, she set sixty dollars in chips before him, each in its own twenty-dollar pile.

"Take it," Silas said.

"It's yours," the boy said, barely speaking above a whisper.

"I gave it to you."

"I don't gamble," the boy said.

"Well, for someone who doesn't gamble, you did pretty well. Take your winnings."

The boy looked at them as if they'd bite him. "I . . ."

"Are you leaving them for the next round?" the dealer asked.

The boy's eyes widened. He was clearly horrified at the very thought. With shaking fingers, he collected the chips, then leaned into Silas. The boy smelled of sweat and wet wool.

"Can I talk to you?" he whispered.

Silas nodded, then cashed in his chips. He'd racked up ten thousand dollars in three hours. He wasn't even having fun at it anymore. He liked losing, felt that it was appropriate—part of the game, part of his life—but the losses had become fewer and farther between the more he played.

The more he lived. A hundred years ago, there were women and a few adopted children. But watching them grow old, helping three of them die, had taken the desire out of that, too.

"Mr. Silas," the boy whispered.

"If you're not going to bet," the dealer said, "please move so someone can have your seats."

People had gathered behind Silas, and he hadn't even noticed. He really didn't care tonight. Normally, he would have noticed anyone around him—noticed who they were, how and when they would die.

"Come on," he said, gathering the bills the dealer had given him. The boy's eyes went to the money like a hungry man's went to food. His one-hundred-and-twenty dollars remained on the table, and Silas had to remind him to pick it up.

The boy used a forefinger and a thumb to carry it, as if it would burn him.

"At least put it in your pocket," Silas snapped.

"But it's yours," the boy said.

"It's a damn gift. Appreciate it."

The boy blinked, then stuffed the money into the front of his unwashed jeans. Silas led him around banks and banks of slot machines, all pinging and ponging and making little musical come-ons, to the steakhouse in the back.

The steakhouse was the reason Silas came back year after year. The place opened at five, closed at three AM, and served the best steaks in Vegas. They weren't arty or too small. One big slab of meat, expensive cut, charred on the outside and red as Christmas on the inside. Beside the steak they served french-fried onions, and sides that no self-respecting Strip restaurant would prepare— creamed corn, au gratin potatoes, popovers—the kind of stuff that Silas always associated with the modern Las Vegas—modern, to him, meaning 1950s–1960s Vegas. Sin city. A place for grown-ups to gamble and smoke and drink and have affairs. The Vegas of Sinatra and the mob, not the Vegas of Steve Wynn and his ilk, who prettified everything and made it all seem upscale and oh-so-right.

Silas still worked Vegas a lot more than any other Nevada city, which made sense, considering how many millions of people lived there now, but millions of people lived all over. Even sparsely-settled Nevada, one of the least populated states in the Union, had ten full-time Death employees. They tried to unionize a few years ago, but Silas, with the most seniority, refused to join. Then they tried to limit the routes—one would get Reno, another Sparks, another Elko and that region, and a few would split Vegas—but Silas wouldn't agree to that either.

He loved the travel part of the job. It was the only part he still liked, the ability to go from place to place to place, see the changes, understand how time affected everything.

Everything except him.

The maitre d' sat them in the back, probably because of the boy. Even in this modern era, where people wore blue jeans to funerals, this steakhouse preferred its customers in a suit and tie.

The booth was made of wood and rose so high that Silas couldn't see anything but the boy and the table across from them. A single lamp reflected against the wall, revealing cloth napkins and real silver utensils.

The boy stared at them with the same kind of fear he had shown at the blackjack table. "I can't."

The maitre d' gave them leather-bound menus, said something about a special, and then handed Silas a wine list. Silas ordered a bottle of burgundy. He didn't know a lot about wines, just that the more expensive ones tasted a lot better than the rest of them. So he ordered the most expensive burgundy on the menu.

The maitre d' nodded crisply, almost militarily, and then left. The boy leaned forward.

"I can't stay. I'm your substitute."

Silas smiled. A waiter came by with a bread basket—hard rolls, still warm—and relish trays filled with sliced carrots, celery, and radishes, and candied beets, things people now would call old-fashioned.

Modern, to him. Just as modern as always.

The boy squirmed, his jeans squeaking on the leather booth.

"I know," Silas said. "You'll be fine."

"I got—

"A big one, probably," Silas said. "It's Christmas Eve. Traffic, right? A shooting in a church? Too many suicides?"

"No," the boy said, distressed. "Not like that."

"When's it scheduled for?" Silas asked. He really wanted his dinner, and he didn't mind sharing it. The boy looked like he needed a good meal.

"Tonight," the boy said. "No specific time. See?"

He put a crumpled piece of paper between them, but Silas didn't pick it up.

"Means you have until midnight," Silas said. "It's only seven. You can eat."

"They said at orientation—

Silas had forgotten; they all got orientation now. The expectations of generations. He'd been thrown into the pool feet first, fumbling his way for six months before someone told him that he could actually ask questions.

"—the longer you wait, the more they suffer."

Silas glanced at the paper. "If it's big, it's a surprise. They won't suffer. They'll just finish when you get there. That's all."

The boy bit his lip. "How do you know?"

Because he'd had big. He'd had grisly. He'd had disgusting. He'd overseen more deaths than the boy could imagine.

The head waiter arrived, took Silas's order, and then turned to the boy.

"I don't got money," the boy said.

"You have one hundred and twenty dollars," Silas said. "But I'm buying, so don't worry."

The boy opened the menu, saw the prices, and closed it again. He shook his head.

The waiter started to leave when Silas stopped him. "Give him what I'm having. Medium well."

Since the kid didn't look like he ate many steaks, he wouldn't like his rare. Rare was an acquired taste, just like burgundy wine and the cigar that Silas wished he could light up. Not everything in the modern era was an improvement.

"You don't have to keep paying for me," the kid said.

Silas waved the waiter away, then leaned back. The back of the booth, made of wood, was rigid against his spine. "After a while in this business," he said, "money is all you have."

The kid bit his lower lip. "Look at the paper. Make sure I'm not screwing up. Please."

But Silas didn't look.

"You're supposed to handle all of this on your own," Silas said gently.

"I know," the boy said. "I know. But this one, he's scary. And I don't think anything I do will make it right."

After he finished his steak and had his first sip of coffee, about the time he would have lit up his cigar, Silas picked up the paper. The boy had devoured the steak like he hadn't eaten in weeks. He ate all the bread and everything from his relish tray.

He was very, very new.

Silas wondered how someone that young had gotten into the death business, but he was determined not to ask. It would be some variation on his own story. Silas had begged for the life of his wife who should have died in the delivery of their second child. Begged, and begged, and begged, and somehow, in his befogged state, he actually saw the woman whom he then called the Angel of Death.

Now he knew better—none of them were angels, just working stiffs waiting for retirement—but then, she had seemed perfect and terrifying, all at the same time.

He'd asked for his wife, saying he didn't want to raise his daughters alone.

The angel had tilted her head. "Would you die for her?"

"Of course," Silas said.

"Leaving her to raise the children alone?" the angel asked.

His breath caught. "Is that my only choice?"

She shrugged, as if she didn't care. Later, when he reflected, he realized she didn't know.

"Yes," he said into her silence. "She would raise better people than I will. She's good. I'm . . . not."

He wasn't bad, he later realized, just lost, as so many were. His wife had been a God-fearing woman with strict ideas about morality. She had raised two marvelous girls, who became two strong women, mothers of large broods who all went on to do good works.

In that, he hadn't been wrong.

But his wife hadn't remarried either, and she had cried for him for the rest of her days.

They had lived in Texas. He had made his bargain, got assigned Nevada, and had to swear never to head east, not while his wife and children lived. His parents saw him, but they couldn't tell anyone. They thought he ran out on his wife and children, and oddly, they had supported him in it.

Remnants of his family still lived. Great-grandchildren generations removed. He still couldn't head east, and he no longer wanted to.

Silas touched the paper, and it burned his fingers. A sign, a warning, a remembrance that he wasn't supposed to work these two days.

Two days out of an entire year.

He slid the paper back to the boy. "I can't open it. I'm not allowed. You tell me."

So the boy did.

And Silas, in wonderment that they had sent a

rookie into a situation a veteran might not be able to handle, settled his tab, took the boy by the arm, and led him into the night.

Every city has pockets of evil. Vegas had fewer than most, despite the things the television lied about. So many people worked in law enforcement or security, so many others were bonded so that they could work in casinos or high-end jewelry stores or banks that Vegas' serious crime was lower than most comparable cities of its size.

Silas appreciated that. Most of the time, it meant that the deaths he attended in Vegas were natural or easy or just plain silly. He got a lot of silly deaths in that city. Some he even found time to laugh over.

But not this one.

As they drove from the very edge of town, past the rows and rows of similar houses, past the stink and desperation of complete poverty, he finally asked, "How long've you been doing this?"

"Six months," the boy said softly, as if that were forever.

Silas looked at him, looked at the young face reflecting the Christmas lights that filled the neighborhood, and shook his head. "All substitutes?"

The boy shrugged. "They didn't have any open routes."

"What about the guy you replaced?"

"He'd been subbing, waiting to retire. They say you could retire, too, but you show no signs of it. Working too hard, even for a younger man."

He wasn't older. He was the same age he had been when his wife struggled with her labor—a breech birth that would be no problem in 2006, but had been deadly if not handled right in 1856. The midwife's hands hadn't been clean—not that anyone knew better in those days—and the infection had started even before the baby got turned.

He shuddered, that night alive in him. The night he'd made his bargain.

"I don't work hard," he said. "I work less than I did when I started."

The boy looked at him, surprised. "Why don't you retire?"

"And do what?" Silas asked. He hadn't planned to speak up. He normally shrugged off that question.

"I dunno," the boy said. "Relax. Live off your savings. Have a family again."

They could all have families again when they retired. Families and a good, rich life, albeit short. Silas would age when he retired. He would age and have no special powers. He would watch a new wife die in childbirth and not be able to see his former colleague sitting beside the bed. He would watch his children squirm after a car accident, blood on their faces, knowing that they would live poorly if they lived at all, and not be able to find out the future from the death dealer hovering near the scene.

Better to continue. Better to keep this half-life, this half-future, time without end.

"Families are overrated," Silas said. They look

at you with betrayal and loss when you do what was right.

But the boy didn't know that yet. He didn't know a lot.

"You ever get scared?" the boy asked.

"Of what?" Silas asked. Then gave the standard answer. "They can't kill you. They can't harm you. You just move from place to place, doing your job. There's nothing to be scared of."

The boy grunted, sighed, and looked out the window.

Silas knew what he had asked, and hadn't answered it. Of course he got scared. All the time. And not of dying—even though he still wasn't sure what happened to the souls he freed. He wasn't scared of that, or of the people he occasionally faced down, the drug addicts with their knives, the gangsters with their guns, the wanna-be outlaws with blood all over their hands.

No, the boy had asked about the one thing to be afraid of, the one thing they couldn't change.

Was he scared of being alone? Of remaining alone, for the rest of his days? Was he scared of being unknown and nearly invisible, having no ties and no dreams?

It was too late to be scared of that.

He'd lived it. He lived it every single day.

The house was one of those square adobe things that filled Vegas. It was probably pink in the sunlight. In the half-light that passed for nighttime in this perpetually alive city, it looked gray and foreboding.

The bars on the windows—standard in this neighborhood—didn't help.

Places like this always astounded him. They seemed so normal, so incorruptible, just another building on another street, like all the other buildings on all the other streets. Sometimes he got to go into those buildings. Very few of them were different from what he expected. Oh, the art changed or the furniture. The smells differed—sometimes unwashed diapers, sometimes perfume, sometimes the heavy scent of meals eaten long ago—but the rest remained the same: the television in the main room, the kitchen with its square table (sometimes decorated with flowers, sometimes nothing but trash), the double bed in the second bedroom down the hall, the one with its own shower and toilet. The room across from the main bathroom was sometimes an office, sometimes a den, sometimes a child's bedroom. If it was a child's bedroom, there were pictures on the wall, studio portraits from the local mall, done up in cheap frames, showing the passing years. The pictures were never straight, and always dusty, except for the most recent, hung with pride in the only remaining empty space.

He had a hunch this house would have none of those things. If anything, it would have an overly neat interior. The television would be in the kitchen or the bedroom or both. The front room would have a sofa set designed for looks, not for comfort. And one of the rooms would be blocked off, maybe even marked private, and in it, he would find (if he looked) trophies of a kind that made even his cast-iron stomach turn.

These houses had no attic. Most didn't have a basement. So the scene would be the garage. The car would be parked outside of it, blocking the door, and the neighbors would assume that the garage was simply a workspace—not that far off, if the truth be told.

He'd been to places like this before. More times than he wanted to think about, especially in the smaller communities out in the desert, the communities that had no names, or once had a name and did no longer. The communities sometimes made up of cheap trailers and empty storefronts, with a whorehouse a few miles off the main highway, and a casino in the center of town, a casino so old it made the one that the boy found him in look like it had been built just the week before.

He hated these jobs. He wasn't sure what made him come with the boy. A moment of compassion? The prospect of yet another long Christmas Eve with nothing to punctuate it except the bong-bong of nearby slots?

He couldn't go to church anymore. It didn't feel right, with as many lives as he had taken. He couldn't go to church or listen to the singing or look at the families and wonder which of them he'd be standing beside in thirty years.

Maybe he belonged here more than the boy did. Maybe he belonged here more than anyone else.

They parked a block away, not because anyone would see their car—if asked, hours later, the neighbors would deny seeing anything to do with Silas or the boy. Maybe they never saw, maybe their memories vanished. Silas had never been clear on that either.

As they got out, Silas asked, "What do you use?"

The boy reached into the breast pocket. For a moment, Silas thought he'd remove the IPod, and Silas wasn't sure how a device that used headphones would work. Then the boy removed a harmonica—expensive, the kind sold at high-end music stores.

"You play that before all this?" Silas asked.

The boy nodded. "They got me a better one, though."

Silas' banjo had been all his own. They'd let him take it, and nothing else. The banjo, the clothes he wore that night, his hat.

He had different clothes now. He never wore a hat. But his banjo was the same as it had always been—new and pure with a sound that he still loved.

It was in the trunk. He doubted it could get stolen, but he took precautions just in case.

He couldn't bring it on this job. This wasn't his job. He'd learned the hard way that the banjo didn't work except in assigned cases. When he'd wanted to help, to put someone out of their misery, to step in where another death dealer had failed, he couldn't. He could only watch, like normal people did, and hope that things got better, even though he knew it wouldn't.

The boy clutched the harmonica in his right hand. The dry desert air was cold. Silas could see his breath. The tourists down on the Strip, with their short skirts and short sleeves, probably felt betrayed by the normal winter chill. He wished he were there with them, instead of walking through this quiet neighborhood, filled with dark houses, dirt-ridden yards, and silence.

So much silence. You'd think there'd be at least one barking dog.

When they reached the house, the boy headed to the garage, just like Silas expected. A car was parked on the road—a 1980s sedan that looked like it had seen better days. In the driveway, a brand-new van with tinted windows, custom-made for bad deeds.

In spite of himself, Silas shuddered.

The boy stopped outside and steeled himself, then he looked at Silas with sadness in his eyes. Silas nodded. The boy extended a hand—Silas couldn't get in without the boy's momentary magic—and then they were inside, near the stench of old gasoline, urine, and fear.

The kids sat in a dimly lit corner, chained together like the slaves on ships in the nineteenth century. The windows were covered with dirty cardboard, the concrete floor was empty except for stains as old as time. It felt bad in here, a recognizable bad, one Silas had encountered before.

The boy was shaking. He wasn't out of place here, his old wool jacket and his dirty jeans making him a cousin to the kids on the floor. Silas had a momentary flash: they were homeless. Runaways, lost, children without borders, without someone looking for them.

"You've been here before," Silas whispered to the boy, and the boy's eyes filled with tears.

Been here, negotiated here, moved on here— didn't quite die, but no longer quite lived—and for who? A group of kids like this one? A group that had somehow escaped, but hadn't reported what had happened?

Then he felt the chill grow worse. Of course they hadn't reported it. Who would believe them? A neat homeowner kidnaps a group of homeless kids for his own personal playthings, and the cops believe the kids? Kids who steal and sell drugs and themselves just for survival.

People like the one who owned this house were cautious. They were smart. They rarely got caught unless they went public with letters or phone calls or both.

They had to prepare for contingencies like losing a plaything now and then. They probably had all the answers planned.

A side door opened. It was attached to the house. The man who came in was everything Silas had expected—white, thin, balding, a bit too intense.

What surprised Silas was the look the man gave him. Measuring, calculating.

Pleased.

The man wasn't supposed to see Silas or the boy. Not until the last moment.

Not until the end.

Silas had heard that some of these creatures could see the death dealers. A few of Silas' colleagues speculated that these men continued to kill so that they could continue to see death in all its forms, collecting images the way they collected trophies.

After seeing the momentary victory in that man's eyes, Silas believed it.

The man picked up the kid at the end of the chain. Too weak to stand, the kid staggered a bit, then had to lean into the man.

"You have to beat me," the man said to Silas. "I slice her first, and you have to leave."

The boy was still shivering. The man hadn't noticed him. The man thought Silas was here for him, not the boy. Silas had no powers, except the ones that humans normally had—not on this night, and not in this way.

If he were here alone, he'd start playing, and praying he'd get the right one. If there was a right one. He couldn't tell. They all seemed to have the mark of death over them.

No wonder the boy needed him.

It was a fluid situation, one that could go in any direction.

"Start playing," Silas said under his breath.

But the man heard him, not the boy. The man pulled the kid's head back, exposing a smooth white throat with the heartbeat visible in a vein.

"Play!" Silas shouted, and ran forward, shoving the man aside, hoping that would be enough.

It saved the girl's neck, for a moment anyway. She fell, and landed on the other kid next to her. The kid moved away, as if proximity to her would cause the kid to die.

The boy started blowing on his harmonica. The notes were faint, barely notes, more like bleats of terror.

The man laughed. He saw the boy now. "So you're back to rob me again," he said.

The boy's playing grew wispier.

"Ignore him," Silas said to the boy.

"Who're you? His coach?" The man approached him. "I know your rules. I destroy you, I get to take your place."

The steak rolled in Silas' stomach. The man was half right. He destroyed Silas, and he would get a chance to take the job. He destroyed both of them, and he would get the job, by old magic not new. Silas had forgotten this danger. No wonder these creatures liked to see death—what better for them than to be the facilitator for the hundreds of people who died in Nevada every day.

The man brandished his knife. "Lessee," he said. "What do I do? Destroy the instrument, deface the man. Right? And send him to hell."

Get him fired, Silas fought. It wasn't really hell, although it seemed like it. He became a ghost, existing forever, but not allowed to interact with anything. He was fired. He lost the right to die.

The man reached for the harmonica. Silas shoved again.

"Play!" Silas shouted.

And miraculously, the boy played. "Home on the Range," a silly song for these circumstances, but probably the first tune the boy had ever learned. He played it with spirit as he backed away from the fight.

But the kids weren't rebelling. They sat on the cold concrete floor, already half dead, probably tortured into submission. If they didn't rise up and kill this monster, no one would.

Silas looked at the boy. Tears streamed down his face, and he nodded toward the kids. Souls hovered above them, as if they couldn't decide whether or not to leave.

Damn the ones in charge: they'd sent the kid here as his final test. Could he take the kind of lives he had given his life for? Was he that strong?

The man reached for the harmonica again, and this time Silas grabbed his knife. It was heavier than Silas expected. He had never wielded a real instrument of death. His banjo eased people into forever. It didn't force them out of their lives a moment too early.

The boy kept playing and the man—the creature—laughed. One of the kids looked up, and Silas thought the kid was staring straight at the boy.

Only a moment, then. Only a moment to decide.

Silas shoved the knife into the man's belly. It went in deep, and the man let out an oof of pain. He stumbled, reached for the knife, and then glared at Silas.

Silas hadn't killed him, maybe hadn't even mortally wounded him. No soul appeared above him, and even these creatures had souls—dark and tainted as they were.

The boy's playing broke in places as if he were trying to catch his breath. The kid at the end of the chain, the girl, managed to get up. She looked at the knife, then at the man, then around the room. She couldn't see Silas or the boy.

Which was good.

The man was pulling on the knife. He would get it free in a moment. He would use it, would destroy these children, the ones no one cared about except the boy who was here to take their souls.

The girl kicked the kid beside her. "Stand up," she said.

The kid looked at her, bleary. Silas couldn't tell if these kids were male or female. He wasn't sure it mattered.

"Stand up," the girl said again.

In a rattle of chains, the kid did. The man didn't notice. He was working the knife, grunting as he tried to dislodge it. Silas stepped back, wondering if he had already interfered too much.

The music got louder, more intense, almost violent. The girl stood beside the man and stared at him for a moment.

He raised his head, saw her, and grinned.

Then she reached down with that chain, wrapped it around his neck, and pulled. "Help me," she said to the others. "Help me."

The music became a live thing, wrapping them all, filling the smelly garage, and reaching deep, deep into the darkness. The soul did rise up—half a soul, broken and burned. It looked at Silas, then flared at the boy, who—bless him—didn't stop playing.

Then the soul floated toward the growing darkness in the corner, a blackness Silas had seen only a handful of times before, a blackness that felt as cold and dark as any empty desert night, and somehow much more permanent.

The music faded. The girl kept pulling, until another kid, farther down the line, convinced her to let go.

"We have to find the key," the other kid—a boy—said.

"On the wall," a third kid said. "Behind the electric box."

They shuffled as a group toward the box. They walked through Silas, and he felt them, alive and vibrant. For a moment, he worried that he had been fired, but he knew he had too many years for that. Too many years of perfect service—and he hadn't killed the man. He had just injured him, took away the threat to the boy.

That was allowed, just barely.

No wonder the boy had brought him. No wonder the boy had asked him if he was scared. Not of being alone or being lonely. But of certain jobs, of the things now asked of them as the no-longer-quite-human beings that they were.

Silas turned to the boy. His face was shiny with tears, but his eyes were clear. He stuffed the harmonica back into his breast pocket.

"You knew he'd beat you without me," Silas said.

The boy nodded.

"You knew this wasn't a substitution. You would have had this job, even without me."

"It's not cheating to bring in help," the boy said.

"But it's nearly impossible to find it," Silas said. "How did you find me?"

"It's Christmas Eve," the boy said. "Everyone knows where you'd be."

Everyone. His colleagues. People on the job. The only folks who even knew his name anymore.

Silas sighed. The boy reached out with his stubby dirty hand. Silas took it, and then, suddenly, they were out of that fetid garage. They stood next to the van and watched as the cardboard came off one of the windows, as glass shattered outward.

Kids, homeless kids, injured and alone, poured out of that window like water.

"Thanks," the boy said. "I can't tell you how much it means."

But Silas knew. The boy didn't yet, but Silas did. When he retired—no longer if. When—this boy would see him again. This boy would take him, gently and with some kind of majestic harmonica music, to a beyond Silas could not imagine.

The boy waved at him, and joined the kids, heading into the dark Vegas night. Those kids couldn't see him, but they had to know he was there, like a guardian angel, saving them from horrors that would haunt their dreams for the rest of their lives.

Silas watched them go. Then he headed in the opposite direction, toward his car. What had those kids seen? The man—the creature—with his knife out, raving at nothing. Then stumbling backward, once, twice, the second time with a knife in his belly. They'd think that he tripped, that he stabbed himself. None of them had seen Silas or the boy.

They wouldn't for another sixty years.

If they were lucky.

The neighborhood remained dark, although a dog barked in the distance. His car was cold. Cold and empty.

He let himself in, started it, warmed his fingers against the still-hot air blowing out of the vents. Only a few minutes gone. A few minutes to take away a nasty, horrible lifetime. He wondered what was in the rest of these houses, and hoped he'd never have to find out.

The clock on the dash read 10:45. As he drove out of the neighborhood, he passed a small adobe church. Outside, candles burned in candleholders made of baked sand. Almost like the churches of his childhood.

Almost, but not quite.

He watched the people thread inside. They wore fancy clothing—dresses on the women, suits on the men, the children dressing like their parents, faces alive with anticipation.

They believed in something.

They had hope.

He wondered if hope was something a man could recapture, if it came with time, relaxation, and the slow inevitable march toward death.

He wondered, if he retired, whether he could spend his Christmas Eves inside, smelling the mix of incense and candlewax, the evergreen bows, and the light dusting of ladies' perfume.

He wondered . . .

Then shook his head.

And drove back to the casino, to spend the rest of his time off in peace.

DRUSILLA

Ed Gorman

In twenty-five years of full-time writing, Ed Gorman has published more than thirty novels and six collections of short stories. Kirkus Review called him "one of the most original [talents] around." Late this year his collected stories, *The Long Silence After*, will be published in two volumes.

NOT EVEN THE heavy pelts Aarak wore could keep the wind from whipping through him, nor the snow from soaking him. At this point in his three-day trip, Lord William's warrior wasn't even sure he was heading in the right direction. His horse had stumbled in the thigh-high snow and broken a foreleg. Aarak had had to put him down with the tenderness that most warriors felt for their mounts.

Moonless nights. Screaming winds. Crude lean-tos built with frozen hands for a few hours' rest. He ate whatever dead things he could find in the snow. One morning he came upon a frozen man in a small cave, but after resting there a few hours, he kept on going. He was not religious, something Lord William constantly criticized him for, but even he would not partake of human flesh, as some warriors were known to do.

Demons in his dreams. The demons that guarded the amulet that William's brother Lord Stephen wore on a bloodstained chain around his neck. In the dreams, the demons ripped Aarak's flesh the way vultures did the flesh of a corpse. He writhed with pain, cried out against the unending indignity, flailed fists in the snow-stabbed air. And then woke to the wind-screams. So cold in the middle of the moonless night that his golden stream of piss froze before it reached the snow.

Lord William was paying him well for this journey. No assassin in the realm had ever been paid so much. Aarak had assumed that killing Lord Stephen would be the difficult part of the task. He hadn't counted on the hellish blizzard.

The village was a typical one. A tall, stone castle overlooking the walled village proper, carts, horses, people constantly going in and out of the guarded gates. Villagers never strayed too far because there were still raiding parties to contend with, fierce warriors who valued above all young girls who could be sold at high prices in the cities of England.

Aarak saw all this from the back of a rumbling wagon filled with reeking, bloody animal carcasses. The stench was only partially alleviated by the chill but not freezing wind. Aarak couldn't remember when or how he'd gotten in the wagon, but he was thankful he had. And thankful that the blizzard hadn't reached this far. Yes, it was cold here, and both the plains and the hills were winter-gray with death. But there was only a dusting of snow, and even that was mitigated by the merry streams of smoke curling upwards into the air. Chimneys, fireplaces, warmth.

"I thank you, my friend," Aarak said, pulling himself from beneath the reeking pile of carcasses. The wagon had slowed so much that Aarak was able to jump off and walk beside the driver.

"You're a lucky one," said the man driving the wagon. He wore a double set of tunics over a set of heavy woolen clothes that fit his ample form tightly, and on his head was a squirrel-skin hat. At his side was an ax so huge it looked fit for slaying giants. "When I found you, you were near dead. All you could say was 'Lord Stephen.' Another piece of luck for you. Lord Stephen is the lord of my own village here."

Inside the walls of the village, on battlement walkways, sword-wielding guards watched the wagon that brought Aarak to the long main street off which ran several much narrower side streets.

Aarak was strong enough to gather himself and jump down to the ground. Shops of every description crowded this section of the village. Thatched-roof houses stretched in all directions on the off-streets.

Aarak quickly joined the crowd moving toward the northernmost part of the village. He had the coins necessary to making himself presentable. A barber could clean him up and, with his medical skills, help Aarak stand up to the cough the elements had inflicted on him.

Two hours later he wore the familiar sleeved tunic of the village. The woolen clothing underneath was footed so that all but his neck and head were covered. He was shaved and clean as well. He ate a spare meal of rye bread, gruel, and ale. He felt sorry for the peasants of this place. As Lord William's official assassin, he was allowed to eat in the manor house, where the meals consisted of lamb, bacon, beef, cheese, and bread made from milled flour. Nobody at Lord William's table ever drank ale. Expensive wines were always at hand.

Dusk came early, just after four, though the merchants and the craftsmen would work until the curfew bell that rang at eight o'clock in the evening. He left the village—making sure to talk to the guards on his way out, leaving them with a good impression of him—and walked to the Norman castle resting above it.

In the deepening shadows, Aarak saw that this was one of the newest types of castles. Built of stone because it could be made taller, less inclined than the wooden ones to be gutted by fire, and sturdy enough to repel most kinds of attacks. Melancholy lute music came from a lighted window in one of the towers, and laughter could be heard from somewhere within the lower regions.

The bridge was down over the moat, and it was from this opening that three horses charged from the castle and stormed directly toward him. Weapons were drawn. Shouts covered the sweet music and the guttural laughter. The three soldiers swept down on Aarak like hungry beasts.

He knew not to run or to offer any resistance. One soldier stayed in the saddle as the other two jumped to the ground and came at him, one with his sword, the other with his club.

"I am a peaceful man," Aarak said, the wind chilling him suddenly.

"That is not what the castle's seer says of you," said the one with the club. "He believes you mean to do the lord great harm."

And with that, he swung the club so that it connected perfectly with the left side of Aarak's skull. Aarak's last thought was that he could not remember ever being knocked out with such precision or speed. He slumped to the ground.

The seer, as seers often were, was blind. Or at least pretended to be. Even indoors, he kept the cowl of his silken gown tight against his bald scalp as he leaned over the cot, where Aarak was just now coming to.

"They should not have clubbed you so hard," said the seer, a scrawny man of great age who smelled of herbs and bad wine.

After feeling Aarak's face—apparently searching for his mouth—the seer began pouring wine into where he thought Aarak's mouth was. He missed by several inches. The red wine ran down the assassin's jaw and neck.

"Does that taste good?" the old one said.

"Let me lick some off the floor and I'll tell you."

"The floor?"

"Yes, unfortunately you didn't get any in my mouth."

The seer laughed. "Being blind does have its limitations, I'm afraid."

Aarak sat up and eased himself off the cot, placing his feet on the floor. His head pounded. He seized the wine bottle from the seer's frail hand and took a swig that would have caused a normal man to vomit. He handed the bottle back and looked around the small room. Aarak enjoyed reading, but was not in any sense educated. But he recognized the symbols drawn on the wall. Druidic. This was the part of England where the Druids had once prospered. The symbols, heavily black, took on a menacing sheen in the jittery light of the three candles that lit the room.

The seer used his long, narrow cane to find a wooden stool. He sat down and said, "There is no use trying to deceive me. Your name is Aarak and you are here to steal Lord Stephen's amulet. You know that the castle wizard showed him how to trap Drusilla inside the amulet so she could never flee back to your lord again."

Aarak thought of telling the old man how much humiliation and agony his own lord had suffered the two times Drusilla had left him for his brother. But then he decided against it. The humiliation and the agony for Stephen had to be just as deep. No lord could look strong and masculine to the people of his village if he could not control his woman. And Drusilla had gone back and forth, unable to make up her mind between the two brothers.

Until Lord Stephen's wizard found a way of magically trapping her inside the amulet. True, Stephen could never set her free, could never allow her to come to full and sumptuous size. She would flee him if he freed her even for a few moments. It was the possession of her that mattered to the brothers. There were many maids they could have in their villages. But there was only one Drusilla, so far beyond everyday beauty as to be ethereal, an erotic phantom on a starry night who could bring a man carnal pleasures that almost cost him his sanity.

No wonder both brothers wanted her with such longing. To possess her was to possess the loveliest woman who had ever graced the countryside. Lord William expected Stephen to be killed and the amulet to be his.

"I can hear by your silence," the old seer said, "that I am speaking the truth. That when I told my lord that an assassin would attempt to kill him and reclaim his amulet, I was right." For the first time, malice shone in the dark, ruined eyes of the old man. "But I am not finished telling you about your own reason for coming here."

"The money. I'll be rich."

But the old man shook his cowled head. "Not the money, no, my killing man. The woman herself is what brought you here. You guarded her for more than a year. Your lord wanted to make sure that she never sneaked out of the castle when he was away. He was afraid that she had other lovers in the countryside. He even had you sleep outside the door to her chambers so escape was impossible."

"I was only doing my duty."

"Your duty? Did that also include being as smitten with her as the two lords are? Did that also include sneaking into the baths to watch her bathe naked? And making all these foolish plans in your head to kidnap her and run away with her, even though you knew that she found you repellent?"

"That's a lie!" Aarak whirled on the seer, his enormous hands already fitting themselves to the size of the seer's scrawny neck.

"You think I didn't foresee this moment," the seer said, backing up. "I am weary, so I don't care if you kill me or not. But let me tell you, you will be a fool to steal the amulet. You won't be able to resist her any more than the brothers did. And this time she is prepared—"

The attack came on so suddenly that for the first few minutes it looked like bad playacting. The old man clutched his chest and fell back against the wall. Only when his skull cracked the stone did Aarak realize that the old man was not putting on a show. Aarak had seen his share of heart attacks on his killing missions—people so afraid of the death he brought that they denied him the satisfaction of his profession by dying of a heart attack instead.

By the time Aarak got the old man laid straight out on the floor, he recognized that he was already too late. The seer had passed over, taking his secrets with him.

No time to waste. Aarak ripped the blind man's dagger from its scabbard. He would have to collect better weapons than this on his way to find Lord Stephen.

He blew out the candles, crept to the door, opened it, and peeked out. A heavyset guard stood a few feet away, leaning against the wall as he looked over something directly beneath the hall sconce. A spear leaned against the wall near him, only a quick grab away. Fortunately, he was facing away from the assassin.

Many years ago, Aarak had been in an army where the leader regularly timed his soldiers on their abilities to perform deadly tasks quickly. Among all the freelance killers, Aarak had been the quickest at jumping a slave from behind and then giving his neck so violent a wrench that the slave was dead before he could even fall over.

Aarak hoped his timing was just as good now as it had been then. He estimated that he would need to take two quick steps toward the guard and then fling himself on the man's back. The two steps would be the danger. The guard would have time, if he heard Aarak, to raise the alarm.

Aarak's timing held. He took his two steps and launched himself on the guard before the man could even turn around. He had apparently been engrossed in whatever he was holding in his hand. Aarak had no trouble seizing the man's head and twisting with such fury that blood shot from the man's mouth and nostrils before the crack of neck bones could be heard.

Aarak dragged the dead guard into the seer's chambers and stripped him of his weapons. Now a sword and a small ax filled Aarak's hands as he began working his way to the lord's chambers, one floor above.

Two more guards had to be murdered before Aarak was able to creep inside the heavily fortified door that led inside the lord's chambers. His forearms and hands were soaked with blood. He liked the stench of it. He even put his tongue on a particularly thick splash of it. He believed in the warriors' tales that the blood of others only made you fiercer. And he wanted to be especially fierce with Lord Stephen.

Seven winding stone steps led to the lord's chambers. Torches lit the way. The stench of the burning oil filled Aarak's nostrils. He despised that smell. Better blood than oil any day.

Another door, huge and wooden, confronted

him. Was it locked? And if it was, what could he do about it? And even if it wasn't locked, what would happen when he sneaked inside the chambers? Would guards be waiting for him there? Or knife-toothed dogs, starved for flesh of any kind? Or Lord Stephen himself, waiting with his weapon?

The door was not locked. It yielded to him with the ease of a prostitute.

He passed beneath the arched doorway, locking the door behind him, the bloody sword he'd taken from one of the guards he'd killed held tightly in his barbarian hand.

Darkness. The scent of incense and tobacco smoke. The heady odor of good whiskey. Only slowly did his eyes trace the outlines of the spare chamber. An enormous pile of cleaned animal pelts dressed up as a bed sprawled in the center of the room. A large wooden table took up much of the north wall, with the remains of a meal, a loaf of bread, and a bottle of wine on it. Books, scrolls, and clothing were piled sloppily on another table. And the darkened fireplace, big enough for a man to stand in, performed the function of a wind tunnel—eerie, ghoulish windcries chased each other up the stone chimney.

Aarak had just spied a second door sunken into the wall itself when it opened and out stepped Lord Stephen himself. He wore the military clothes of his realm, with a broadsword in a scabbard on his belt.

Aarak had no trouble seeing the lord because

just to Stephen's right walked what appeared to be a short troll-like being so ugly of face that Aarak felt his stomach knot. The little creature wore the pointed hat and comic green suit of the leprechaun. But it was the twisted stubby features and absurd little gray goatee and bulging, angry eyes that held Aarak's attention. He couldn't recall ever seeing a being of any kind this repellent. There was even an odor wafting from the ugly little man that was as angry as his eyes.

"Stay where you are, assassin. Or I will curse you dead," the little man growled.

"I didn't know leprechauns knew magic."

"He's assured me he does," said Lord Stephen. "He said he can protect me against any kind of intruder—including one sent by my brother."

"I just want the amulet. I don't care about killing you."

Lord Stephen smirked. He looked eerily like his brother. "Lord William isn't strong enough to keep her inside the amulet. And if she ever escapes, she has the strength and will to be rid of both of us. She feels we have defiled her youth. So all I can do is keep her—" He raised a large metal amulet the color of silver, jagged sun rays bursting from the center of the piece. In the center, Aarak saw the beautiful Drusilla pounding against the glass of the amulet. She was shrieking something, but no sound was coming from the jewelry. And—she was completely naked. Aarak felt his mouth go dry with lust and his nervous system begin to crackle and burn. She had always had this effect on him.

Lord Stephen laughed. "You can barely restrain yourself, can you, Aarak? And I don't blame you. I'm tempted to let her out, too. How long can any sane man gaze upon a woman so beautiful and not want to make love to her? But I know what she's up to. That's why I've forbidden the amulet to carry any sounds she makes. At night when I was trying to sleep next to my wife, I kept the amulet on my table, and Drusilla would whisper the carnal things she wanted to do with me if I'd only let her out of the amulet. But I can't. All I think about is making love to her. But if I do— she'll be gone from me forever."

"So you're as much in a prison as she is."

"That's one way to put it, I suppose. Yes, both of us prisoners. So you see, I'm doing my brother a favor by keeping her here within the amulet. That way she won't break his heart as she has broken mine."

"She's already broken his heart. Many times over."

Lord Stephen drew and flourished his broadsword. "She won't be going with you, if that's why you're here. I have Fitzpatrick here to defend me. I bought him yesterday at a marketplace that had nothing but magical people for sale."

"He may be a good pickpocket, perhaps a good arsonist because he can climb in and out of tight places, and maybe even a good burglar for the same reason. But he's not magic, Lord Stephen. No matter what he tells you, he's not magical.''

Lord Stephen's face flushed with rage and his burning gaze fell to the twisted face of the tiny man. ''Is this true? You can't cast a spell that will protect me from him?''

But he was foolish to let his rage distract him. It made him reckless. For a moment, he forgot that the man standing in front of him was an assassin. And so it was that Aarak made his move. He quickly ripped the seer's stiletto from his belt and flung it with such precision that it pierced the exact center of Lord Stephen's right eye. And then, leaping to the man, Aarak swept the broadsword from his hand and cleanly cleaved the man's head from his neck. The head went flying across the room to smash against a wall and then fall to the floor.

Aarak scowled at the little man. ''I thought you could protect him with one of your magical spells.''

The ugly little man shrugged. ''I didn't have time to summon my powers.''

''I'll have to remember that the next time somebody runs a blade through me.'' He shook his head at the little man's bold lie.

He then walked over, knelt down on one knee and snapped the amulet from the chain around Lord Stephen's stump of a neck. Blood still pulsed from the raw wound.

''You and your master haven't thought this through,'' Fitzpatrick said.

Aarak stood up, stared down at the naked woman screaming inside the window of the amulet. Her sexuality was diminished somewhat by her rage. But only somewhat.

"Neither you nor your master will be able to set her free unless you know the proper words."

"Lord William has many wizards in his realm. One of them will be able to figure this out."

Now it was Fitzpatrick's turn to smirk. "You are an arrogant man, Aarak. Not even you and all your self-confidence can free her. Only I now know the words."

"You only worked for him one day."

"Yes, but he kept the words in his book on magic and the supernatural. I tore the page out unbeknownst to him. I memorized them and then burned the page. Lord Stephen, I'm sorry to say, was not in danger of becoming a genius. Wine would have made him forget the words—so he would have had to depend on me."

Aarak was forced to look at the little man in a different way. Comic as the twitchy little bastard was, his eyes now gleamed with a smug knowledge that Aarak desperately needed.

"I wouldn't set her free anyway," Aarak said. "You heard Lord Stephen. She'd just run away."

"Those words were for your ears only. He wanted to dissuade you from killing him. She simply wants to enjoy life. And she can hardly do that while trapped in this amulet. I know you want to free her—I can see it in your eyes. Were I in your position, I would do the same."

Aarak brought the point of the broadsword over so that it rested under the leprechaun's chin. "You seem to forget that I have the medallion, not you. But you can write those words down for me."

The hideous man shook his head. "If I do, you'll kill me."

Aarak's grin was mirthless. "If you don't, I'll cut off one of your fingers every minute until you change your mind."

"Swear that you will let me live if I do as you ask, and I'll show you a secret way out of the castle."

Aarak raised an eyebrow. The little man was cleverer than he looked. "You have my word that you will live if you give me the words to control the amulet and show me a way out of here."

The little man sprang to the small table, sweeping clothes and papers aside, and found an inkpot and quill. He scratched down a few words, sanded the ink and paper, then rolled it up. "Here you go." He handed the small scroll to Aarak and cocked his head. "It's a long way back. Why don't you take this food, too? After all—" He nodded in the direction of Lord Stephen's body. "He won't need it anymore."

"Why are you being so helpful all of a sudden?"

"Like Stephen said—he did buy me. But you've just given me my freedom. Why shouldn't I help you?"

Aarak thrust the broadsword into his belt and examined the bread carefully, smelling it and taking a small nibble. It seemed fine. The bottle of wine was still sealed, so he grabbed it as well, shoving the bread and wine into a sack. "Now show me the way out of here."

The little man went to the second door and opened it. "This way."

Aarak, his blade at the ugly man's back, followed him down a narrow, winding staircase. They came to a narrow passageway that led to what appeared to be a blank wall.

"This is your way out?" Aarak advanced on the little man, sword poised to run him through.

"Wait! Look." The little man pushed on a rock, and a section of wall swung open, tall enough for a man to crawl through. "As I said, Stephen wasn't a genius, showing this to me."

"Thanks." Aarak shoved the little man out of the way with a boot to his back. The wee one went back to being comic again, doing two perfect somersaults and finally slamming up against the stone wall. He cursed Aarak in a language Aarak had never heard before. And it was probably just as well. Aarak was sure that Fitzpatrick was damning him most profanely as he left.

The night held no mercy. The amulet burned against Aarak's chest, thumping back and forth on the crude leather necklace he'd fashioned. With his cape thrown around his shoulders, at least the amulet was safe and warm.

Hungry wolves cried even louder than the witch winds that swept the acid, stinging snow across the midnight lands. He knew he needed to stop soon, and he knew where that would be—or hoped he remembered, anyway—that cave where the frozen man was, a cave deep enough to hide a man from the blizzard that had befallen this realm like a curse fulfilled.

He needed to find it quickly, but he had two problems. The lashing snow had rendered him virtually blind, and the moonless white hills and glens and crevices all looked the same by now. The second problem was his exhaustion. He had been riding for almost five hours. Which would give out first—his stolen steed or himself? Early on, the snow on the ground had been but a few inches deep. By now it reached the top of the struggling horse's flanks. It couldn't go much longer.

Fitzpatrick had left the castle not long after Aarak. He had no trouble following the assassin, especially since the depth of the snow would slow a horse to a crawl, but the top layer of the snow had hardened into an icy crust that the leprechaun could run on top of with ease.

Fitzpatrick wondered if the man were daft. How much further could he go on? Didn't he know that he could die out here? Had possession of the amulet cost him his good sense?

Of course, the leprechaun could say the same thing about himself. Though he'd been exposed to Drusilla for barely twenty-four hours, he was already in her thrall. What kind of common sense had led him into this vengeful night to do battle with a gigantic killer in order to possess a woman trapped inside an amulet?

He could die out here just as easily as Aarak could.

He thought of something ironic: what if both of them died out here in this savage night? Who would possess the amulet? Would it ever be found?

The cave ran long and narrow into a hillside. A ragged corner of it provided a barrier against the endless wind. Aarak was so exhausted he forgot all about the amulet for the time being. He needed rest. His horse had died some time back and he'd had to force himself forward through the whipping winds and freezing snow to find shelter.

He made a small fire, his numb fingers clumsy and awkward as they struck flint and steel. Somebody else—maybe the frozen man—had sought shelter here not too long ago and had been cordial enough to leave wood behind. Even without the wind battering him, his body still felt ice-cold. He huddled close to the fire, gnawing on the loaf of bread he'd stolen from the castle, and washing it down with wine, wishing he'd had the time to carve a haunch from the dead horse. The bones of dead animals were strewn across the cave floor, as were feces from a half dozen species.

As the fire began to warm him a little, his thoughts returned to the amulet. He took the sunburst from around his neck and stared at the woman inside. Drusilla wore a white dress and sat near a summer stream, watching the swans swim by. He knew this to be some other dimension. Not only had the wizard imprisoned her in an amulet, he'd also imprisoned her in another realm.

When she became aware of him, she angled her elegant head so that their eyes could meet. Her gaze jolted him. All his love and all his passion grabbed him, literally shook him to his core, so that he had to clutch the amulet to keep it from falling into the fire.

I knew we would be together someday, Aarak. I've prayed for it every night. You not only loved me, you protected me.

He remembered that from time to time she'd been able to communicate with him through mindthoughts. She'd always told him that mindthoughts were the purest form of expression, that speech was often vile and vulgar.

I want to be with you the rest of my life, Aarak. I want you to be my protector again.

Is that all I'll be? Your protector?

A shy laugh. You know better than that. This time we will be lovers, too. The kind of lover I've never had before. A man who respects me as well as loves me.

Ridiculous glee such as the kind he hadn't felt since being a boy filled his heart. A rhapsody in equal parts love and lust. This time she would be his in every sense. Protector *and* lover, she'd promised. Protector *and* lover.

I'm assuming you got the release words for this amulet when you killed Lord Stephen.

Of course I did—I made the leprechaun write them down for me.

Then release me from this prison, and we can be together again.

By now Aarak had forgotten about his mission for Lord William, forgotten his duty, forgotten everything but the face and the body of the woman who now captivated his every thought. He fumbled for the scroll and unrolled it—

There were two lines of text there, and Aarak read them to himself, sounding them out to be sure he pronounced them correctly. Then, with a flourish, he spoke the words out loud, his breath pluming in the cold air of the cave.

Nothing happened.

Aarak said the words again, louder this time. Still Drusilla remained in her prison. *I don't know why it isn't working.* Then the truth hit Aarak, and his face tightened. The rhapsody was no more. He saw in her face his own disappointment. *That little leprechaun bastard tricked me!*

The leprechaun? You let a leprechaun outwit you? Where is your pride?

He'd forgotten that she didn't take bad news well. Not at all. He knew that some might say that she behaved like a spoiled child at moments like these. But when one is in love as Aarak was in love, even objectionable traits can seem endearing. Love deludes just like wine.

I'm going to find him, I promise you that. All I need is some rest and then we'll go after him. He can't be that hard to find. Maybe he's even at the castle. Aarak pried the cork out of the wine bottle and took a long swallow.

You know he wants me, don't you?

That's pretty obvious.

Just imagine those grubby little hands pawing my white pure skin—

Let's not talk of such things, m'lady. Let me rest a bit, and then we will hunt him down. Together.

Fitzpatrick spent an hour just inside the cave entrance. He saw the firelight flicker on the walls and smelled the pleasant smoke wafting out.

He also heard Aarak settling in back there. When silence came, Fitzpatrick would make his move. His small hand held a knife so sharp the blade could cleave thick leather. A human throat would be much easier to cut.

For the first time in many lonely years, Aarak did not sleep alone. He filled his hands with the amulet and held it close to his heart as he drifted peacefully to sleep knowing that one fine day he and his true love would ride golden steeds into the palaces of the mighty, and all men would envy Aarak not only as a great warrior, but as the only man worthy of such a beauty.

Thus wrapped inside the warmth and tenderness of such thoughts, he fell asleep, snoring soon after, snoring that was a joke to those who'd had to sleep anywhere near him on his travels.

Fitzpatrick himself fell asleep, though only in a

shallow way. The sound, whatever in holy hell it was, raised him a good three inches off the ground. His pinched little face showed pure terror as he tried to recognize the noise that seemed to come from the rough stone walls themselves.

And then he smiled. It was Aarak. Snoring. Good Lord, had anyone but the giants of myth snored with such incredible force? The damned cave might collapse under such a sonic assault.

Now was the time to make his move. The drugged wine the assassin had taken had been intended for Stephen, so that Fitzpatrick could steal the amulet and leave the castle, but the big oaf had changed everything. However, the leprechaun would soon have Drusilla to himself, and the human would be as dead as his former master.

He crawled into the cave, keeping to the shadows as much as possible. The fire burned warmer as he got closer and the sounds Aarak made caused the little man to stop a few times and cover his ears in pain.

When he reached the rear of the cave, he found Aarak spread out on the floor, sound asleep, the empty wine bottle lying beside him. And the fire crackling merrily.

Now he had to move fast.

In three steps he was at Aarak's side, sweeping down with his blade to cut the man's throat and make the amulet his own.

But the amulet was not around Aarak's neck.

Panic.

What would Aarak have done with it?

And then he saw it clasped in the enormous hands of the assassin.

Only when he reached for the amulet did the little man realize how deep Aarak's sleep was. He didn't even stir as Fitzpatrick eased the amulet from the massive hands. The snoring, so close to the little man's ears, threatened to deafen him forever. And Aarak had the habit of seasoning his snoring with spittle.

But the little man had what he wanted. The amulet.

No time to waste.

He took the real paper from his pocket and read the wizard's words that would open the amulet and bring the woman to full and beautiful life.

And then there she stood, every inch a woman.

"I thank you for that," Drusilla said, smiling at him with such warmth and tenderness that Fitzpatrick felt like his heart would burst. "You know the real meaning of chivalry."

"And I hope you know the real meaning of gratitude," said Fitzpatrick as he stood before her and winked. "*My* kind of gratitude."

"I would hope so, too," she said.

He was so completely into his fantasy, that he didn't notice her slipping his knife from his hand. Bringing the blade up to his throat.

Opening a deep and bloody gash across that throat until it was too late. He was instantly spitting blood from the mouth below his nose and the new mouth across his throat. Fitzpatrick's last vision before he fell forever into darkness was of Drusilla, bloody blade in hand, and a look of absolute hatred on her face.

Even before he opened his eyes, Aarak knew that something was wrong. The air, the smells, the very texture of existence felt—wrong.

Some other realm.

"You slept for a very long time," said the radiant Drusilla. She peered down at him as if she was a giantess and he was some kind of tiny animal in a cage.

It took till this very moment to realize that he was in fact in a cage—the cage of the amulet. She had hexed him into the realm she had recently inhabited.

"I thought I was going to be your protector and your lover," Aarak said, knowing that the whine in his voice pleased neither of them. Few things are more unmanly than large men whining.

"Well, you are," she said. "Whenever we wish to spend the night together, I will hex my way into the amulet and we will spend nights you will never forget, Aarak. Never."

"But I won't be free."

"You said that I was the only thing you wanted."

"Yes, but—"

"Then count your blessings. Think of all the men who would give up everything to have what you have. When the storm dies, I want to go to Winiver Castle. There is a prince there who should now be king. I'll seduce him out of his fortune and then we'll be off.''

"Seduce him? But you said *we* would be lovers.''

"We will be, silly. But that doesn't mean I won't sleep with other people now and then when necessary. After all, *you* certainly don't have any fortune.''

She tapped her nail on the glass circle of the amulet. "Now you get some sleep, you grumpy old bear. And when dawn comes, we'll be off. We'll find some riders and take their horses—or rather you will.''

"You're going to let me out of here to do battle?''

"Well, of course. How else will you be my protector?''

"But what if I don't want to come back inside?''

"Oh,'' she said sweetly, touching the glass of the amulet in a way that made him almost feel her fingers on his thigh. He gasped with anticipated pleasure. "I think you'll want to come back inside.'' And then she kissed him gently on the cheek.

His smile did not come immediately, but when it did he looked like a small boy who'd been granted the finest gift in the land. He'd wanted nothing more than to be beside her the rest of his life. It had taken a moment to realize that that was exactly what she'd given him. Herself. And in a way nobody else could ever have.

THE HUNDREDTH KILL

John Marco

John Marco is the author of six novels of epic
fantasy, many of which have been translated into
various languages throughout the world. His first
book, *The Jackal of Nar*, was published in 1999
and won the Barnes and Noble Maiden Voyage
Award for best first fantasy novel. His most recent
novels, *The Eyes of God*, *The Devil's Armor*, and
Sword of Angels, are all available in DAW edi-
tions. John writes full time from his home in
Kings Park, NY, a North Shore Long Island sub-
urb, where he lives with his wife Deborah and his
young son Jack. He is currently at work on a
brand new epic fantasy project, as well as a few
smaller projects.

TEN-YEAR-OLD CHARLIE Mason had long
watched the ships from his spot in Foochow's

harbor, waiting for his chance to board one of the grand clippers. Along with his lordly father, Charlie had been on ships before, but now that steamers were taking over, he had never had a chance to board a real sailing vessel until heading for home. They had always seemed so beautiful to him, like big white eagles, but now, halfway through his three-month journey, Charlie was bored.

There were no other children his age or otherwise aboard the *Cairngorm*, and no one really for Charlie to talk to. His father was already home in England, and his governess Priscilla—who accompanied him everywhere—was nearly thirty. To Charlie's thinking, thirty was very nearly dead, and Priscilla had already worn him out with her stories. Most nights, Priscilla and Charlie ate with the rest of the passengers, listening to outdated gossip about the goings-on back home, where a man named Disraeli was struggling as Prime Minister, or to the troubles of the Spanish Queen Isabella or the American President Johnson. But Charlie wasn't interested in this talk, and six weeks of it had left him numb. He missed his tutors back in Foochow, where his father had left him to learn the tea trade. It was tea that filled the holds of the *Cairngorm*, and it was tea that was the only reason the clippers still existed. Charlie understood this and appreciated it, knowing that the slow steamers could not get the goods back to the home markets quickly enough. Charlie had learned a lot from his year in China, and it had all been a great adventure. Hong Kong, Macau, Foochow . . . Charlie had seen them all, but he longed for home now, and even the swift clipper ship could not speed him back to Wiltshire fast enough.

Each night aboard the ship was like the one before, and when the passengers finished their meals they talked and played games, and sometimes the men wagered at cards. All of them were kind to Charlie, and all of them were like his parents. English, mostly, they had purchased passage back to Britain full of stories, their pockets packed with Chinese wealth. There was only one passenger who never ate with the others, an Oriental woman who kept to herself and spent almost every evening at the bow of the ship, sitting in her strange and colorful clothes, knitting or reading, always alone. Her name was Lady Kita. She had dark hair and dark eyes and she looked different from the women Charlie knew in China. Priscilla had explained to Charlie that Lady Kita was standoffish and cold, and that was why the rest of the passengers ignored her. Tonight, however, Charlie had heard his fill of politics, and so left the supper table before the tea was served. Knowing he could not get lost aboard the ship, Priscilla let him go with a warning to be careful, then turned back to the charming man named Hawthorne who Charlie knew she fancied.

Six weeks at sea had made Charlie an expert seaman. He knew the *Cairngorm* nearly as well as any of its crew, who had spent hours teaching him about the vessel. He had no trouble making it across the deck, not even this night, when the sea was choppy and the deck tossed him about. It was summer, late July, and the sun was just dipping below the ocean, blazing on the horizon. Waves crashed against the vessel's hull. The busy crew—there were thirty of them—went about their usual work, smiling at Charlie but mostly ignoring him as he made his way to the bow.

Lady Kita had taken her usual spot, sitting in a deck chair facing the clipper's wake. Her hands were empty, clasped in her lap. She wore a fine robe of patterned silk, cinched around her waist by a wide, elaborate belt. She wore her hair pinned up in the back. Charlie slowed as he neared her, spying her. He had explored every inch of the *Cairngorm* except for this strange woman, but now he grew afraid of her. Was she a baroness, Charlie wondered, or a duchess perhaps? She was called "lady," and where Charlie was from that meant nobility. His father had spent months in Japan and had dined in the court of the nobles there, but Charlie himself had never been.

"Come out," said the woman suddenly, making Charlie jump. He stood very still, hiding himself in the shadow of a crate. "Come out," the woman repeated. "It is rude to stare."

Charlie's face grew hot. "Sorry," he stammered. He stepped out from his hiding spot. "I wasn't staring. Honest."

"What were you doing, then?" The lady finally

turned to face him. Charlie didn't know how to answer.

"We were having supper. My governess is waiting for me . . ."

Lady Kita pretended to look around. "I don't see her."

"She's back in the galley," Charlie managed.

"Where you should be," said the lady, not unkindly. "Never mind. It is good to see you. You are Charlie Mason."

"Yes," said Charlie brightly. "How do you know that?"

"There is little to do onboard. I learned the names of everyone."

She spoke in a courtly voice, with the hint of an accent. Charlie was used to the Chinese women and the way they spoke, fast and loud. Lady Kita's voice was neither of those things. She reminded Charlie of the women back home.

And then, to Charlie's great surprise, she invited him to sit. Since the lady occupied the only chair, Charlie took to the deck, captivated by her. She seemed to sense his boredom, something that they shared, perhaps.

"Do you like this ship?" she asked. "I have seen you with the crew, full of questions for them."

Charlie nodded. "It's my first time on a ship like this. I've traveled with my father before, but only on a steamer. This is better. It's faster."

"For now," said the lady. "The world is changing."

Her expression darkened. Charlie puzzled over her words.

"You're Japanese," he pronounced. "I can tell. My father went to Japan. He met the emperor."

Lady Kita raised her brows. "Did he? That is wonderful."

"It is," said Charlie proudly. "My father told me about him. He went all over Japan meeting important people. He's a diplomat." He looked at her. "Do you know what that is?"

"Yes," said the lady, smiling. "How much do you know about Japan, Charlie? I can tell you stories if you like. Do you like stories, Charlie?"

Charlie loved stories. Best of all, he loved stories of places he had never been before.

For the next week,. Charlie went every night to Lady Kita's side. Sometimes she had treats for him, strange confections from her homeland that she had lovingly packed for her long journey. She regaled him with tales of the emperor, explaining to him about the warlords she called *daimyos* and how they had battled with the emperor for control of Japan. Japan was changing, she explained to Charlie, and this she told him over and over again. The old ways—the things she cherished—were quickly fading. But Lady Kita kept them alive, at least onboard the *Cairngorm*, bringing them to life with her stories. Most of all, Charlie loved to hear her talk about the samurai, the warriors of Japan, and that strange group of mysterious men she called the nin-sha.

"They are shadows of the samurai," she had explained to him. "We have words for them. We call them *shinobi-no-mono*. That means they are the unseen people. But you know Chinese better, Charlie, so we will say what the Chinese call them. *Nin-sha*."

Now Charlie was truly fascinated. Lady Kita's stories about the samurai were good, but her tales about the nin-sha were astonishing. She had filled his mind with tales of the nin-sha so that Charlie could barely sleep, so excited was he to hear more. This night, as they settled in to their deck chairs over a pot of steaming tea, Charlie insisted she tell him more.

"Where did the nin-sha come from?" he asked. That was still a mystery she had left unsolved. Charlie knew she had deliberately held back the best bits of her story. Just as she had explained everything about the daimyos and their samurai, he wanted now to know everything about the nin-sha.

Lady Kita held her teacup in both hands, savoring its warmth, her white face lit by a nearby lantern. "A long time ago, when my country first began, there was a man named Jimmu who wanted to be emperor. Jimmu was a powerful man. He had armies, but he had enemies, too, and he needed the favor of the gods to defeat them. Jimmu prayed mightily for help, and the gods answered him. They told him to fetch some clay from the holy mountain of Amakaga, but Jimmu could not do this alone. He needed help from men who could sneak their way past his enemies and reach the mountain."

"Nin-sha?" asked Charlie excitedly.

"The first of the nin-sha," the lady explained. "Their names were Shinetsuiko and Otokashi. They dressed themselves up as peasant women and sneaked past Jimmu's enemies to reach Mount Amakaga. They fetched the clay from the holy mountain and returned it to Jimmu, who fired the clay into a bowl as an offering to the gods. The gods were pleased with Jimmu and gave him victory over his enemies. He became emperor."

"What about the other two? What happened to them?"

"Shinetsuiko and Otokashi disappeared into the mountains. They taught others what they had learned. And Shinetsuiko established his clan." The lady paused. "Do you know what a clan is, Charlie?"

"A family," Charlie replied.

"Yes," said Lady Kita brightly. "Shinetsuiko's clan was the first nin-sha family. They settled in Iga, where Shinetsuiko was born, and they became the finest of the nin-sha clans. There were many clans once, but none were as fine as Shinetsuiko's. They were a proud people. They made schools, like you go to school, Charlie."

"I have tutors," Charlie corrected.

"But you learn, yes? And so others learned what Shinetsuiko and his clan taught them, and the knowledge was passed on. And they cherished the bowl that Jimmu had made from the holy clay.

It was their symbol. It was their strength. It was not fabulous to look at, and those who saw it said it looked like the work of peasants." Lady Kita laughed. "But it was made by an emperor! It gave Shinetsuiko and his clan power. The nin-sha became like magic folk."

"They can pass through walls, that's what you said. Tell me about that."

"Some nin-sha can do these things, it is true. Some nin-sha are very powerful." Lady Kita leaned forward over her teacup. "Some nin-sha are not people at all."

Charlie blanched. "Not people? What are they?"

"Ghosts," said Lady Kita.

Charlie laughed. "There's no such thing!"

"But there is, Charlie. In my country there are many spirits, and many things that the outside world does not know or understand."

"My father never saw any ghosts in Japan."

"And how would he see a ghost anyway?" asked the lady tartly. "Nin-shas are never seen or heard, not unless they choose to be."

"But I thought they were men," Charlie protested. "How can they be ghosts?"

"Not all were ghosts, Charlie. Only the best of them ever became ghosts."

Charlie's mind began to reel, and he knew that his father would never believe these tales. But Charlie believed, because he trusted Lady Kita. She had no reason to lie to him.

"Are there still nin-sha?" he asked.

"Some," replied the lady. "In old Japan there

were many, but the daimyos are fading now, and with them fade the samurai and nin-sha, too. There are masters, though, who still keep nin-sha as their servants." Lady Kita smiled. "But that is a tale for tomorrow night."

That night, Charlie dreamed of the nin-sha ghosts Lady Kita had told him about, and all the next day he waited to find out more. He rarely saw Lady Kita in the daytime, and, besides, he didn't want to share her with anyone else. He spent time with Priscilla and the other passengers, and sometimes with members of the crew, because Charlie knew his lordly father wanted him to take every opportunity to learn and would ask him questions when he returned home. Nighttime, though, was Charlie's great respite from the drudgery of day. He rushed through supper with the others in the galley, begged off the desserts offered by the staff, and made his way to the bow of the ship where, as usual, Lady Kita was waiting. This time, though, the woman's demeanor was different. She smiled when she saw Charlie, as though he was a ray of sunlight striking through some gloom. She had dressed beautifully, too, more so than usual, in a dazzling robe of red and blue that Charlie had never seen before.

"What's the matter?" Charlie asked.

Lady Kita stiffened. "I have been thinking, Charlie, about the stories I have told you. They make me sad, these stories."

Charlie did not understand. "But they're great stories. I love your stories, Lady Kita."

"You are a little boy, Charlie. When you are old like me, stories will mean more to you. Sometimes, they will be all that you have left."

Charlie sidled closer to her, wanting to comfort her. "I've been thinking," he began, "about what you told me about the ghost nin-sha. I'm not afraid of them."

Lady Kita broke into a smile. "No?"

"No. I know they kill people and all, but they're not bad. That's right, isn't it? You told me that nin-sha aren't bad people."

"That's right, Charlie. The nin-sha were as good as the samurai. Better, even. A samurai might kill for the pleasure of it. A nin-sha would never do such a thing."

"I like them better," said Charlie. "Will you tell me more about them?"

"Yes," said Lady Kita, "but first, why don't you tell me a story?"

"Me?"

"Yes. I have told you a story every night for weeks now. It is your turn."

Charlie thought hard about this. "I can tell you about my father."

Lady Kita brightened immediately. "Yes. Yes, that would be good."

So Charlie told the lady about his father, Sir Ernest, the diplomat and traveler, who had made a fortune importing tea and who insisted that his young son learn the trade. His father was an important man, Charlie told the lady, and had been to many foreign lands. He had been to Japan to meet the emperor, of course, and he had lived among the nobles who had taken him into their homes. One of them, a man named Okaga, had once been a friend to Charlie's father.

"Okaga is well known in Japan, Charlie," said Lady Kita. "He is a daimyo. Do you remember? He is one of the great men. He has a castle in Iga, where the nin-sha come from."

"I remember," said Charlie. He remembered every small detail of Lady Kita's tales. "Is Okaga a nin-sha?"

"No," said the lady flatly. "He is Lord of Iga, but he is no nin-sha. He is just like other powerful men of his kind. Like the samurai class, Charlie. It is Okaga's birthright to rule Iga, that is all. And he is loyal to the emperor."

Charlie didn't know if that was a good thing or bad. Not all the daimyo were loyal to the emperor, he remembered. But Okaga had once been his father's friend. "My father is only friends with good men," said Charlie. Then, his expression flattened. "He hasn't been to Japan for a long time, though. He doesn't talk about it much anymore, or about Okaga."

Lady Kita took note of this, then urged Charlie to tell her more. Charlie continued with his story, telling of the gifts Okaga had given his father, all of which had been taken home to Wiltshire where they adorned Charlie's house in the country. Charlie missed the house, but he missed his father more.

"My father left me in Foochow to learn, and I have learned," he insisted. "I learned from my tutors and the men aboard this ship, and I've learned from you, Lady Kita." He smiled, hoping to coax her into finishing her tale. "Will you tell me more about the ghosts?"

Lady Kita smiled. "Yes, I will tell you. But you must listen closely, so that you understand everything. Make me that promise, Charlie."

Charlie promised without really knowing why, then settled comfortably into his deck chair. Night had fallen quickly and they were alone on the bow, the perfect setting for a ghost story.

"All of the nin-sha come from their own clans," the lady began. "They do the bidding of their masters. And sometimes, the best of nin-sha remain here after they die, and are bound to their masters. Do you know the story of Aladdin and his magic lamp, Charlie?"

Charlie nodded. "The lamp with the genie."

"Yes, that is right. It is like that for some of the nin-sha. They are like the genie of the lamp. They remain with their masters and they cannot be freed until they do his bidding one hundred times." Lady Kita grimaced. "That means one hundred kills, Charlie. They may kill ninety-nine men for the master, and still be forever in his service. Until they kill that hundredth person, they can never leave this world."

Charlie's jaw went slack with awe. "Why do

they have to serve their masters?'' he asked. "Why are they servants?"

"Mostly because they were sold into it," said the lady sadly. "The daimyos have always been powerful. And the nin-sha clans were always poor. Sometimes they give away things that are precious to them so that they may be protected by the daimyo. Sometimes the things they give away are people. Sometimes not."

"But they don't have to serve forever," Charlie pointed out. He pretended to wield a sword, waving it in the air before him. "They could kill a hundred people easily!"

"No," laughed the lady. "That is not the way of things. The master must give the order, Charlie. Remember what I told you? The nin-sha are not like samurai. When they were strong, the samurai trod the earth like princes. They enforced the law however they wished. Woe to you if you displeased them, Charlie! The nin-sha, though, they were not like that. They were not butchers. They would not kill for the sport of it."

"Oh," said Charlie darkly. "So they're stuck. That's doesn't seem fair."

Lady Kita continued. "You asked me if there are still nin-sha in the world, and I told you that there were. But there are very few of them left. As the world changes, the clipper ships will sail away. The samurai will all vanish. The only nin-sha who exist now are the ghosts, Charlie, who are bound to the last of the daimyos."

She looked profoundly sad. Charlie nudged her with a question.

"Why won't the masters let the nin-sha ghosts go?" he asked. "Why are they so cruel?"

"Oh, there are many reasons, Charlie. Some of them you will not understand until you are older."

"What happens then?" Charlie asked. "What happens after they kill a hundred people?"

"They go to heaven, Charlie," said Lady Kita serenely. "Like everyone else."

For the rest of the voyage, Charlie saw Lady Kita almost every night, and she continued to regale him with stories. But she no longer spoke about the nin-sha. Their story, she explained, was already told and there was nothing more for Charlie to know. Charlie did not badger his friend about it, but simply enjoyed her company and the tales she told about other things. She knew a lot about Japanese history, which Charlie thought was strange for a woman. She was a scholar, far smarter than any of his tutors had been. She knew so much about the world that she reminded Charlie of his father back home.

Eventually, the *Cairngorm* reached its destination, and Charlie and the other passengers of the clipper disembarked at the London docks. Because most of them were Englishmen, the passengers sung the praises of their homeland, glad to be home after so many weeks at sea. At the docks,

Charlie said good-bye to Lady Kita, who did not offer to write the boy or ever see him again. She shook his hand politely, said nothing to the other passengers, then disappeared into the crowded port. Charlie held Priscilla's hand as he watched Lady Kita go. For a moment, he thought he would cry.

It was early in September.

The season rolled from summer into fall. The autumn chill crept into the English air. In Wiltshire the leaves were changing early, and the estate of Sir Ernest burst with color. The lord of the manor had servants who milled about the green lawns, keeping the hedgerows trimmed and the animals fed, and pruning back the flowers for the coming winter. Sometimes, horses clip-clopped across the pretty hills. At night, when the estate was quiet, the windows winked with oil lamps and the chimneys spouted smoke. The animals fell silent. Sir Ernest and his only son got under the covers of their soft beds and slept.

All of these things Kita had watched while she waited. She had always been endlessly patient. After months aboard ship, tracking Charlie Mason to his father, there was no real rush to do the thing she had come to do. She enjoyed Wiltshire, though it was nothing like home, and seeing Charlie with his father pleased her. It was easy for Kita to spy from the woods or to walk the grounds when the sun went down. She was like the nin-sha of old, soundless when she walked, able to leave the grass undisturbed beneath her feet.

Tonight, Kita moved like a breeze, her slippered feet barely grazing the earth, her face obscured beneath wraps of black cloth. The sun had gone down long ago, and the moon had dimmed, too. A gentle wind buffeted the leaves of the yard. Sir Ernest was a widower and slept alone. He had only one child but a score of servants, all of whom would be asleep and none of whom—Kita was sure—would see her if they weren't. In the weeks he had spent at Okaga's castle, Sir Ernest had talked incessantly about himself and his collections, and Kita had seen some of these things when she'd spied through the windows. He was not an unkind man, though, and her master had liked him. Charlie, of course, loved him.

Kita paused, thinking of Charlie. Then, like a tiny flame, she snuffed out the image of his face, focusing instead on her task.

Her target was in the upper bedroom. Kita drifted to the doors. In the days before the restoration, men and women like herself ruled the night and made the daimyos tremble. They were servants now, those who "survived," but they still had the skills, and being what she was made the doors no obstacle at all. With merely a thought she passed through them. She wore no weapons and her body was like ether, but when she willed it so, she could make her hands like steel. Kita did not will that now, though, and so floated her way through the silent house, admiring the things Sir Ernest had collected. He had many things from China, and items from the dark continent, too. Of course, the things her master Okaga had given him were well displayed in his enormous home, gracing the walls and tiny walnut tables, showcased by crystal chandeliers that must have been grand when lit. Kita allowed herself only a moment to admire these treasures.

Like the doors, the stairs posed no problem. Kita willed it and she ascended, carried aloft by an unseen force. On the second floor were the bedchambers, and the largest of these belonged to Sir Ernest. Not far from his own was Charlie's room. Kita paused and looked at Charlie's door. For a moment she was frozen. For a moment, she hesitated. How much did she truly want to do this thing? She had come on a mission, but now all she wanted was to see Charlie one more time.

No.

That could never be. Never again.

Resolute, Kita pushed on toward Sir Ernest's room. This time she did not move through the portal, but opened it silently, and through the darkness she saw the chamber, large and—what did the English say? Posh. Sir Ernest slept upon his enormous bed, little sounds of sleep bubbling on his lips. The velvet curtains of his window hung open, letting in stray beams of moonlight. Kita scanned the room and its riches, and saw a sword near his mantle, a beautiful katana resting on a silver stand, perfect and unblemished. Other treasures rested near it. Kita's eyes went at once to the object of her mission. Looking plain and valueless, the clay bowl sat atop the mantle. The thing that had called her across the seas, the one holy relic her people treasured.

Her eyes darted between the clay bowl and the man in the bed, and then to the katana on the mantle. Sir Ernest began to stir. Kita smiled. In a blur she went to the sword, pulling it free of its ornate scabbard. Quickly, she took the bowl in her other hand. Standing over Sir Ernest, she put the tip of the katana to the startled man's throat. Sir Ernest gasped as he saw her, the blade nipping his skin. She shook her head, bidding him to silence. Half-asleep, Sir Ernest obeyed. He looked terrified to Kita, and also very brave. Other men had begged for their lives. Sir Ernest, she knew, would not beg.

"This," said Kita, holding up the bowl, "is mine."

Sir Ernest moved only his mouth as he spoke. "It was a gift," he explained steadily.

"It did not belong to the giver to give," said Kita. She pushed on the sword ever so gently, making her point. "Do not follow me."

Backing away, Kita dropped the sword to the floor and sped from the room. With the bowl tucked safely in her arms, she raced down the stairs and through the house. This time, she unlocked the great doors before fleeing, no longer soundless as she held the earthly item. Still a ghost, the holy bowl bound her to the world of men. Outside, she cursed the moonlight as it lit her black garb, speeding toward the trees and their protective darkness.

Up in his chamber, Sir Ernest sat stupefied by what had happened. Then, when at last he had collected himself, he ran to Charlie's room to check on his son.

Lady Kita returned to Japan in January, following a tumultuous return voyage aboard a modern steamship. Just as she had during her voyage aboard the *Cairngorm*, she kept to herself and spoke to almost no one. This time, she did not befriend anyone, for there was no one she needed to befriend to lead her to her goal. She had not expected to like Charlie as much as she had, and she was surprised that even now she remembered him so fondly. But she had accomplished what she had set out to do, and when she arrived in Japan, she did not return at once to the court of her master at Iga Castle, but instead went to the mountains in the south, and returned the clay bowl to her clan. Lady Kita's people were no longer practitioners of the unseen arts. They had seen the changes coming and became blacksmiths and farmers instead, and this saddened Kita because she was stuck in a world that no longer existed. Then, when she was done, Lady Kita went to Iga Castle to face her master, Okaga.

Word spread quickly of Kita's return. She knew her master would be displeased, but there was very little he could do to her. She was already his servant. She had been so for decades. She was too beautiful for him to ever release. Her beauty was a curse. It had made Lord Okaga love her.

Like all of the daimyos, Okaga's castle—a modern *hirayamajiro*—was remarkable, rising up from the side of a small mountain so that he could oversee the land of Iga—the land of Kita's people. Upon her return, Okaga summoned Lady Kita to the *donjon*, the tower of his castle, where vassals attended him, kneeling upon the big wooden floor. Okaga himself sat upon a bamboo chair, his youngest children playing at his feet. Lady Kita did not dare meet his eyes. She knelt before him, her gaze downcast. There was no need to explain what she had done. Lord Okaga had already figured that out months ago.

"The bowl," said Okaga. "You have returned it to your people?"

Kita nodded. "Yes."

Lord Okaga already knew this as well, and yet still seemed disappointed. "Are they not my people, too? I am the Lord of Iga."

"Yes, my lord."

"So the bowl is mine, too."

Kita hesitated. "No, my lord. The bowl is holy to my clan."

Okaga's attendants stayed very still, shocked by her disagreement. It was Kita's clan who had made the bowl, and all of them knew it. But like sheep, they were afraid. Kita, though, was not afraid. She could only die once.

Lord Okaga rose from his chair to stand before

her. "You have offended my friend, Sir Ernest, and you have disgraced me, Kita."

"I am lower than dust, master," said Kita. "I am unfit to serve your house."

"True," said Okaga. "I should send you away, yes? Release you?"

"Yes, master."

Even as she said it, she knew her master would laugh. And laugh he did.

"No, Kita, my beautiful one. There will be no hundredth kill for you. For what you have done, I will never release you. I will pass you on to my sons and they will pass you on to their sons, and you will be our servant for all of time."

His verdict did not shock her. "Yes, master," she replied.

"Go. Walk the nights as a ghost and return to me in the daylight so that I can look at you in pleasure."

Lady Kita rose and, head bowed, began backing out of the room. There would be no hundredth kill for her, not ever. She could kill a thousand men, but without her lord's sanction those deaths would mean nothing. She would never join her ancestors in heaven or meet the gods who had made the holy clay. Instead she would steal for Okaga and spy on his enemies, never to kill in his name again. She was more than his servant. She was his slave.

"Kita," said Okaga before she left the room. "Was this worth it?"

Kita did not need to think before giving her

answer. The bowl belonged to her people. It was never truly Okaga's, and never his to give.

"Yes, master," she replied, and left the donjon.

The world would continue to change. Lady Kita took comfort in this. It was just like she had explained to Charlie all those months ago. Someday, there would be no more clipper ships. The samurai would fade away. And all the daimyos and all their castles would one day fall to dust. And then, perhaps, she would be free.

Tanya Huff

Tony Foster—familiar to Tanya Huff fans from her *Blood* series—has relocated to Vancouver with Henry Fitzroy, vampire son of Henry VIII. Tony landed a job as a production assistant at CB Productions, ironically working on a syndicated TV series, "Darkest Night," about a vampire detective. Tony was pretty content with his new life—until wizards, demons, and haunted houses became more than just episodes on his TV series...

"An exciting, creepy adventure"—*Booklist*

SMOKE AND SHADOWS
0-7564-0263-8 $6.99

SMOKE AND MIRRORS
0-7564-0348-0 $7.99

SMOKE AND ASHES
0-7564-0415-4 $7.99

Tanya Huff

The Finest in Fantasy

To Order Call: 1-800-788-6262
www.dawbooks.com

DAW 21